"I've been thinking about this since the first day you walked into the gym," Jack admitted raggedly.

Maureen looked up into the bottomless darkness of his eyes and could no more lie than she could fly. "Me, too."

His right hand slipped to her ribs, his left cupped her hip, bringing her firmly against his hard thigh. "God, you feel good."

"So do you," she whispered, running her fingers along corded muscles at the back of his neck.

"This'll never work," he said hoarsely.

She swallowed hard. "I know."

"You'll be gone as soon as you get your money."

"You'll be busy with the boys at the gym after you fight."

Jack nuzzled her throat, her earlobe, her temple, leaving hot spots in his wake. "So, what do you think?"

Maureen tilted her head invitingly as she realized that she'd been waiting a lifetime for a man who was strong enough to be gentle. "I think I'd like another kiss. . . ."

THE LADY AND THE CHAMP

THE
LADY
AND THE
CHAMP

FRAN BAKER

BANTAM BOOKS
NEW YORK · TORONTO · LONDON
SYDNEY · AUCKLAND

THE LADY AND THE CHAMP

A Bantam Fanfare Book

PUBLISHING HISTORY
Doubleday Loveswept edition published January 1993
Bantam paperback edition / April 1993

FANFARE and the portrayal of a boxed "ff" are trademarks of Bantam Books, a division of Bantam Doubleday Dell Publishing Group, Inc.

ISBN 0-553-29655-8

Published simultaneously in the United States and Canada

Bantam Books are published by Bantam Books, a division of Bantam Doubleday Dell Publishing Group, Inc. Its trademark, consisting of the words "Bantam Books" and the portrayal of a rooster, is Registered in U.S. Patent and Trademark Office and in other countries. Marca Registrada. Bantam Books, 666 Fifth Avenue, New York, New York 10103.

For those fabulous Baker boys—
Vincent and Shane

THE
LADY
AND THE
CHAMP

PROLOGUE

March 1963

She raised her hand, released her breath and knocked.

"Come in," Seamus Sullivan called.

She did, stepping into the office he kept on the second floor of Kansas City's most famous fight gym. He sat at his desk with his back to the door, feet up on the broad windowsill, reading a copy of *Ring*. The familiar sight hit her like a fist in the stomach, and she sucked in a small, sharp breath.

He glanced over his shoulder, and in his eyes flared a pure, unguarded joy. Until he saw the look on her face. Then it disappeared, just like that, and the excruciatingly polite expression he had adopted with her since their divorce took its place. He tossed the magazine aside and turned to confront her.

"Hello, Laura," he said quietly.

"Hello, Sully." She closed the door behind her and crossed the room.

He rose, motioning toward a chair. "Have a seat."

She declined with a shake of her carefully coiffed head and remained standing. "I can only stay a minute," she said, wanting to get this over with as quickly and painlessly as possible.

The incessant *thwack* of a punching bag being pummeled on the balcony level punctuated the tense silence that suddenly seized the cluttered office.

Looking around her, Laura was relieved to see that nothing had changed since she'd left him. Contracts and newspaper clippings still littered Sully's desk. Posters of fierce-faced fighters still passed for wallpaper. A foul-smelling cigar still sent smoke signals from the beanbag ashtray sitting on the windowsill.

All of these things made the papers burning a hole in her purse that much easier to present to him.

"You look great, Slim." Sully's use of the affectionate nickname he'd bestowed upon her during their whirlwind courtship upset her almost as much as the way his admiring gaze swept from her pink cloth coat to her matching pillbox hat. "Just like a blond Jackie Kennedy."

Even as she nodded her thanks, Laura felt a guilty flush creeping up her face. She'd dressed and done her hair very deliberately, remembering that Sully considered the President's wife the perfect wife. But now she wondered if she hadn't gone a bit overboard in trying to put him in a receptive mood.

"How's Maureen?" he asked her then.

"She's beautiful, Sully, just beautiful."

His smile took a grim turn. "You never bring her around anymore—"

"A fight gym is no place for a little girl."

Sully opened his mouth as if to argue the point, then sighed resignedly and changed the subject. "Did she get that doll I sent her for her birthday?"

The porcelain-faced doll belonged on a display shelf, not in the arms of a five-year-old girl. But Laura's relief that another battle had been avoided spilled over into generous truth. "She takes it to bed with her every night."

He ran a hand through the thick red hair that their daughter had inherited. "I meant to bring it out to your

2

folks' house myself, but I signed a new fighter that day—a real comer—and the time just got away from me."

Same old Sully, Laura thought, stung anew by the way he'd always put his surrogate sons first and his wife and daughter second. Forcing the bitter memories to the back of her mind, she broke her news before she lost her nerve. "I'm getting married again next month."

"Well, congratulations." His face fell but his voice remained doggedly buoyant. "Who's the lucky guy?"

"His name is Paul Bryant."

"Sounds familiar."

"You might have seen his picture in the paper."

"In the society section, right?"

"Financial," she corrected, refusing to rise to the bait of his caustic tone. "He's a banker."

Sully gave a humorless laugh. "With bankers' hours."

Laura hesitated, but there was no way to say it except straight out. "Paul wants to adopt Maureen after we're married."

Sully staggered as if he'd just been hit with a sucker punch. "No!"

"He couldn't love her more if she were his own." And Laura wouldn't be content until the three of them were a family in the eyes of the law.

"But she's my daughter." He thumped his chest with his closed fist to emphasize his claim. "*Mine!*"

"She barely remembers you!" That was a desperate lie, told by a desperate woman whose little girl's emotional wounds always seemed to break open at bedtime.

It was also a low blow. Sully's eyes glazed over with pain and he sank to his chair in slow motion. The *ssh-ssh-ssh* of someone skipping rope drifted in through the window overlooking the gym.

Laura opened her clutch purse, got the consent forms out and laid them on his littered desk. She turned and started toward the door, then paused to look over her shoulder. Dry-eyed, for she adamantly refused to shed any more tears over the man who'd fathered her daughter, she delivered the decisive punch. "If you love her, Sully—really love her—you'll let her go."

THE
MAIN
EVENT

―――――

ROUND 1

Sullivan's Fight Gym was no place for a lady, either.

It wasn't just the Northeast area neighborhood—once home to the city's upper crust, now habitat of so many urban hopeless—that caused Maureen Bryant to circle the block twice before pulling over to the curb in front of the old brick building.

Nor was it necessarily the motley crew of males—some with their hair spiked to the mid-June sky, others with their shirts open to the navel—who made their way inside while she sat outside with the engine idling and her heart racing.

It was, more than anything, her own soul-wrenching ambiguity that had her stalled.

Maureen reached to cut the motor, then retracted her hand and left it running. She usually wasn't this wishy-washy. Then again, she rarely had reason to venture this far north of the Country Club Plaza.

A siren wailed in the distance, reinforcing her doubts. She didn't *have* to do this herself. Her family's attorney had practically pleaded with her to let him send the eviction notice by registered mail. And Mr. Marks, the fast-talking commercial developer who'd called her last week and expressed an interest in buying both this leaning tower of pugilism and the weed-infested lot next door, had sounded almost eager to serve it on her behalf.

Over the years she'd let other people's feelings and her own fear of being rejected again dictate her actions—or rather, her lack of action. The least she could do now was see this through to the bitter end.

Besides, she admitted as she cut the engine with a decisive flick of her wrist, she was dying of curiosity.

Dying could be the operative word here, she realized when five teenage boys made camp on the gym's crumbling front stoop. Gang slang embellished their red ball caps, crude tattoos scarred their forearms, and leather strips bound their knuckles. Their expressions, as angry as the streets that had spawned them, would have inspired Spike Lee to crank up his camera.

Adding to her concern for her personal safety, they cast covetous eyes at the silver Mercedes SEL that was her pride and joy.

Individually, she knew, they might not be so bad. But together, propelled by a pack mentality and the possibility of chop-shop money for the car she suddenly wished she'd left at home, they could be dangerous. Maureen was sensible enough to keep her doors locked as she looked for help.

A woman's face, haloed by white hair, peered out timidly from a second-floor window of the redbrick rooming house across the street, then promptly pulled back. The man who stumbled out the door of the corner bar looked as though *he* could use a hand. And the sidewalk, which only moments before had been crowded with wanna-be boxers, now seemed stripped of humans.

Failing to find someone to come to her aid, she weighed her other options. She could call the police on her cellular telephone and have the gang arrested for trespassing. That would not only remove them from her property, but it would also eliminate the risk of their tampering with the Mercedes. Or she could start her engine and head south. Return tomorrow with her lawyer—in his car, of course.

But that would mean admitting defeat, a galling prospect after she'd made such a big deal out of going it alone.

"Never let them see you sweat." Maureen couldn't remember where she'd heard that before, but it seemed to bear repeating as she got out of the car.

Not that anyone in recent memory had seen her sweat. Her clients marveled at how calmly she handled their crises, her colleagues admired her discipline under the fire of a deadline, and a contractor whose crude passes she routinely ignored called her "The Ice Princess." Even her ex-fiancé had frequently commented that she had the coolest skin he'd ever touched.

That glacial exterior served her well as she mentally catalogued her car's contents for the insurance company. Her carpet and drapery samples were in the trunk, the back seat was empty, and her car phone was bolted to the console. As an extra precaution, though, she activated the burglar alarm before she closed the door. If nothing else, she mused as she eyed the hooligans holding up the front of *her* building, they'd go deaf if they tried to steal it.

Maureen took comfort from the thought. She also took a moment to smooth down the skirt of the crisp beige suit she'd paired with a single strand of pearls and earrings to match, and to touch up the sleek French twist that so effectively tamed her mind-of-its-own red hair.

Normally she felt as fresh at the end of the day as she had at the beginning. But between the architect whose blueprints had proven to be an interior designer's nightmare and the antiques dealer who'd suddenly raised his wholesale prices, she was starting to wilt. And something told her she was in for a total meltdown.

"Fo-xy la-dy," one of the gang members drawled to approving laughter.

His crony drew more guffaws when he added, "Fresh Mer-ce-des."

If they thought they were frightening her, they were

right. She was literally shaking in her ivory eelskin pumps. But if they thought she'd take flight, they were wrong. In a staccato rhythm that matched her escalating pulse rate, her heels beat on the weed-cracked sidewalk as she started toward the entrance.

Perhaps it was her out-of-my-way walk that made them move. More likely, it was the police car that happened to cruise down Independence Avenue just as she approached the stoop. Whatever, when she marched into the building, the teenagers parted as the Red Sea must have parted for Moses.

Having survived the gang's verbal gauntlet, Maureen was ready for anything. But in truth, nothing she'd ever experienced could have prepared her for what she found as she made her way down the narrow hall.

Empty chip bags and dead cigarette butts littered the floor. Spray-can murals of tigers, their eyes glowing a sinister amber, glared down at her from the walls. A sign over the open door at the end of the hall warned NO GLOVE, NO LOVE.

A potato chip crumb crunched underfoot—or was it a bug? Maureen shivered but stayed the course. She told herself that her imagination was running wild, that those tigers' eyes were *not* following her. That didn't keep the skin at her nape from prickling, though.

She'd had a pretty good idea of what to expect, thanks to her attorney pushing the panic button when she told him she wanted to handle this herself. "You can't be serious!" he'd all but shouted at her. "The neighborhood is the pits, the people are lowlifes, and you could film *Rocky Meets Rumble Fish* in that dump!"

What she hadn't expected, she discovered when she paused in the doorway of the dusty old palaestra, was this dizzying sense of déjà vu.

The smell of Omega Oil and stale cigar smoke sparked vague memories. Spurts of locker room laughter and the steady *whappity, whappity, whappity* of punching bags from up on the balcony rang distant bells. The men's faces—contorted with no-pain-no-gain expressions as they lifted weights and ran laps—might have belonged to family or friends, so familiar did they seem.

Maureen told herself that her reaction was ridiculous at best. She couldn't possibly remember anything. Yet even as she shook off that startling burst of phantasm and stepped inside, she couldn't quite shake the feeling that she'd finally come home.

But home was never like this.

A regulation-size ring, empty at the moment, dominated this circus of spars. Ropes as big around as her fist encircled it, posts as rigid as palace guards cornered it, and the photoflood lamp that dangled above it threw its illumination onto a canvas that appeared more gray than white.

Her moue of distaste didn't even begin to express what she thought of the decor. The walls were painted industrial-green, the floors resembled rough seas, and the wavery full-length mirror looked like something out of a fun house.

The equipment had nothing on Nautilus, either. A rowing machine, minus the oars, sat beached upon an exercise mat. Target bags with the stuffing bursting from the seams lay piled in a corner. Metal folding chairs held an assortment of items ranging from convenience-store water bottles and soiled towels to jump ropes and—she closed her eyes in mortification—a jockstrap.

Well, what did she think she'd find—a pair of panty hose draped over the back of that chair? This was a fight gym, not a sorority house. And she was a woman in a man's world. Perhaps the most chauvinistic world of all. If she balked now, she would never forgive herself.

Her mental pep talk helped. She opened her eyes and gave the athletic supporter that had so unnerved her a second ago a good long look. There, that wasn't so bad.

Then, spotting a hand-printed sign reading OFFICE with an arrow pointing up, she started toward the stairs.

The man who climbed into the ring at that very same moment stopped her cold.

He wore a white plastic headguard, black satin trunks, and nothing in between. His smooth, sun-bronzed neck flowed into shoulders that were about a yard wide and biceps that looked as round and firm as green apples. His red-gloved hands flashed like thunderbolts when he started shadowboxing, pummeling his invisible opponent with a furious flurry of rights and lefts.

Maureen abhorred violence, and she found no redeeming social value in blood sports of any kind. Standing ringside, though, she suddenly saw a brutal Renaissance beauty in the boxer's sculpted physique and athletic prowess, a beauty that was as frightening as it was fascinating to behold.

"He's all yours," said a gravelly voice just beside her.

Startled, she jumped, then spun to find she'd been joined by a balding little man with a big smile.

Thoroughly shaken by the way he'd snuck up on her, Maureen returned his wide grin with a wary eye. In a go-for-broke plaid sportcoat and a pair of shiny polyester slacks he'd pulled up practically to his armpits, he looked as if he'd stepped right out of a Damon Runyon short story. He also looked perfectly harmless—a relief, considering what she'd encountered thus far.

She tilted her head, the better to hear him. "I beg your pardon?"

The gnome of a man standing next to her pointed the unlit cigar he was carrying toward the muscular giant in the center ring. "I said, 'He's all yours.' "

"*Mine?*"

"You're Maureen, aren't you?"

Momentarily taken aback, she could only nod.

"Then you own his contract."

Now she shook her head. "But—"

"And he owes you a fight."

Puzzled, she swung her gaze back to the subject of this bizarre discussion. The commercial developer had mentioned something to the effect that she would probably have to buy out some old boxer's contract when she sold the gym. But the man in the ring looked to be in his prime.

"How old is he?" she asked, still grappling with this surprising news.

"Thirty-eight."

"That's not old!" Only three years older than she, in fact.

"It is for a fighter."

Maureen examined the boxer a little closer, looking for flaws. He hadn't gone to fat, as aging athletes are wont to do. To the contrary, his inverted triangle of a chest tapered to a trim waist and, judging from the way that black satin fabric draped itself over them, taut hips.

Nor did he seem to have "lost his legs," to quote a former Royals' baseball player whose trophy room she had recently redecorated. Quite the opposite, in fact. The boxer's powerful thighs and balustrade calves provided the perfect blend of balance and leverage as he danced backward and forward and sideways across the canvas in a pugilistic ballet that literally left her breathless.

She fanned her face, which suddenly felt warm, with her flat ivory clutch purse. Then she caught herself and, quickly dropping her hand, asked a question off the top of her head. "How much does he weigh?"

"One-ninety." Her sidekick hitched up his pants, and she was surprised he didn't strangle himself. "That's stripped, of course."

Her voice, when she managed to find it again, came out in a squeak. "Of course."

"You oughtta put another fifteen pounds on him before you fight him again."

Maureen pointedly ignored that piece of advice. "Has he ever won anything?"

"The Golden Gloves title."

"I thought that was for amateurs." Even as she said it, she wondered what hidden corner of her mind that tidbit had popped out of.

"It is."

"Well, I meant professionally."

"Seventeen KO's in eighteen fights."

"KO's?" She frowned, trying to put words to the strangely familiar térm.

"Knockouts."

"Right." Now she smiled, inordinately pleased to have that clarified. "What happened in the eighteenth fight?"

For the first time since he'd walked up and started talking to her, the man hesitated. He clamped the cold cigar between his teeth with fingers that were short and stubby and stained tobacco-brown. Then he chewed the stogie from one side of his mouth to the other before removing it and flicking the nonexistent ash onto the floor.

"Technical knockout," he said in a clipped tone.

She tipped her head inquiringly. "Which means?"

"The referee called the fight in the second round."

"Why?" She saw the reluctance in his pale blue eyes and realized she probably wasn't going to get an answer.

He proved her right when he gestured toward the ring and said with gravelly pride, "Now, was that sonofagun bred for battle, or what?"

Maureen responded more to the tone of his voice than to the visual impact of the boxer's shadow falling across the canvas like a double dare. "He's tall."

"Six foot one."

Her stomach fluttered as a gloved hand flashed through the air like heat lightning. "And he's certainly got long arms."

"Seventy-seven-inch reach."

A gruesome thought occurred to her. "He doesn't take steroids, does he?"

That earned a chuckle. "He's so anti-drug, he'd give an aspirin a headache."

"Well, he's"—she faltered slightly at the sight of that naked back—"extremely well-built."

"He works out every day, rain or shine."

"I see." Michelangelo's *David*, come to life and clad in black satin trunks—that's what she saw.

"Feel his biceps if you get a chance, and you'll find he's ninety-two percent muscle."

The man's suggestion brought Maureen back to earth with a bang. She had no intention of feeling the boxer's biceps. Or any other portion of his anatomy. But her palms —those traitors!—had a mind of their own. They just itched to feel the softness of his bare flesh, the heat and steel that rippled beneath.

Clutching her purse before her with both hands, she steered the discussion to safer ground. "What's his name?"

"Jack Ryan." No sooner had he filed that away for future reference than he added, "But Sully—God rest his soul—always carded him 'The Irish Terror.'"

The moment Sully's name came up, Maureen's heart slid down the cellar door of her childhood fantasies. She'd thought she'd outgrown these feelings—the secret wonderings and the silent yearnings for this absentee father despite a constant shower of affection from her adoptive father. But deep inside the woman who presented such an icy façade in her personal and professional dealings, there burned a desperate longing for something she could never have. Sully's love. It was too late for that.

Somehow, she managed to keep her voice composed and the conversation on track. "'The Irish Terror' being the name Mr. Ryan fights under, I presume?"

"His ring name, right."

"It sounds like a play on Irish tenor."

"Knowing Sully, it probably was."

Her heart took another dip, and she wondered if it was destined to do so with every mention of his name. Overriding her concern, however, was a natural curiosity about the man who, until his will was filed after a second, fatal heart attack, had seemingly forgotten she even existed.

"He enjoyed word games?" She decided this was as good a time as any to begin satisfying that gnawing need to know.

"He was no English major, if that's what you're asking."

"Oh, no, I just—"

"But if he came up with a nickname for you—and he came up with some doozies in his day—it stuck."

"Give me an example," she prompted.

"Well, take me for instance." The grizzled man poked himself in the chest with the butt of his cigar. "He called me Duck for so many years, I've clean forgotten my given name."

Maureen did a double take, wondering if she'd heard him correctly. "Duck?"

His milky blue eyes, submerged beneath bushy gray brows, twinkled mischievously. "As in 'Sorry, Sully, I forgot to duck.'"

"You were a boxer?"

"With a glass jaw."

She wasn't sure what that meant, but it didn't sound good. "That's too bad."

Duck shrugged pragmatically. "Trainers last longer than flyweights, anyway."

Maureen looked at him with new respect. "So you're a trainer now?"

He puffed up with masculine pride. "A cut-man too."

"And everyone calls you Duck?"

"Only if they want me to answer 'em."

She threw her head back and laughed.

"When you were a baby, Sully called you Carrot Top."

Duck's revelation drove the smile from her lips. She knew that Seamus Sullivan was responsible for both the red of her hair and the green in her eyes. But out of fairness to Paul Bryant, she'd refused to dwell on any physical resemblance to the man who'd given her life and then given her up in a court of law.

So why did she suddenly feel so moved by the simple fact that he'd given her a nickname? Even a silly nickname like Carrot Top?

"Is that how you knew me?" she demanded. "By the color of my hair?"

"That, plus the fact I've seen your picture," Duck said, as if that explained everything.

It didn't, of course, and Maureen shook her head, more confused than ever. But before she could ask him when and where he'd seen her picture, he turned to hail four teenage boys who came tearing into the gym.

From their flattops and buzz cuts to their hightops and motorcycle boots, they looked to be in their mid-teens—about the same age as the gang who'd confronted her outside. But where those boys had flaunted their street colors and looks of surly defiance, these boys wore green satin starter jackets bearing SULLIVAN'S FIGHT GYM logos and exuded an air of excitement.

"We'll talk later, up in the office," Duck promised over his shoulder. "But right now, I've gotta collect their homework."

"Homework?"

"To prove they've been to school today."

"But school's out." At least it was for her secretary's children.

"Not for them."

Maureen opened her mouth to ask why, then closed it again and let him go without further comment. Considering his age, Duck was surprisingly light on his feet as he hustled over to the street door she'd entered a few moments ago. Once there, he put up his dukes and bumped shoulders with each of the teenagers in some ridiculous macho greeting ritual.

The clean-cut quartet finally settled down and opened the schoolbooks they carried. One by one, they unfolded the looseleaf notebook pages inside and handed them over. Like a checker in a parking lot, Duck traded their papers for small, shiny keys that he fished from the pocket of his gaudy sportcoat.

Keys in hand, the boys raced each other to the door marked LOCKER ROOM and clambered noisily down the stairs. Their laughter and friendly shouts reverberated back up to the gym as Duck cleared the clutter off a metal folding chair with a sweep of his arm. He sat down and began browsing through the stack of papers in his possession.

Maureen, realizing she was on her own for the time being, turned her attention back to the boxer.

She'd yet to get a good look at his face, but she could just picture the cauliflower ears and flattened nose—not to mention the ugly scars—that were the inevitable result of such a violent career. To top it off, a little voice inside her said, he was probably so punch-drunk that trying to talk business with him would be a waste of both her time and her breath.

If she had an ounce of sense, she thought, she'd walk out of here now and let her lawyer handle this. Yet she stood transfixed, awed by the beauty of the beast.

The reflection of the overhead light flickered across the rippling musculature of his torso. Sweat sheened his sun-baked skin and dampened the dark pelt of hair that bisected his massive chest. Veins mapped his biceps like the road to ruin for his hapless opponents.

He was the ultimate hard body. A lean, mean fighting machine, honed to perfection by years of rigorous training.

And to think, he was all hers . . .

• • •

She looked as delicate as a butterfly, but she was as dangerous as a bulldozer.

Jack Ryan unleashed a mental stream of curses and a potent flurry of jabs when the willowy redhead didn't go on up to the office after Duck went to check the boys in.

It wasn't bad enough that she'd waited thirty years before deigning to grace the place with her presence. Or that once she finally did come around, she'd kept up a running dialogue with the gabby trainer that had ruined his concentration. Now she was just standing there staring at him as if he'd grown an extra head or something.

Jack knew who she was. Hell, he'd have to be blind not to, after the way Sully used to collar him every couple of months and shove the latest picture of his precious Maureen in his face. That she was even more of a knockout in person, with her father's Celtic coloring and her mother's classic features, didn't change his opinion of her for the better.

Because he knew damned good and well why she was here.

That lounge lizard who passed himself off as a commercial developer had seen to that. After failing to persuade Sully to sell him the gym so he could raze it and replace it with a go-go bar, Lenny Marks had strolled in here last week and announced that the long-lost daughter had all but signed on the dotted line.

Jack had ached to wipe that grin off Marks's smug face. Or maybe even wipe the floor with him. But rather than risk a lawsuit for assault and battery, he'd just smiled and said, "Your toupee's crooked," sending the asshole scurrying out the door in search of some more glue and a mirror.

It was funny in retrospect but not in reality. The neighborhood had enough trouble now; the last thing it needed was another damn bar.

Anger—a lifetime's worth—fueled the next punch Jack threw. It sang in his veins like a savage refrain and pumped adrenaline through his system as he delivered a vicious roundhouse right that hit nothing but air.

But like a blast from the past, he could suddenly feel the crunch of bone and gristle through his glove. Could see the blue-white lights of the flashbulbs popping all around him. As crazy as it sounded, he could hear the roar bursting from the collective throat of the crowd as his opponent crumpled to the canvas. Could smell the metallic odor of blood oozing from the other fighter's nose and mouth and —oh Christ, no!—his eyes and ears. Bitter as bile, he could taste the satisfaction of a good punch gone bad as the referee shoved him into his corner and called for a doctor.

Jack blinked the present into focus and realized he'd just suffered another flashback. It hadn't lasted but a few seconds. They never did. Yet, as always, it left him sweating and shaking and swearing like a drunken sailor.

Irrationally, perhaps, he blamed the elegantly dressed wrecking ball who'd yet to take her eyes off him. She'd revived times better forgotten and differences best remembered. A couple of one-two combinations later, he decided he should probably thank her. She'd also reminded him that there were still some things in life worth fighting for.

The boys came barreling up out of the locker room and into the gym, ready to begin their warm-ups and raring to get into the ring with the champ.

Former champ, Jack amended, his pride stinging as he fired a four-punch fusillade that said he still had his stuff. But, hell, it was better to be a former somebody than a friggin' nobody. And a nobody with a number across his chest was exactly what he would've been without Seamus Sullivan's gruff but affectionate guidance.

He'd been a high-school dropout with nothing but a rap sheet to his name and nowhere to go but jail when Sully broke his fall by convincing the judge to release him into his custody on one condition. The condition being that he join the neighborhood fight club.

If Jack thought he'd gotten off easy—and in the back of his mind, he did—he was in for a real shock when he reported to the gym that first day.

"Boxing is hard work," Sully had said through a cloud of cigar smoke. "And trying to be a contender—the man coming up—is even harder."

"What's in it for me?" he'd demanded selfishly.

"A title, if you've got the legs and the brains and the heart to go the distance." Sully had sat back in his swivel chair and put his feet on the desk, looking at him long and hard. "What you've got now—nothing—if you don't."

Jack had balked at that. Who wanted to get up at five-thirty in the morning and jog in that mugger's paradise that was euphemistically called a park? Jump rope like some stupid sissy, then do sit-ups and deep-knee bends until his muscles quivered and screamed for relief? Sweat and bleed and sacrifice with no promise of a payoff in the long run?

But he really hadn't had much choice in the matter. It was either the fight club or the county jail. So he'd decided to play around with boxing for a while, figuring he'd at least have the freedom to come and go as he pleased, only to find himself working harder than he'd ever dreamed possible. And enjoying every minute of it.

As he'd built up his wind, Jack had discovered that the park was different by day. The grass, what there was of it, was spongy with dew. The air was still sweet at dawn, before gasoline fumes polluted it. To top it off, the drunks he used to roll under cover of darkness had disappeared with the rising sun.

And when he'd bulked up his body, he'd found that people in the neighborhood respected him. Not only on the strength of his physical appearance, but because they recognized him as a genuine contender. Even the cops who used to haul him down to headquarters at the first hint of trouble just smiled and saluted when he sprinted by.

There weren't any shortcuts for getting into the ring, though. There were rules, something he'd rarely had at home and never had on the streets. And there were temptations, seeing his old friends smoking and drinking and staying out all night and sleeping in all day.

A month into his training schedule, Jack had rebelled. Screw this early-to-bed-early-to-rise crap! he'd thought. He wanted to catch up with the guys, then he wanted to pick up a girl—the hotter the better. Screw the meat-vegetable-milk diet, too. He wanted a beer—the colder the better. And screw that old man for making him wait until he was "ready" to get into the ring. He wanted to tear someone's head off—the sooner the better.

He'd gotten everything he wanted, all right. The guys had greeted him like a brother, the girl had gone down as smoothly as the beer, and someone had come up missing two front teeth in a back-alley brawl. But at some point during the smoky, sticky blur of that lost weekend, somewhere between Friday night's anarchy and Monday morning's agony, he'd realized he wanted something else.

He wanted to be somebody. Somebody special. He wanted to be a champion. But he sure as hell wasn't going to win any titles lying on the kitchen floor in a pool of ice-cold sweat and regurgitated regrets.

Sully hadn't berated him when he'd dragged his errant butt back to the gym. Neither had he babied him. He'd simply met Jack's hangdog expression with flat green eyes and jerked his head in the direction of the balcony.

Another month of torturous self-discipline, of pounding the heavy bag for power and the peanut bag for speed and timing, had finally paid off. One morning Sully had called him up to the office and told him he was ready to get into the ring. Jack could hardly stand still while Duck taped his hands.

That had been the beginning of his reign. He'd scaled the amateur ladder at a dizzying pace, taking the National Golden Gloves title with a sensational knockout, only to have it end in tragedy during his professional ascent. Now, twenty years later, he was back where he'd started . . . but for entirely different reasons.

Jack tried to put the past behind him and focus on the footwork patterns he wanted to teach the boys today. Footwork patterns that were an essential part of a fighter's game plan. At practically every turn, however, he caught a glimpse of soft red hair shot through with gold sleeked away from a photogenic face he'd recognized the instant he'd stepped into the ring.

Looking back, he realized that he'd literally watched Maureen Bryant grow up from a pretty little girl in ribbons and lace into the designing woman she now was. She'd been a regular media darling, given her parents' social prominence and her own numerous accomplishments. And her biggest fan had been a sad old man whose only contact with her was a scrapbook full of lovingly preserved clippings.

Certain pictures stuck out in Jack's mind, mainly because they marked some major rite of passage in his own life.

Around the time she'd paraded her first pet, a shaggy black Scottie, past the dog-show judges, he'd made his first appearance in juvenile court. The same year she'd started ballroom dance classes, he'd entered reform school. While she'd been taking riding lessons at the Saddle & Sirloin Club, he'd been taking the name of the Marquis of Queensberry in vain at this very gym.

He doubted she even realized that the night she'd made her bow to society on Paul Bryant's proud arm, he'd made his professional debut under Sully's tongue-in-cheek ring name. Or that the summer she'd interned with one of the top decorators in town, he'd trained on a shoestring budget for his first televised bout. He doubted she'd care, either, that a couple of years before she'd opened her own shop to a splash of publicity, he'd quietly hung up his gloves and gone back to school.

On the one hand, Jack found it amazing that he knew so much about Sully's precious Maureen. On the other hand, he thought it amusing that she probably knew precious little about him.

Actually, he reflected as he took a final turn around the ring, that could work to his advantage. If she thought she was dealing with some punchy palooka with scrambled eggs for brains, she was in for a surprise. And surprise, as he'd learned during his streetfighting days, often resulted in a successful attack.

The boys, having finished their warm-ups in record time, began crowding around the steamroller in silk stockings who'd come to crush their dreams of going the distance.

Standing at the ropes, Jack wondered how Ms. Gucci Two-shoes would react if she knew she'd just been surrounded by a bunch of kids who still thought "designer" was a word that preceded "drugs." Or was it *Mrs.* now? He remembered Sully showing him the press announcement of her engagement a couple of years ago, but he couldn't recall ever seeing a follow-up article on her wedding.

Not that he cared, of course. Single or married, she was out of her element. A society decorator in a den of reformed thieves and recovering substance abusers. Worse yet—in his opinion, anyway—she was her mother's daughter.

A muscle flexed in Jack's jaw as he glared down at Maureen Bryant's upturned face. He wanted to grab her and shake her until her perfect teeth rattled. Rub that aristocratic nose in the lives that Sully had reclaimed before he died. He wanted, somehow, to force her to focus those sloe green eyes on the real legacy that her father had left her.

Instead, he propped his hands on his hips and inclined his head in a curt gesture that didn't even begin to express the contempt he felt for her kind. Then, addressing the boys but keeping his gaze riveted on the pearl-draped powder keg standing ringside, he growled, "Who's first?"

ROUND 2

Maureen snapped out of her daze and saw Jack Ryan, his legs braced apart in a fighting stance and his gloved hands buttressed upon his hips, scowling down at her from just inside the ropes.

Surely, she thought as she dredged herself up to a level of consciousness where his churlish "Who's first?" finally registered, he wasn't talking to *her*?

But his fearsome demeanor said otherwise. His curled lip told her he was serious. His flared nostrils echoed the sentiment. And when she met the twin brown flamethrowers of his eyes, she felt their impact like a blow to the abdomen.

"Me first!"

"Bull!"

"You went first yesterday!"

Maureen whirled at the sound of the scuffle taking place behind her. She'd been so lost in thought a few moments ago that she hadn't heard the boys come up from the locker room. Nor had she noticed how they'd crowded around her, trapping her between them and the ring.

Like Jack Ryan, they were decked out in boxing trunks and training gloves. Unlike the former champion, however, they'd yet to grow into their bodies. Their bones protruded like arrow tips from their shoulders, elbows and knees. And their feet, shod in black lace-up shoes, were so big that they were tripping all over them in their puppylike haste to reach their hero.

"Wait a minute, guys." Duck's ground-glass voice put an end to the shoving match. He'd vacated his metal folding chair and, homework papers in hand, was elbowing his way through the melee. "I'm missing an algebra assignment here."

"So?" one of the boys said belligerently.

The balding trainer was a head shorter than the blond teenager who'd just challenged him, but he wasn't taking any of his guff. After laying the looseleaf pages on a nearby chair, he straightened and said, "So you know the rules, Frankie."

"Algebra sucks!"

"Watch your language, boy."

The softly spoken warning sliced through the tension-filled air like a broadsword. All but one of the teenagers fell back. He stood alone in "The Irish Terror's" formidable shadow, his fair skin flushing with sudden blood.

Apparently everyone else in the gym sensed the sudden shift in the atmosphere too. Runners came to a dead stop. Weight lifters set down their barbells. Heads turned curiously from every corner of the facility.

Feeling as if she'd just entered a revolving door with no exit, Maureen pivoted back to the man in the ring.

"I believe you owe the lady an apology." Jack hitched his chin in her direction, but kept his gaze glued on the boy. He understood Frankie's frustration because he'd flunked algebra himself the first time around. Empathy aside, his job was to teach these kids some of the things their parents and teachers either couldn't or wouldn't. Things like self-discipline and perseverance and—Lord help him—manners.

The beleaguered Frankie seemed inclined to argue with the boxer's suggestion. His eyes flashed blue fire. His nostrils narrowed on an indrawn breath. But what finally came out of his mouth was a mumbled "Sorry, ma'am."

Maureen felt a peculiar tightness in her chest as she accepted his apology with a small nod and a gracious smile. She had a sudden urge to put her arm around his bony shoulders and give him a hug. Tell him that she'd heard worse—much worse—from the construction crews she worked with. Because she wasn't used to acting on impulse, though, she held back. Then immediately regretted doing nothing.

"See you tomorrow, Frankie." Jack spoke in the same temperate tone he'd used to elicit the apology, though there was no mistaking that he meant what he said. He just hated sending a kid out that door, knowing the dangers that lurked beyond. But rules were rules. And if he didn't enforce them, there was no sense in having them.

When the boy turned and started for the locker room, Duck gave him a friendly wallop between the shoulder blades to show him there were no hard feelings. "I'll be along in a minute to help you unlace your gloves."

"I can do it myself," Frankie asserted, rebellious to the last.

Peace restored, Jack smiled down at the remaining teenagers. "Now, who's first?"

Three gloved hands shot up in response.

"Jamal, Tony, Deron." Duck ticked off their names in the order they were going to fight as he strapped protective headguards on each of them.

Maureen's relief that Jack Ryan no longer posed a threat to her congealed into horrified disbelief when she realized that the teenagers had been his target from the beginning. She hadn't opened her mouth even once during the earlier exchange, a sin of omission on her part. But now, determined to prevent disaster from taking place before her very eyes, she grabbed hold of Duck's gaudy jacket tail to keep him from taking off.

"You can't let those boys get into the ring with that man!" she cried.

He looked at her as if she'd grown horns. "Why not?"

She pointed out the obvious. "They're half his size, for heaven's sake!"

"And growing like weeds," he said proudly.

"But he's a professional boxer."

"Who still owes you a fight."

She set her teeth. "He'll hurt them."

"He never has before."

"Are you saying this is something that happens on a regular basis?" She gaped at Duck, aghast.

"Five days a week, year-round." He took advantage of her slack grip to smooth down his jacket tail.

"Who came up with this crazy idea, anyway?"

"Sully."

Maureen bit her lip, finding it easier to hear his name but difficult to believe he'd been so deliberately cruel. "Why would he do something like that?"

"Like what?" Duck sounded genuinely puzzled.

She gestured toward the ring, where Jamal, his black eyes shining with excitement, was climbing through the ropes that Jack Ryan was holding open for him. "Pit teenage boys against a professional fighter."

A wide smile sprang to Duck's face as Jamal headed for his corner to prepare for the fight and Tony and Deron cranked up their gloved fists and called out words of encouragement. "To keep 'em out of trouble."

"By putting them in the hospital?"

"By getting 'em off the streets."

Thinking back to the gang on the stoop, she could see a certain logic in that.

"Between school and boxing," he added, "our boys don't have time for jacking."

"Jacking?"

"Street talk for stealing."

Her heart sank as her beautiful silver Mercedes streaked before her eyes. At the same time, the two fighters came out of their respective corners and met in the center of the ring. She decided to forget about her car, figuring it was probably gone by now anyway, and waited to see what happened next.

Jack Ryan and Jamal stood immobile for a moment, their bodies poised at full height and the overhead light pouring down upon them. One was larger of limb and bone, the epitome of masculine grace, while the other exuded a youthful vigor that promised a good showing. Yet both reminded Maureen of superb statuary, molded in bronze to last through the ages.

When they raised their hands and touched gloves, challenging each other to combat like gladiators of old, she was profoundly moved by the formality of the sportsmanship. There was—for lack of a better word—a gentleness there that seemed totally out of keeping with the violence that was to follow.

And follow it did.

Standing right up against the ring, unaware that she'd even stepped forward, Maureen heard every grunt and groan as the former champion and the fearless teenager went toe-to-toe.

"Head down . . . guard up." Duck bounced on the balls of his feet as he urged both fighters on in a gravelly patois that was probably indigenous to any dingy gym. "Snap it out . . . now spin . . . spin!"

"Awwwright!" Tony and Deron cheered collectively when Jamal slipped a jab by bobbing to his left.

Awwright! Maureen echoed silently, caught up completely in the fervor of the moment.

But her excitement turned to revulsion when Jamal took it on the chin. It happened so fast, she had no warning of it, was unprepared for the lightning bolt of Jack Ryan's gloved right connecting with the boy's lower jaw. Jamal staggered backward, then bent over and spit something white out of his mouth.

"His *teeth!*" she shrieked hysterically.

Everyone in the gym, Jamal and Jack Ryan included, looked at Maureen as though she'd gone stark, staring mad. But she had eyes only for the man in the ring.

"You knocked out his teeth, you . . . you animal!" she screamed at him.

"Wait a minute—" Duck began.

But his warning fell on deaf ears. Intent on rescuing the injured teenager, Maureen dropped her purse and, her high heels and confining skirt be damned, scrambled up onto the apron of the ring and slipped between the ropes. The canvas was surprisingly springy as she stalked toward Jack Ryan with both hands fisted, prepared to take him on herself if he tried to prevent her from taking Jamal out.

"Why don't you pick on someone your own size, you overgrown neighborhood bully?" she taunted, never stopping to think that, at five-eight in her stocking feet and one-hundred-thirty pounds fully dressed, she didn't even remotely resemble that someone.

Maureen was almost within striking distance of her rock-hewn target when Jamal reached down and picked up a waxy white mouthpiece. The realization that it wasn't his teeth he'd spit out, after all, brought her to an abrupt standstill. And the ripples of laughter floating up from her ringside audience had her wishing that the canvas would simply open up and swallow her.

"I'm sorry, Mr. Ryan." She began backing toward the ropes, wondering how she would ever live this down. "Really, I am." She continued to babble her apologies while trying to make a graceful exit. "I just thought . . . I mean, from where I was standing . . ."

How she got caught up in the ropes was a complete mystery to Maureen. One minute she was holding the bottom two down and the top two up so she could slip through them. The next, she was riding the bottom ones, with her legs astraddle the black-taped hemp and the hem of her linen skirt creeping up to Lord knows where, and hanging on to the top ones for dear life.

As she jockeyed to keep her balance, she felt a hairpin slide down the back of her neck. It joined several others that seemed to have found a home inside her suit jacket. The heavy curls she'd so carefully confined that morning tumbled free, spilling past her padded shoulders.

The men outside the ring were no help. Duck was so slack-jawed he was in danger of losing his cigar. Tony and Deron were, quite simply, bug-eyed with astonishment. And everyone else seemed too engrossed in her show of leg to realize she was in serious trouble.

As a last resort, she looked to the man inside the ring, whom she'd castigated so unmercifully—and, yes, she admitted it, unfairly—just a few moments ago.

"Please," she whispered, begging both his forgiveness and his help.

Except for spitting out his mouthpiece, Jack hadn't moved a muscle since she'd gone ballistic on him. He wanted to think she'd gotten exactly what she deserved. That she was hoisted by her own petard. But then he remembered how fearlessly she had come to Jamal's defense, jumping into the fray as if common sense and care for her own safety were the last things on her mind. And most of all, he remembered that she was Sully's daughter.

"Hang on," he said grudgingly as he started toward her. "I've got to take my gloves off."

Maureen shuddered, endangering her precarious position, as she watched him tear at the leather laces with his strong white teeth. He was like a wild animal trying to free himself from a hunter's trap. Then she shuddered again, feeling her sweaty palms beginning to slip and fretting that she was going to end up falling onto the hard floor below. He was also her only hope.

Jack tucked his hands under opposite arms and pulled off his gloves, letting them drop to the canvas with a dull thud. Knowing that time was of the essence, he didn't bother removing the gauze and tape wrapped between his fingers and over his knuckles. He simply reached to extricate this feisty redheaded nemesis from the cat's cradle she'd made of the ropes.

She froze, afraid that after the terrible names she'd flung at him he would probably just push her over the edge.

But his left hand slid under the top ropes, lending support to her clammy fingers, and his corresponding foot stabilized the bottom ones. "When I tell you to, I want you to let go."

Too relieved to argue, she could only nod.

"First, though, I want you to swing your leg over the bottom ropes so that you're sitting facing me."

She lost one of her shoes and what remained of her modesty when she brought her leg up and over and down. At the same time, she swiveled—and found herself staring at the sculpted bulge behind the front seam of his black satin boxing shorts. The memory of the jockstrap she'd seen earlier emblazoned itself across her mind, and she felt a flush begin to creep up from her navel.

"Now let go of the ropes and grab hold of my . . ."

Maureen shut her eyes and cringed, waiting for him to finish his crude suggestion.

"Hand."

Blinking her eyes open, she saw his right hand extended down to her. Dumbstruck, she released the ropes and laid her damp palm in his partially taped one. His strong fingers closed over hers, and she caught a whiff of his musky male scent as he pulled her to her feet.

She listed before him, a pitiful figure with one shoe off and one shoe on, while he let the tautly strung ropes *thwang* back into place. Then she was lifted above him, his hands clamped firmly around her waist and her arms flailing wildly about his head as he prepared—or so she presumed—to throw her out of the ring.

Their eyes, hers a terrified green and his a turbulent brown, met at the same moment he elevated her over the ropes. She went down, down, down then, just knowing he was going to drop her. But her fear proved unfounded when he gently deposited her onto the gym floor.

"Thank you," she whispered, trying to forget the feel of his hands on her body even as her skin tingled a reminder beneath her clothes.

"My pleasure," he declared in a husky voice, his expression both troubled and tender as he continued to stare down into her eyes.

Amenities exchanged, they finally broke their visual bond.

That might have been that. But as Jack gazed out over the gym, he realized that Maureen Bryant's backside had become the center of attention. And with good reason too. For no sooner had she finished shaking her jacket out, smoothing her skirt down, and slipping her shoe on than she bent over to pick up her purse and hairpins.

Somewhat disgruntled to discover that he didn't like the way the other men were ogling her, he whipped off his headguard and barked, "Show's over, guys."

Maureen glanced up, wondering what *that* was all about, and got her first really good look at his face. She also got the shock of her life. In spite of the violent career path he'd chosen, Jack Ryan was virtually the most handsome man she'd ever seen.

He had a magnificent head, beautifully shaped like a bust from the Periclean Age in Greece and capped with curly, close-cropped brown hair. She took in the strong lines of his face, the stubborn jaw and spare cheekbones, the surprisingly sensual mouth and not-so-surprisingly bent nose. Except for the white scar above his left eyebrow, his skin was smooth and glistening with perspiration.

"I need a shower."

She realized he was talking to her and wondered how she was supposed to respond. By offering to wash his back? She felt an adolescent blush bathe her face as she suddenly saw her lathered hands gliding over his lean nakedness, saw her soapy fingertips tracing the steel column of his spine down to his taut . . .

The misty romance of the image sent her temperature rising. Her temper too. Fantasies were for foolish women with nothing better to do, not for businesswomen with places to go, people to see and eviction notices to serve.

"Shall I meet you up in the office in, say, ten minutes?" she asked, her tone unnecessarily sharp.

"Suits me," Jack agreed with a grin. He had to admit, she had the princess act down pat. Even with her fiery hair falling into her shamrock eyes and her freckles defying their artful camouflage job, she was every inch the lady.

But he was no gentleman. Had never claimed to be. So he felt absolutely no compunctions about checking out the body by *Vogue* and the legs that seemed to stretch from here to Chicago. Nor did he suffer even the teeniest twinge of conscience as he wondered if she wore something pretty and lacy under that prim linen suit.

"I'll see you shortly, then." Maureen wanted, badly, to escape his bold perusal. In the last few minutes he'd had either his eyes or his hands on more parts of her body than she cared to recall, and now—now he'd had the unmitigated gall to let his gaze move over her as if he were mentally undressing her.

Her posture book-on-the-head perfect, she turned on her heels and hurried toward the stairs. She bypassed the balcony level, where a lone boxer was punching a huge bag that hung from the ceiling, and took the last few steps at a near run. Her blood thundered in her ears as she reached for the office doorknob.

She told herself it was because she was out of shape, that

she needed to start going to her health club on a regular basis again. Then she told herself it was a combination of hunger and heat that caused her to feel this way. She'd worked on finishing up a design proposal for that new office complex instead of eating lunch, not knowing how long she'd be stuck down here, and then she'd walked into this blast furnace.

Her real problem, though—the reason her breath was backing up in her lungs—was that Jack Ryan had knocked her for a loop. Coming in, she'd assumed he was just some ugly old palooka for whom the bell had already tolled. All beef and brutality, with a brain wattage inversely proportional to his muscle power.

What next? she wondered now. A Phi Beta Kappa key? The "Jeopardy" Tournament of Champions? She didn't think so, but she couldn't say for sure. And it was that uncertainty, more than the lack of exercise, food or air-conditioning, that made her such a Nervous Nellie.

The office was the first pleasant surprise she'd had since she'd set foot in this house of ill dispute. Oh, the walls were painted that same industrial-strength green and were papered with posters of Golden Boys past. But someone had swept the floor and dusted the top of the scarred but still-serviceable desk. While they were at it, they'd even washed the windows, both the one that fronted the street and the one overlooking the gym.

She opened the first of two doors along the far wall, hoping to find a bathroom where she could repin her hair and pull herself together, only to discover it led to a closet.

A bare light bulb dangled from the ceiling and a folded cot stood in the corner. Flannel shirts and work pants hung from the wooden rod. A pair of brown leather shoes, scuffed at the toes and worn down at the heels, sat beneath them. Books and towels and papers were neatly stacked on the shelves above them.

"What're you looking for?"

Startled, Maureen spun and saw that Duck had followed her upstairs. Along the way he'd rid himself of the cigar. She answered his question with one of her own. "Whose clothes?"

"Sully's."

"Why are they here instead of his home?"

"This *was* his home."

She drew in a sharp breath. "He lived *here?*"

Duck nodded. "He moved in after the divorce."

A lump of sadness formed in Maureen's throat at the thought of Sully bedding down every night on that awful cot and waking up every morning in this airless room. She'd come here in search of the truth. But this truth was almost more than she could bear.

The steady *boom-boom-boom* echoing up from the balcony level played counterpoint to the soft click of the closing door.

She cleared her throat and eyed the other door ambivalently.

"What're you looking for?" Duck asked her a second time.

"A bathroom."

"In there."

"I'll only be a minute."

The bathroom wasn't fancy by any stretch of the imagination. Both the white porcelain commode and the matching pedestal sink were cracked with age. Like the office, though, they were relatively clean, and that was all that really mattered.

Maureen almost died when she saw herself in the beveled medicine-chest mirror. She had eaten off her lipstick, her hair was flying every which way, and her freckles were sending an SOS from the bridge of her nose. Fortunately, she had time to repair the damage before she got down to business.

She attacked her hair first, managing to restore it to

some semblance of its sleeked-back neatness. A touch of lip gloss and a dusting of powder, and she almost looked like herself again. Finally, she tore a paper towel off the roller, wet it and held it to her nape in the hope it would help cool her off.

Just remembering what a fool she'd made of herself in front of all those men made her flush anew with embarrassment. Her only comfort was that, after today, she would never have to see any of them again. "The Irish Terror" included.

Maureen suppressed an absurd pang of regret at the latter. Despite the fact he was a walking work of art, the man was a Philistine. He made his living beating up on other men. Teenagers too. He probably treated women even worse, roughing them up just for the fun of it.

That being her reasoning, why did she have to forcibly eject the memory of Jack Ryan's gently mocking grin from her mind?

"Are you all right?" Duck called through the closed door.

She started guiltily. No, she wasn't all right. Her imagination was behaving completely out of character, and she didn't know how to deal with it. She couldn't tell him that, of course, so she tossed the paper towel into the trash, picked up her purse and scurried out of the bathroom.

"Feel better?"

"Much." She walked purposefully to the window that fronted the street and looked out. Then she breathed a sigh of relief at the sight of her car still parked at the curb. She recalled Duck's words about getting the boys in the gym off the streets, and found herself wondering if it was too late for the gang that had accosted her.

Ridiculous, she thought, and definitely not her problem.

She caught a glint of metal from the corner of her eye and glanced at the clean beanbag ashtray sitting in a corner of the windowsill. Its plaid bottom had faded to a muddy brown and its brass bowl had tarnished slightly over time.

The image of a fat hand-rolled cigar resting there, smoke rising from its glowing red tip, suddenly flickered in the back of her mind.

More ridiculous yet, she decided, turning back to Duck.

He waved his arm, encompassing the room. "Look familiar?"

"Should it?" she asked blankly, the smell of that phantom cigar smoke still pungent in her nostrils.

"Considering you used to drag all your dolls up here and play tea party with 'em, I should say so." He indicated Sully's old swivel chair behind the desk.

Maureen sat, too stunned to speak, as a memory she hadn't even realized she'd retained came back with haunting clarity. In her mind's eye she could suddenly see a little girl clutching a fragile porcelain doll and crying into her pillow for the daddy who'd missed her birthday party. Determined not to disgrace herself any more than she already had, she dammed up those tears before they could burst through the years and slipped her polite social mask back in place.

"You mentioned something earlier about having seen my picture," she reminded him.

Duck hooked his thumbs in his waistband and hitched up his pants. "In the scrapbook, right."

"What scrapbook?" she asked, her interest piqued.

"The one Sully kept."

"He kept a scrapbook with my picture in it?"

"With a whole bunch of your pictures."

She shook her head incredulously. "But where would he get pictures of me?"

He shrugged. "From the newspaper—usually the society section—and from brochures for those designer showcases you've done for charity."

"You're kidding!"

"He even had a couple of clippings of you and that yuckie stockbroker you got engaged to."

"Yuckie?" She was too busy trying to figure out what he meant to tell him she'd broken her engagement.

"I think he means *yuppie*."

Maureen almost jumped out of her chair at the sound of that deep masculine voice. Then she whipped her head around and saw Jack Ryan filling the doorway.

His brown hair, still damp from the shower, curled like a crown of laurels upon his head. His blue warm-up jacket was partially unzipped, revealing entirely too much of his coppery chest for her comfort, while the matching shorts displayed his long muscular legs to perfection. His white athletic shoes were, she realized numbly, the largest she'd ever laid eyes on.

"Yuckie, yuppie," Duck said amiably, recapturing her attention. "The only picture Sully was missing was one of you getting married to the guy."

"That's because I didn't get married," she said shortly.

"Why not?"

"Because," she said through clenched teeth, "I didn't want to live and die by the Dow Jones Average."

"Well, that explains that," the balding trainer replied with a satisfied nod.

She didn't dare look for Jack Ryan's reaction to her news. "Where's the scrapbook?"

"On the closet shelf, I suppose." When she rose, Duck waved her off and reached for the doorknob. "I'll check."

Maureen remained standing as Jack Ryan came all the way into the office. She refused to be intimidated by either his size or his clean, spicy scent wafting across the desk— *her* desk now, she reminded herself. He might look sharp on the outside, but he was probably a little dull in the brains department.

With that in mind, she spoke in a tone she would use with her secretary's second-grader. "You know why I'm here, don't you?"

"You're going to sell the gym," he lashed back.

41

"I have a buyer."

"A slimeball."

Reflexively, she pressed her hand to her chest and demanded, "What would *I* do with a fight gym?"

"Probably paint it pink and turn it into one of those fancy fitness clubs," he scoffed.

"Well, you have to admit it could use a paint job," she responded in kind.

"Nope." Duck came out of the closet with a large stack of towels in his arms. "The scrapbook's not in there."

"It was on the top shelf the last time I saw it," Jack said.

"Somebody must've moved it, then." Duck hit for the door that led downstairs, almost losing the top two towels in the process. "I'll look around the locker room after I hang these up for the boys."

"I was just in the locker room," Jack called after him, "and it wasn't there."

"That you know of," the trainer said as he closed the door.

Maureen felt as if she'd just joined a Keystone Kops movie in mid-reel. "Seriously, now, Mr. Ryan—"

"Jack."

She blinked. "I beg your pardon?"

"Around here, I'm just plain Jack."

With those dark chocolate eyes and that disarming grin, he was anything but plain. She cleared her throat and started again. "Okay, Jack—"

"Or Champ."

She counted to ten. "Fine."

"I answer to either one."

"Now that we've got that settled," she said, thinking her teeth were going to be ground to nubs before this was over, "would you mind telling me what you think I would do with a fight gym?"

"Make a difference in people's lives."

"That's a pretty vague statement."

Jack spun and stalked to the window overlooking the main floor. He was enough of a realist to know he couldn't save the world by running the gym. He was just one guy. But if he could save just one kid, the way Sully had saved him, then his work was worth the effort.

"Come here, Maureen."

She'd neither asked him to use her name nor given him permission to do so. "Why?"

"You want specifics, right?"

"Not really."

He recalled the use-'em-and-abuse-'em example set by a violent father and successfully resisted the urge to drag her over by her hair. "Well, I'm going to give you some anyway."

With an impatient sigh, she joined him at the window.

Jamal had left the ring and now the boy whom Duck had called Tony was taking his turn against a tall man who wasn't cutting him any slack. Her face paled when a right to the stomach caused poor Tony to back off and bend over, much as Jamal had earlier. Then the teenager shook it off and came back swinging.

"I don't understand it," she said softly.

"What?" Jack glanced down, saw how upset she was and gentled his voice.

"Why those boys want to come here."

"It's their chance to hit back."

She looked up at him inquiringly. "Hit back?"

He could smell her perfume. Something cool and appealing and expensive. Just like her. Angry with himself for even noticing, he pointed to Jamal, who was giving Tony the Arsenio Hall wave. "At the people who've hurt them."

"Like who?"

"Abusive parents, for one."

"Jamal's parents are abusive?"

"To punish him, his mother used to take him to the basement, tie one end of a rope around his neck, throw the

43

other end up over one of the supporting beams and leave him standing on tiptoes." Jack raked aggravated fingers through his hair. "If he tried to stand flat-footed, he'd hang himself."

Maureen, whose sole experience with corporal punishment was being swatted on the bottom with a carpet slipper, shivered at the image that suddenly reared its ugly head. She read the newspapers and watched television, so she knew that child abuse was a problem of epidemic proportions in this country and in these times. She'd just never known anyone who'd lived through it. Until now.

"Where was his father when this was happening?" she asked.

"Who knows?" he answered with a slow shrug.

"He doesn't live with the family?"

"He probably doesn't even know he has a son."

Maureen wasn't sure how much more of this she could take. Against her better judgment, she pointed to Tony. "Who's he hitting back?"

Jack's eyes followed the elegant length of her finger. "The entire English-speaking world."

"That doesn't make much sense."

"Unless you've been raised by migrant parents who don't speak English and you're a pupil in a school district that demands you read and write it."

She remembered Tony's jubilant "Awwwright!" when Jamal slipped that jab. "I assume he's in bilingual classes."

"Going on two years now."

"And Deron?" she prompted finally.

He fed her the full load. "Booze for breakfast, lunch and dinner, crack for snacks."

Her stomach tied itself in knots. "It's a wonder he's still alive."

"He's taking it a day at a time now that he's in training."

"I'm assuming he got the drugs on the street," she said. "But where would someone his age buy liquor?"

"Same place you and I bought it when we were his age."

Maureen pursed her lips primly. "I didn't even attempt to buy liquor until I was twenty-one."

Jack snorted and almost slipped. "Then you, Ms. Gu— Goody Two-shoes, are the rare exception."

Frankie came out of the locker room. Dressed in a T-shirt and jeans, he stood by himself, watching as Tony finished up in the ring and Deron got ready to take his place. His pale face contorted, first with longing and then with loathing. Finally losing the battle with his own private demons, he spun on his heels and stomped out the door.

"He forgot his jacket," Jack muttered under his breath.

Maureen was surprised by the concern in his voice. "I figured you'd say 'good riddance.' "

"To tell you the truth," he admitted reluctantly, "he reminds me of myself at that age."

"A chip on his shoulder?" she ventured.

"The Rock of Gibraltar."

"A smart-aleck?"

"Rudest mouth west of the Mississippi."

She turned away from the window and started toward the desk. "Sounds bad."

He trailed behind her, studying the no-nonsense switch of her slender hips. "It's worse than you think."

Maureen did an about-face and caught him in the act. "How so?"

Jack felt like a clod, but grinned unrepentantly. "Armed robbery."

"Him or you?"

"Both."

She waited until she had the desk between them again to ask, "Who were you hitting back?"

"All of the above."

"Abusive parents?"

"Let me put it this way," he said as he flipped a metal chair around and straddled it so he was facing her. "Until I was big enough to stand up to him, my father never gave me anything but his beer breath and the back of his hand."

"And your mother?" she asked quietly.

"She died of internal bleeding and total despair when I was ten," he answered just as quietly.

She wanted to weep for the broken-hearted boy she suddenly saw in the man's brown eyes. She sat, suspecting he didn't want her sympathy, and folded her shaking hands on the scarred desktop. Desperate to keep it light, she said, "Funny, you don't look foreign."

"Dyslexia creates language barriers all its own."

"You couldn't read?"

"Not till Sully enrolled me in a remedial program."

Maureen felt a stab of resentment at the thought of Sully taking so much interest in a stranger's ability to read. *She* was his flesh and blood. But for all he seemed to have cared, she might as well have lived on the moon.

She realized it wasn't Jack's fault that her father had neglected her and nurtured him. He was just lucky enough to have been in the right place at the right time. Still, it hurt to acknowledge she'd been so easily replaced in Sully's affections.

"What about the drinking?" she asked then.

Jack's smile was just short of devilish. "I'll take the Fifth on that one."

Maureen laughed. "Sounds like you already did."

"Several of them, until I started training."

She sobered instantly. "And the drugs?"

"A joint now and then, but no Jones."

"Jones?"

"Addiction."

Her brow furrowed. "You said 'now and th—' "

"I haven't had a hit since—"

"You started training," she finished for him.

His eyes looked into hers across the desk. "God's truth."

She believed him with every fiber of her being. "So what

you're telling me, in essence, is that the gym was your salvation?"

He nodded. "That's it in a nutshell."

"And you, in turn—"

"Want to give these boys the same break Sully gave me."

"You must spend a lot of time here."

"I've spent my fair share of nights on that damned cot."

Maureen waffled for a moment, then took the plunge. "How does your wife feel about sitting home alone?"

Jack moved his shoulders in the way she now recognized as habit. "To quote Sully, 'A fightin' man's got no business being married.'"

"Too bad he didn't take his own advice." She meant to sound blithe, but knew she came off brittle.

"If he had," he said pointedly, "you wouldn't be sitting here today."

She rose and reached for her purse. "I'll admit there's a need for a place like this. I'll even admit your purpose is noble. But I have a business of my own to run."

He stayed put, wanting to play it cool. "You could maintain ownership of the gym and I could manage it for you."

"I have enough to do without the extra responsibilities of a fight gym and a bunch of troubled boys."

He waggled his eyebrows suggestively, and the white scar did a belly dance on his brow. "You could even paint the office pink."

"Brighter colors really would be better. More energetic, you know?" She realized what she was saying and wanted to bite her tongue. "I'll pass my suggestions along to Mr. Marks."

Jack stood up so fast, his chair fell on its side. He stepped over it, placed his hands on the desk and leaned forward. "Lenny Marks plans to tear down the gym and build a bar."

Maureen knew how badly that must upset him. "I'm

sorry to hear that," she said in all sincerity. "But maybe you can talk to him. Convince him to reconsider."

"When donkeys fly."

"Well, then, maybe I can talk to him."

"Have at it," he said agreeably. Then added for spite, "If you feel like wasting your breath."

A spasm of frustration crossed her face. "What do you want from me, anyway?"

He eyed her meaningfully.

Maureen shook her head. "No. Absolutely not."

A wintry smile came and went on Jack's lean visage. "Sully was afraid you'd feel that way."

"Then why did he leave me the gym?" Maureen's voice was as stiff as her back.

"You're his daughter."

"Not legally."

"He loved you."

"Oh, right." Deep inside the grown woman, a little girl suddenly wanted to cry. "He loved me so much, he gave me up for adoption."

Jack saw the tears welling in her eyes and felt like a world-class heel. "He loved you enough to want you raised in the proper atmosphere."

The *smack* of a fist hitting that huge bag on the balcony level, followed by a loud curse, punctuated his point.

Maureen controlled herself with effort. "If you're so committed to saving the gym, why don't you buy it?"

"I would if I had the money."

She glanced at her watch and realized she was running late for that house call in Mission Hills. "I read somewhere that fighters are among the highest paid athletes in this country."

His mouth twisted in a torque of exasperation. "I'm not denying I made some bucks in my day, but—"

"Excuse me," she said in a condescending tone as she cut around the desk, "I really do have to leave."

He stepped in front of her, blocking her exit. "Do you always do that?"

"What?"

"Cut people off in mid-sentence."

Her eyebrows vaulted into haughty arches. "I said, 'Excuse me.'"

His voice lowered to a dangerous level. "So it's not bad manners, just a good old-fashioned brush-off."

Their eyes met in a silent battle of wills. Sizzled in a scorched-earth clash of tempers. Then the door squealed open and they pulled back by tacit agreement.

"Nope," Duck said as he shuffled in, "the scrapbook's not in the locker room, either." He splayed his empty hands and smiled guilelessly at Maureen. "I guess you'll just have to come back tomorrow and see if we've found it yet."

She gaped at him in dismay. "Tomorrow?"

Jack remembered the inordinately large stack of towels Duck had carried out of the closet a little while ago and had a gut feeling he knew what that wily old fox was up to. He seriously doubted it would work, however. "Frankly, I think we've seen the last of our Ms. Bryant."

She was tempted to ask him what had become of the more-familiar *Maureen*. "It just so happens I'm busy tomorrow."

"Running your business, of course."

She replied to Jack's snide remark with a serene, "I'll leave my offer open until the end of the week, Mr. Ryan."

"What offer?"

Jack ignored Duck's question and demanded of her, "And just where am I supposed to get the money to buy the gym?"

"That's not my problem," she declared.

"From the fight you still owe her," Duck interjected.

"There you go," Maureen said, smiling down at the short

but spirited man who'd taken her side. "Put on a fight and use the proceeds to buy the gym."

Trapped between the beautiful redhead and the buttin-sky trainer, Jack gave serious thought to putting his fist through the wall. "It costs a small fortune and takes two months minimum to properly stage a fight."

But Duck was too far gone to listen to reason. He grabbed his beltless waistband with both hands and hiked up his pants. "I can see the headline now: Former Golden Gloves Champ Fights To Save Inner-City Gym."

"And think what good publicity it would be for the work you're doing with the boys," she added.

"Better yet," he said to Jack, "just think what good experience it'd be for 'em, sparring with you for a real fight."

"Please call me when you find the scrapbook," she told Duck by way of taking her leave.

"Will do," he promised.

She smiled dismissively at Jack as she opened her purse and reached for her car keys. "If I haven't heard from you by the end of the week, my attorney will contact you about buying out your contract."

"Fine."

Her fingers latched on to the eviction notice, which she'd forgotten to give him earlier. "Feel free to consult with your own attorney if there's anything in here that you don't understand."

His eyes flashed from the legal document she proffered to her face. The patronizing expression he saw there was the last straw. "Are you going to be embarrassed if I tell you that *I'm* an attorney?"

Maureen, realizing too late how badly she'd misjudged this man, could do nothing more than nod in reply.

For all his victories both in and out of the ring, Jack couldn't recall a single one he'd ever enjoyed as much as this. "Then start blushing."

ROUND 3

"*Then* what did you do?"

Maureen gave her secretary a rueful look across the storeroom worktable. "What do you think?"

"I think you turned . . ." Donna Martin pulled a binder of drapery samples off a wall peg and flipped through it until she found the one she wanted—a swatch of deep rose silk. "This color."

"If not darker," Maureen admitted, remembering all too well how her face had heated up after Jack Ryan had dropped his bombshell yesterday afternoon. If he had intended to make a fool of her—which she was certain he had—he could have succeeded no better. She'd let the eviction notice flutter from her fingers while she'd groped for words. Then, finding herself at a complete loss, she'd turned on her heel and stomped out of the office, slamming the door on his rogues'-gallery grin.

Now, determined not to dwell on her own gullibility, she reached for the shipping list that lay atop the new carpet samples. They had arrived from one of her suppliers last week, but between making house calls and drawing up design plans, she hadn't had time to inventory them until today. Eager to see what fresh colors and creative piles she could incorporate into her work, she pulled the top deckboard toward her and began browsing through it.

"Actually, I think it's kind of exciting."

Maureen looked up from the velvety, hunter green plush she couldn't wait to find a home for and nodded at the older woman across the table from her. "Me too."

Donna's eyes twinkled with laughter behind the lenses of her stylish tortoiseshell glasses. "Not the carpet samples."

"Then what?"

"Owning a fighter."

Now Maureen shook her neatly coiffed head. "I don't own Jack Ryan. He owes me . . . I mean, he still owed Sully—"

"Boxing is a very disciplined sport, you know," the other woman said as she hung up the drapery binder and went back to inserting replacement pages into a furniture catalogue.

"Do tell," Maureen shot back flippantly.

But Donna took her seriously. "It's the art of action over reaction. You either hit or get hit."

Maureen could hardly believe her ears. She propped an elbow on the deckboard, rested her chin in her palm and looked at her secretary as if she'd never seen her before.

Donna was forty-five going on thirty-five, living proof that a woman really could get better as she got older. She had a pixie haircut and a petite figure that belied she'd given birth to four children and the fact that she ate like a harvest hand. Her wardrobe was upscale and chic, which made a good first impression on Maureen's walk-in customers, and her ultimate goal was to become an interior designer herself. Toward that end, she was enrolled as a part-time student at the Kansas City Art Institute, taking classes from some of her boss's old teachers. And making straight A's, to boot.

"Where did you learn so much about boxing?"

"When I was a little girl I used to watch the Friday night fights on television with my father." Memory curved

Donna's mobile mouth into a smile. "I always bet him my quarter allowance, and I almost always lost."

Maureen was flabbergasted. "You *watched* the fights?"

"Then, on my tenth birthday, my father took me to see them in person."

"You *went* to the fights?"

"At Municipal Auditorium, in the Main Arena."

Maureen threw up her hands. "I can't believe it!"

Donna turned the catalogue page. "What?"

"You've worked for me for two years—"

"Almost three now."

"And we've discussed everything under the sun—"

"From PMS to Picasso."

"But you've never once in all that time mentioned that you like boxing."

"A lot of women like boxing," Donna said with a shrug.

"To each her own," Maureen returned wryly.

The telephone rang, and Donna grabbed the wall extension over the worktable, saying into the receiver, "Bryant's Interiors."

Maureen had agonized for months over what to call her shop. She'd thought of a dozen names, everything from the catchy By Design to the cutesy Designing Woman, in the singular, after the popular TV show. Finally she'd settled on the self-explanatory.

"Just a moment, Mr. Marks, I'll see if Ms. Bryant is available," Donna said, and put him on hold.

Lenny Marks was the last person on earth Maureen wanted to talk to right now. She hadn't promised to sell him the gym, only to consider his offer. She had, on the other hand, promised Jack Ryan the rest of the week to decide what he was going to do.

"Tell him I . . ." She didn't want to lie, so she slid off her stool and went to the delivery door. Then, standing in the alley out back, she smiled at Donna. "Stepped out for a moment."

"I'm sorry, Mr. Marks, but Ms. Bryant stepped out for a moment. . . ."

The alley, which was wide enough to accommodate the large delivery trucks turning in off hilly Broadway, was one of the reasons Maureen had been willing to pay through the nose for the two-story duplex where she lived and worked.

The unobstructed view from the front was the other. Her duplex faced south and overlooked the Country Club Plaza. Day or night, summer or winter, she never tired of looking at the stone statues, spraying fountains and Spanish-style architecture that made up the world-famous outdoor shopping area.

She might have appeared the dilettante at times, staring dreamily out the window with a cup of herbal tea in hand, but the artist within was always working. Once she'd drawn inspiration for a client's kitchen island from the mosaic tile work that sided Seville Square. And one dreary December evening she'd watched those miles of Christmas lights wink on and, in the blink of an eye, had realized she could brighten up a dark corner of yet another client's home by stringing small white bulbs on the silk ficus tree standing there.

"All clear," Donna called as she hung up the phone.

Maureen stepped back into the storeroom and closed the heavy metal door behind her. "Was he angry?"

"Actually, he sounded kind of nervous."

"Really?" Maureen had never met the man, but the one time she'd talked to him on the phone he'd come off as cocksure.

"He said he heard you went to the gym yesterday."

"He's got reason to be nervous," Maureen said, remembering Jack's remark about his wanting to build a bar. Then she remembered Jack's hands on her waist, his thumbs pressing on the tender center of her stomach and his fingers encasing her ribs. He'd lifted her as if she weighed no more than a feather, and it made her uneasy to know he could be so strong and yet so gentle.

"I'm starved," Donna declared, startling her out of the unwelcome reverie. "I think I'll call Bo Ling's."

"Is it lunchtime already?" Maureen glanced at her watch and saw that it was, indeed.

"Time flies when you're doing inventory," Donna said drolly. After placing her carryout order for Crab Rangoon, Moo Goo Gai Pan and fried rice, she tipped up the mouthpiece and asked, "Do you want anything?"

"No, thanks." If she ate a heavy meal in the middle of the day, all Maureen wanted to do the rest of the day was sleep. "I stuck a strawberry-and-spinach salad in my office refrigerator when I came downstairs this morning, so I'll eat that if I get hungry."

"Don't work too hard," Donna toodled on her way out.

Maureen conjured up a smile but couldn't bring herself to pick up where she'd left off before Lenny Marks's phone call.

Usually she could lose herself in her work with no trouble at all. She loved fabric—from the slub of fine silk to the slight roughness of French ticking. Color, too, from the jewel tones of garnet and amethyst to the cool tints of blue and green. Yet here she sat, surrounded by the beautiful tools of her trade but unable to eradicate the recollection of all she'd encountered yesterday.

The gang's street colors and sinister mannerisms . . . Duck's unlit cigar and loaded comments . . . The boys' heartwrenching backgrounds and hero-worshiping expressions . . . Jack's Olympian presence and do-the-right-thing philosophy . . .

Not my problem, she'd told herself as she'd left the gym. As long as the gang remained on their own turf, they weren't a threat to her or to those she loved. Even if Jack couldn't come up with the money to buy the gym so he and Duck could continue their work with the boys, he had an extra week to try to relocate. And that, she'd thought as she'd gotten into her car and pulled away from the curb, was the end of that.

But one question would not be quelled. It had hounded her from the economic ghetto of the gym's surroundings to the old-money enclave of Mission Hills. Haunted her through a terribly restless night. And now it had come creeping up on her in the silent storeroom, disrupting her day and forcing her to ask herself: *Whose problem is it?*

"Not mine!" Maureen reiterated aloud, and recoiled from the vehemence of her own voice in the stillness. Then she leaped to her feet and headed for her office refrigerator, hoping that the strawberry-and-spinach salad would get rid of the bad taste she suddenly had in her mouth.

Jack spit out his mouthpiece and smiled at Jamal. "Looking good, dude."

The fourteen-year-old boy laughed, music to his mentor's ears, and held up his own mouthpiece. "Didn't lose it even once today."

Innocent as it was, the remark brought to Jack's mind the picture of Maureen Bryant, her face aglow and her eyes afire, storming across the ring at him just two days ago. He could still see her hair spilling in a riot of wavy disarray to her shoulders and the perspiration glistening like morning dew on her upper lip. The memory of her English-garden perfume lingered stubbornly in his head, drowning out the smell of sweat and old socks and sheer desperation that permeated the gym.

He squelched those recollections as flatly as he would squash a bug. Self-control was the name of the game. The mental edge every fighter strove for, both in and out of the ring. And it made absolutely no sense to get all worked up over a woman who was going to close him down.

"How's school?" he asked as he walked Jamal to the ropes.

"G." Which was his way of saying "great."

"Did you ever finish that history paper on General Douglas MacArthur that Duck was helping you with?"

"I got an A minus on it." Coming from a kid who'd been pulling down a 1.5 grade-point average before joining the fight club last fall, it was nothing short of a miracle.

"Way to go." Jack clapped him on the shoulder with a gloved hand in congratulations, then cut to the heart of the matter. "Have you heard from your mother lately?"

The rope burns on Jamal's neck were nearly invisible now, but there was no telling how deep the internal scars ran. "She's getting out of jail a week from tomorrow."

Jack made a note on his mental calendar. "How do you feel about that?"

"I love Mama," he said, the words stiff and halting. "And she loves me."

"Of course she does."

"I just hope she's got her head on straight, you know?"

"So do I, son," he said softly. "So do I."

Jamal dropped his head and concentrated on the canvas for a long moment. Then he looked up, his face the picture of puzzlement. "Did I tell you what my Aunt Fannie told me the other day?"

"No, what?" Jack silently blessed the woman who, when informed that her battered nephew was being made a ward of the court while his mother was in jail, had immediately moved him into the bosom of her own large and loving family.

"She said their mother used to beat them with an ironing cord until they bled."

That came as no surprise to Jack. Violence begat violence. Abused children usually grew up to become abusive parents, unless they made a conscious effort to break the cycle.

"How does she manage, with her six kids plus you?"

"She prays a lot," Jamal joked. Then he grew serious again. "No matter how bad we get on her nerves, she never hits us when she's mad. Sometimes, she even hugs us."

"Aunt Fannie is a wise and wonderful woman." Jack gave him a friendly poke in the ribs, which had fleshed out considerably in the time he'd been in her care. "A pretty good cook, too, by the looks of it."

Jamal beamed in reply. "She's said she's going to bring supper to our house every night until my mother gets back into the swing of things."

"Sounds like a good idea." Jack held the ropes open so he could slip out.

But the boy shifted from foot to foot, seeming reluctant to leave the ring just yet.

"What's the matter?"

"Word around the gym is, you might be going back into the ring for real."

Jack let the ropes snap closed. "Who told you that?"

"Same person who told me General MacArthur said, 'I'll be right back,' when he left the Philippines and messed up my history paper."

"Duck."

Jamal tucked his chin against his chest and peppered the air between them with a quick series of rights and lefts. "He said you might even let us spar with you if we worked hard enough."

"What else did he tell you?"

"That you're going to buy the gym with the proceeds."

Jack had heard enough. Pulling the ropes open again, he shooed Jamal through them with a jerk of his head before following him out. Then, his temper at a full boil, he headed for the balcony level, taking the steps two at a time, to confront his old trainer about the rumors he was spreading and the false hopes he was raising.

"Have you lost your friggin' mind?" he roared, hitting a

peanut bag so hard with the back of his gloved hand as he passed it that it sounded like a machine gun.

"Who, me?" Duck was alone, having finished timing the boys on the speed bags for the day. He didn't look surprised to see his favorite fighter raging toward him, however. In fact, his eyes lit up and he smiled behind his cigar as if he'd been expecting him.

"Yeah," Jack said between clenched teeth as he stopped just short of crushing the trainer's toes, *"you!"*

"What's the problem?" Duck asked after maneuvering the stogie from one side of his mouth to the other.

"First you smuggle the scrapbook out with the towels—"

"I wondered how long it'd take you to figure that out."

Jack scowled down at the trainer with a ferocity that would have scared the pants off a lesser man. Duck merely hooked his thumbs in his waistband and hitched his polyester slacks a couple of inches higher.

They'd butted heads before, hundreds of times, over boxing in particular and life in general. No one had gotten hurt then. There was no reason to believe that they would now.

"Where'd you hide the damn scrapbook?" Jack demanded.

Duck stood firm. "That's for me to know and Maureen to find out."

"Hell, she's probably forgotten all about it."

"My five to your one says she hasn't."

"What makes you so sure?"

"The expression on her face when she realized Sully kept a scrapbook full of her pictures."

But the expression that was burned into Jack's memory was the one of her looking at him as though he were some functional illiterate who couldn't read the handwriting on the wall, much less an eviction notice.

Anger exploded inside him, demanding an outlet.

Turning his back on Duck, he dug his gloved fist—*boom!*

—into the heavy bag hanging from the ceiling, causing it to twist and groan. He'd gotten her back. But good. And if he lived to see Armageddon, he would never forget how the blood had rushed to her face when he'd told her he was an attorney.

The body that had been accompanying that face into his dreams he would just as soon forget, however.

Leggy and lissome yet curved in all the right places, that body had ruined his sleep for two nights running. Both mornings now Jack had had to remind himself that Maureen Bryant was too uptight for his taste. That he liked his women loose and warm, not starched from knees to throat and cold enough to give a man frostbite.

He raised his fist to hit the bag again, and realized his anger was gone. Kaput. Displaced by the thought of a redheaded fashion plate who'd probably never lifted a hand toward another human being until she'd climbed into the ring to rescue Jamal.

That reminded him why he'd originally come to the balcony level. He dropped his hand and turned back to Duck, his temper staging another full-scale rebellion. "In three words: For Get It!"

"I'm drawing a blank even as we speak," the trainer said agreeably.

Jack couldn't stand still. He spun and stalked from one end of the balcony to the other, fuming every step of the way, "I'm not—repeat *not*—going back into that ring."

Duck stayed where he was, playing devil's advocate like a pro. "You probably can't fight your way out of a paper bag anymore, anyway."

"The hell I can't!" Jack roared, contradicting himself in response to the caustic remark. "I'm in better shape now than I've ever been."

"Maybe, maybe not."

"Even if I wanted to fight again—which I don't—when would I find time to train?"

"You're one busy guy, all right."

"Between appearing in juvenile court and running the diversionary program—"

"And wrestling with that monkey on your back."

Jack came to a screeching halt as the past caught up with him. It didn't nudge him gently from behind; it rear-ended him at ninety miles an hour. He whirled, fully expecting to see the skull that confronted him in the mirror every morning smirking back at him.

But all he saw was Duck, teething on his cigar and bouncing on the balls of his feet. Working side by side with Sully, he'd once taken a delinquent boy and taught him the physical and mental skills to go the distance. Now Sully was gone and the boy was grown. And between the two men who remained there echoed the reminder of how they'd come to be in their present predicament.

Jack looked down at his hands. Lethal weapons gloved in twenty ounces of soft red leather. Then he raised his head and glared at the trainer who'd been his cornerman through triumph and tragedy.

"Anybody ever tell you that you fight dirty, old man?" he growled, only partly in jest.

Duck grinned as if he'd just been handed the deed to the gym. "All the time."

The brick-and-stucco Tudor had stood the test of time.

Maureen smiled, as she always did whenever she pulled up before her parents' home. Then she turned off the engine and sat a moment, steeping herself in the splendor of its steeply pitched roofing and the solidity of the masons' quoins climbing the arched entryway. Forsythia bushes on either side of the front door added eye appeal, as did the neatly trimmed box hedges beneath the windows.

Built in 1927, the house was a beautiful example of Kansas City architect Napoleon Dibble's work in the Sunset

Hills neighborhood where she'd grown up. Even now, twelve years after she'd moved out on her own, Maureen could make her way blindfolded from her old upstairs bedroom down to the kitchen her parents had remodeled twice in the thirty years they'd lived there. And while her mental geography had expanded alarmingly in the last three days to include an aching awareness of Sully's old stomping grounds, this would always be home.

Dread pooled, ice-cold, in the pit of Maureen's stomach. Just as she'd put off going to the gym all those years, not knowing how she would be received, she had delayed telling her parents that she had finally done so. She had given serious thought to taking the coward's way out and simply calling them on the phone, but then she'd decided that this was something she needed to do in person.

"No time like the present," she told herself as she closed her car door and started up the paved brick sidewalk.

Her parents' neighbor, a free-lance writer out for her noon constitutional, waved in recognition. The heart-shaped leaves on the matched redbuds in the manicured side yards rustled a welcome in the equally welcome breeze. Geraniums in the terra-cotta pot on the front step bobbed their pink and white heads like gossiping matrons as she used the key she still carried to unlock the wrought-iron storm door.

Pausing a few feet inside the wide entrance hall, which was dominated by a mahogany staircase, Maureen let the well-mannered familiarity of it all close around her. Ivory stucco walls wore their ingrained swirls with style and grace. The burnished console table boasted a Baccarat vase filled with a spray of colorful gladiolas, while a gilt-edged mirror mimicked the arched doorways that led to a traditionally comfortable living room and a dining room where formality prevailed.

Two black Scottish terriers, tails high and happily wagging, came tearing out the kitchen doorway at the far end of the center hall to greet her.

"Hi, Bonnie. Hi, Clyde." She knelt on the Oriental runner to facilitate petting them. Bonnie was a direct descendant of the championship Scottie she'd had as a child, and Clyde had sired the litter of six pups she'd whelped last year. They sat, eyes shining and ears erect, as she stroked their wiry coats and cooed inanities at them.

"Maureen?"

She felt a twinge of guilt when she looked up at the slender woman with the pale hair and the pleased expression who was following the dogs down the hall, but she managed to inject a cheerful note into her answering, "Hi, Mom."

"What a lovely surprise, seeing you in the middle of the day like this."

"Yes, well . . ." Maureen gave the Scotties a final pet apiece before she stood and released the pent-up breath she'd been holding all morning. "I need to talk to you and Dad."

Everything inside Laura Bryant went as still as death. She had read Sully's obituary in the paper with a terrible sense of foreboding, as if the door she had closed on the past that long-ago day had come suddenly open. And the news that he'd left that damn gym to the daughter for whom he'd never had time had brought the old bitterness seeping through her body with a constant, burning pain.

"You've been to the gym." Even as she said it, Laura couldn't believe she'd ever been so foolish as to think she could change Sully from a fighting man into a family man.

"I went down there on Monday," Maureen admitted with a slight catch in her voice.

"Monday?"

"Yes."

Concern flickered in Laura's teal blue eyes at the three-day gap between Maureen's going there and coming here.

"I thought you were going to let the lawyer serve the eviction notice."

"I decided to do it myself."

"I see."

"No, Mom, I don't think you do." Growing up, Maureen had always been able to internalize her questions and, more often than not, to ignore them. But going down to the gym had brought them roiling to the surface. Reminded her that she had no idea who she was, where she came from, and why she felt so hopelessly lost sometimes.

"I was just fixing your father's lunch." Laura purposely put an emphasis on the words "your father" before she turned and started back toward the kitchen. "I never really ate lunch until he retired. Now, if the weather's nice, I usually serve it on the patio."

"Mom, please—"

"If you're hungry—"

"I ate a late breakfast," Maureen fibbed, the dogs at her heels as she trailed Laura down the hall. There had always been this awful silence between them where Sully was concerned, but now she needed some answers. "I will have a glass of tea, though."

Mother and daughter entered the sun-drenched kitchen within arm's reach of each other yet miles apart.

"I've got a wonderful new recipe for chicken salad." Laura could hardly hear her own voice over the pounding of her heart in her ears, but she was desperate not to leave a vacuum lest Maureen attempt to fill it. "It calls for poppy seed dressing."

"Sounds delicious."

"Your father loves it."

Maureen took a sip of her tea, trying to drown the screams of frustration that were clawing at her throat. "Where is Dad, by the way?"

"He's out in the potting shed."

"I think I'll go talk to him."

Laura spun away from the counter, startling the Scotties at her feet, as Maureen started toward the back door. Maybe if she'd been able to give Paul children of his own, she wouldn't be so frantic about preserving the status quo. One ectopic pregnancy and two miscarriages into their marriage, however, the doctor had advised her to either quit or die trying.

"When you were a little girl," she said, pulling no punches now, "you used to follow your father out there all the time."

Maureen paused at the door and smiled, the musty smells of potting soil and fertilizer still strong in her memory. "He'd say, 'Hoe, hoe, hoe,' and then he'd hand me one."

"I remember watching the two of you working in the flower beds and thinking all was right with the world."

"And I remember how muddy we'd get and how you'd make us take off our shoes before we could come inside."

The strain of this pretense proved too much for Laura, and she finally snapped, "If you hurt his feelings, I'll never forgive you."

Maureen stared at her mother, as shocked by the look on her face as by the words she'd flung. "I have no intention of hurting Dad."

"You're all he has."

"I know that."

Crossing to the door, Laura reined in her runaway emotions and tried a less confrontational approach. "Your father loved you from the first moment he laid eyes on you."

Taking her mother's hands between her own, Maureen held on tightly. "And I love him. You too. And it's *because* I love you both so much that I came here today to tell you the truth about what I've done rather than sneaking around behind your backs and lying to you."

Laura breathed a little easier at that. But only a little. She still had a sense of impending doom. A feeling that

Sully was going to reach out from the grave and snatch their daughter away from her.

Releasing her mother's hands, Maureen opened the door. Halfway out, she stopped and stuck her head back inside. "If it's not too late for me to change my mind, I'll have some of that special chicken salad after all."

"I'll call you when it's ready," Laura said, just as she had a thousand times through the years.

The back yard was Paul Bryant's crowning glory, a virtual riot of color from early spring to late fall. He'd chosen horticulture as his hobby instead of fishing or golf because it kept him close to home and to his "two best girls." Judging from the lush sprays of lavender bordering the patio and the beds of blousy hollyhocks soaking up the June sun, he'd chosen well.

Maureen didn't stop to smell the roses she'd helped her father plant when she was growing up. Or the spicy phlox or sweet verbena, for that matter. She headed straight for the potting shed, which was actually a bump-out on the west side of the detached two-car garage.

The door to Paul's private domain swung open soundlessly. As her eyes adjusted to the gloom, Maureen noticed the small room was as tidy as ever. Then she saw her father and smiled. He was standing at his workbench, his silvery head bent over a pair of hedge clippers he was sharpening before hanging them back on their wall peg. Even in his plaid shirt, chinos and the Wellington boots she'd given him as a retirement present, he had the buttoned-down look of a banker.

"Hoe, hoe, hoe," she said softly, not wanting to startle him and cause him to cut himself.

Paul spun, file in hand. The long, Modigliani lines of his face lifted with both surprise and pleasure as he set the tool down and held out his arms. "Got a hug for your old man?"

"Only for my best man," Maureen said, and stepped easily into his embrace.

The shed grew closer and warmer as father and daughter reaffirmed their love in each other's arms.

"What's my favorite interior designer got on her mind?" he asked after he'd bear-hugged her.

She took a deep breath. "First, I want to say that this has nothing to do with my feelings for you. That you'll always be my father."

Paul braced himself for what he suddenly knew was coming. A lifetime career in the banking business had taught him to read between the lines. And thirty years of holding this beautiful redhead close to his heart told him that the inevitable had finally happened.

"I went down to the gym, Dad." Maureen just blurted it out, not wanting to prolong the agony for either of them.

Oddly enough, his long-harbored fear of her wanting to do exactly that gave way to a flood of relief that the waiting was over. He loved her too much to lay a guilt trip on her for trying to find the years she'd lost. And of all the people she could have turned to, he alone understood that it wasn't really Sully she was seeking . . . it was herself.

"Smart business move," Paul congratulated her now. "Seeing it before you sell it."

"I'm not so sure about that," Maureen said on a sigh.

"Why not?"

"It's a real dump."

"So I've heard." He didn't have to say from whom, since they both knew Laura despised the gym.

"But there's so much good happening there. . . ."

"Do you want to talk about it?" It cost him dearly to ask, but he sensed her confusion, her need to sort things out.

She was close to tears when she replied, "The question is, do you really want to hear about it?"

"If it concerns you," he said quietly, "it concerns me."

Maureen loved him so much at that moment, she ached

with it. She laid a tentative hand on his arm. "Are you sure?"

For an answer, Paul pulled her old stool out from under the bench, dusted it off with his shirtsleeve and said, "Sit."

She sat. And then, just as she always had when she was in need of a sounding board or a sympathetic ear, she crossed her arms on the clean work surface and confided in her father. She told him everything—about the depressing neighborhood and the dangerous gang, about Duck's pants and the boys' pasts. Embarrassing as it was, she even told him about getting caught up in the ropes and having to be rescued.

Last but not least, she told him about Jack Ryan.

"He sounds like a good role model for the boys," Paul said when she finally wound down.

"Father Flanagan in boxing trunks." Though Maureen couldn't even begin to picture Jack in a Roman collar. Or a regular shirt, either, given the broad expanse of his chest.

Paul laughed.

"Anyway, he's got until tomorrow to decide whether he wants to buy the gym."

Finished sharpening the hedge clippers, her father reached for the oil can. "You really put him on the spot, didn't you?"

"What was I supposed to do?" She picked up one of the empty terra-cotta flowerpots lining the back of the workbench, turned it over and stared at the hole in the bottom. "Hand him the deed and tell him to have fun?"

"You could have given him a little more time to make a decision," he suggested.

She turned the flowerpot right side up and put it back with a firm *thump*. "I might have done exactly that if he hadn't made me so damn mad."

Paul's ears perked up. It was the rare man who could rile his unflappable Maureen. He bit back a smile, not wanting to risk her wrath. But there was nothing to stop him from wondering if she had, at long last, met her match.

"What did he do to make you angry?"

"For one thing, he implied that I was rude."

Her father frowned. "Were you?"

"Of course not." Thinking back, though, Maureen realized that she had cut Jack off rather abruptly. "Well, maybe a little."

"What else did he do?"

"He made me look like a complete fool in front of Duck."

Paul hung the hedge clippers on their wall peg. "How so?"

Her eyes flashed emerald fire. "By not telling me he was an attorney up front."

A rare man, indeed, Paul thought. And this time he did smile. "Letting you assume he was just a punchdrunk boxer, you mean?"

She squirmed as if her wooden stool were the hot seat. "I guess I did go in there with some preconceived notions."

"Pa-a-ul, Maur-e-een!" Laura's voice lilted across the yard and into the potting shed like an echo of yesteryear. "It's lunchtime!"

"Have you told your mother yet?" Paul asked as he put the file and the oil can away.

Maureen nodded, then stood and slid the stool back under the workbench. "She's pretty upset."

"Be patient with her."

"I'm trying," she insisted with a wan smile.

He ran a hand through his silver hair. "It was a time in her life she'd just as soon forget."

"I understand."

"Tell you what," he said, making a decision he hoped he wouldn't live to regret. "I'll talk to your mother this evening and tell her you have my full support."

Maureen threw her arms around the man who had always put her happiness above his own and hugged him tightly. "Thanks, Dad."

Paul pressed her head to his shoulder and hid his apprehensive eyes in her hair. "That's what fathers are for, darlin'."

Had he been given a choice of fathers, Jack would've picked Sully. No contest there. That Sully had stepped in after his old man had finally kicked him out of the house never ceased to amaze him. Because the boxing manager had put him on the straight and narrow.

Now, sitting at that ancient office desk and staring down at Maureen's number in the open telephone directory, Jack knew it was payback time. If he wanted to keep the gym and the diversionary program going, he had to put his money where his mouth was. Either that, or pack it in for good.

And the hell of it was, he had to decide today.

"Why me?" Jack had asked that long-ago day.

"I've watched you grow up," Sully had answered around the cigar he'd lit up the minute they left the courtroom. "You've got no self-discipline. No ambition that I know of, either. But you've got one thing that a lot of kids your age don't have."

"What's that?"

"Hate."

Jack hadn't disputed that because it was true. He'd hated having a drunken bully for a father and, until her death, a doormat for a mother. He'd despised wearing ragged clothes to school and then not being able to read when he got there. Worse yet was his own sense of self-loathing, the feeling that he was never going to accomplish any of his secret goals anyway, so why bother to try.

"Your whole life you've let that hate get you into trouble," Sully had continued as they'd walked to his car. "Now I wanna see if I can teach you to let it do you some good."

That was exactly what he'd done too.

Sully had preached discipline and determination while pairing Jack with the meanest SOB's in the club. Duck had patched up his cuts and ice-bagged his bruises, then sent him back for more. Even worse—or so he'd thought that long-ago summer—they'd put him in the hands of a counselor who'd diagnosed his dyslexia and recommended a tutor.

Learning to read at long last opened a whole new world for Jack. It did wonders for his self-esteem, too, knowing he wasn't stupid but that he simply had an invisible handicap he could and did overcome. Still, he'd been reluctant to put his newfound skill to the test because, as he'd contended at the time, he would have been the oldest high-school junior in history.

Arguing with Sully had been as futile as arguing with a fence post. Come September, he'd bought Jack some new shirts and jeans and shoes. Then he'd told him that he couldn't come back to the gym until he went back to school . . . and brought his graded homework papers to prove he'd been there.

By June of his senior year, Jack had been so angry with "Slave-driver" Sullivan—as he'd secretly dubbed him— that he would have done anything to get revenge. Even graduate with honors the week before he took the National Golden Gloves title. But the moment the referee had lifted his gloved hand into the air and declared him champion, he'd realized that the crafty old manager had outfoxed him. He'd realized, too, that the sky was the limit now.

"Champ?" a softly accented voice queried.

Jack blinked at the long-blurred pages of the telephone directory and looked up. Then he smiled at the dark-haired boy standing in the doorway. "Hey, Tony, what's happening?"

Still in his street clothes and starter jacket, the teenager shrugged and said, "If you have a minute, my father would like to talk to you."

"Bring him in." Jack rose, welcoming the distraction, and rounded the desk to greet the man he'd met only once before—two years ago, in juvenile court.

"*Adelante*," the bilingual boy said, then ushered a tall, thin man he was the spitting image of into the office.

"Long time no see, Mr. Sanchez." Jack's regards were out before he remembered that Tony's father didn't speak English.

But he did recognize the universal symbol of fellowship, because he clasped the hand extended to him and pumped it heartily. Then he launched into a rapid-fire spate of Spanish that left Jack's head spinning.

"What did he just say?" he asked when he finally got a word in edgewise.

Tony was only too glad to translate. "My father says he is sorry, he still does not speak English—"

"That makes us even, then," Jack quipped, "because I still don't speak Spanish."

The boy rolled his brown eyes at that, then continued serving as interpreter for his father. "He says he brought his family to America from Mexico because he wanted to make a better life for them. But he soon found that the only job he could get was doing menial labor because he couldn't read or write English.

"His oldest son"—here, Tony pointed to himself and grimaced—"was his hope for the future. Until he dropped out of school, joined a gang and got caught stealing hubcaps. He despaired of ever getting his son out of jail and back in school because he didn't have the money to hire a lawyer."

Mr. Sanchez paused to catch his breath, and began again.

"Then you"—now Tony nodded at Jack—"came to juvenile court and convinced the judge to release his son into your custody. You made him go back to school and arranged for special teachers so he could learn the language of opportunity and success. And with your boxing program, you taught him how to direct his energies away from senseless violence and into the sport.

"So today—two years from the day you gave his son a fighting chance—he decided that it was only right that he come to the gym to thank you in person and to tell you that you are a champion in every sense of the word."

Jack had received his share of thanks through the years, but he couldn't recall ever receiving such a heartfelt tribute. Profoundly moved, he looked at Mr. Sanchez and said to Tony, "Tell your father I appreciate the effort he made to come see me today, and that I know his son will do us both proud."

Tony beamed and did as he was bade.

Mr. Sanchez nodded happily, then stuck out his hand to say good-bye. "*Adiós.*"

"*Adiós,*" Jack repeated, thinking it was probably time he learned a new language.

The swish-slap of a jump rope floated up from the main floor as Tony and his father made their way out the office door and down the stairs.

Jack went to the window overlooking the gym. He slid his hands, palms out, into the seat pockets of his jeans. Then he just stood there . . . watching the boys exchange high fives with Duck, mulling over everything Mr. Sanchez had said, weighing the risks of a comeback against the rewards.

The ring had always been the refuge of the poor. A place where an angry young man with nothing better to do than get into trouble could expend his aggressive energy in positive ways. Not all of them turned out to be champions, of course, but the boxing discipline they developed in the gym helped most of them deal with life outside it.

Unfortunately, the major spawning grounds of yester-year, the urban streets, had become the killing fields of today's young male talent. Instead of putting on the gloves and duking out their differences, kids pulled out their Uzis and blasted each other to Kingdom Come. Now, more than ever, they needed somewhere they could go to work off their steam and walk away alive and feeling good about themselves.

His decision finally made, Jack spun on his heel and headed straight for the telephone sitting on the desk. There would be no requiem for Sullivan's Fight Gym—not if *this* heavyweight could help it. Even, he swore as he dialed Maureen's number from memory, if it meant climbing back into the ring himself.

ROUND 4

"Yo, Mama, you serve fries with that shake?"

Maureen stopped dead on the sidewalk, then turned slowly around. The gang was back, bolder than ever and watching her from behind. She was essentially trapped in the no-man's-land between her car at the curb and the door to the gym.

Thunder rumbled, low and distant, as she made her stand. She wasn't frightened by their rude comments and coarse laughter. Not this time. She'd had all weekend to think about what she should do if they accosted her again. And, between Jack phoning her on Friday and curtly informing her she could pick up his deposit check on Monday afternoon and Lenny Marks calling her at the shop this morning and threatening to sue her for breach of contract, she'd had it up to her eyeballs with belligerent males.

"Don't you have anything better to do than to hang around here bothering people?" Maureen fired her question at the tallest of the five boys—their leader and the one who'd made that crack, judging by the way the other four were still laughing at his cleverness.

He opened a jackknife of a smile on her. One gold tooth glittered menacingly as, to the further amusement of his followers, he drawled, "Whatcha got in mind, Mama?"

She tossed her head back, chin jutting. "And don't call me Mama!"

He blinked in surprise, and his buddies' mouths hung slack.

"What's your name?" she demanded, seizing the moment to begin putting the plan she'd devised for dealing with them into action. She'd seen this done in a detective movie once, and she only hoped it worked in real life.

"Rocstar," he mumbled reluctantly.

"Well, I'm Maureen Bryant—"

"Yo, Mo," he said in all seriousness.

She bit back a smile. "And I've got a business proposition for you and your friends."

He grinned and his posse nodded as if to say this was more like it.

She reached into the side pocket of the geometric print wrap-dress she'd cinched with a black patent belt and pulled out the five-dollar bill she'd placed there for this very purpose. "See my car?"

Five pairs of eyes veered from the money in her hand to the Mercedes on their left.

"I want you to make sure nobody tries to jack it."

The street term for stealing, coming from the mouth of this fly female, brought their eyes right.

Maureen tore the bill in two and made a big production of putting one half back in her pocket and proffering the other one to Rocstar. "If it's still here when I come out, I'll give you the rest."

"That's only a dollar apiece," he calculated aloud.

"That's true." She knew she was setting a bad precedent, paying to park in front of her own building, though that didn't keep her from sweetening the pot. "But I'll probably have to come back again before I'm finished. Several times, in fact. And I'll pay you the same amount every time to watch my car."

Rocstar made the decision for the entire gang. He

stepped forward and snatched the torn bill from her hand, then led the others in forming a ring around the Mercedes. The five of them stood there like Nubian guards, their tattooed arms crossed over their chests and their expressions just daring someone to try jacking it.

Maureen smiled her first real smile of the day, rather pleased with the outcome, and headed inside. Those tigers' eyes on the walls seemed less fierce, the hall floor less littered than before. And when she entered the gym, she even caught herself inhaling deeply of the pungently masculine smells that permeated its every corner.

She saw Duck before he saw her. Which wasn't hard to do, considering that his pants could have doubled as a checkerboard and his sportcoat a stop sign. He was standing ringside, giving her a view of his profile as he chewed on that cigar stub and watched two boxers work out.

"It's legal to hit him back, y'know!" he yelled when one of the men took a hard right to the ribs. "Get ugly. Get *real*—"

The bell sounded, and each boxer retreated to his corner.

Duck gave his waistband a tug and turned away from the ring, looking thoroughly disgusted. Then he spotted her standing just inside the doorway, gave a great big grin and thumbed toward the stairs.

Maureen assumed he was telling her that Jack was in the office. She nodded her thanks. Then, skirting a man jumping rope only to come perilously close to putting her foot in the stomach of one doing sit-ups on a mat, she started toward the sign with the arrow pointing up.

Hearing the steady *rackety-rackety-rackety* of someone hitting a punching bag as she neared the balcony level, she paused and peeked in. She could see why all these half-naked, glistening bodies would have offended her mother's sensibilities. But as a student of art in every form, she frankly found them fascinating.

Jack was sitting behind the desk talking on the telephone when Maureen opened the door. Having already discarded his taupe suit jacket and silk jacquard tie, he waved her into the office without missing a beat in his conversation with Frankie's caseworker at juvenile court.

"I haven't seen him since he walked out of here last week." After freeing his collar button, he cradled the receiver in the crook of his shoulder and put the finishing touches on getting comfortable by rolling up the sleeves of his white shirt. "I haven't had time to try and find him, either."

As Maureen closed the door and crossed to the desk, her sarong-style skirt giving him a tantalizing glimpse of her long, slender legs, Jack felt his gut twist with desire. The man on the other end of the phone said something he could hardly hear over the delicious whisper of one silk-encased thigh moving against the other.

"From what I've been able to gather," he replied, sitting upright after the caseworker repeated the question, "he was having problems at home too. His old man's been on a toot and his mother's in a shelter for battered women."

Indicating the chair on the visitor's side of the desk, he decided Maureen looked different. Looser, somehow. Not until she shook her head and remained standing did Jack realize she was wearing her hair down. It cascaded past her shoulders, forming a soft cloud around her face and setting off her large, liquescent eyes.

"Well, if he doesn't show up again today, I'll start looking for him tonight," he promised the caseworker in conclusion.

"Were you talking about Frankie?" Maureen asked when he hung up the phone.

He answered her with a curt nod.

"Is he in some kind of trouble?"

"What do you care?" Jack snapped, irritated with himself for noticing her legs, her hair, her floral perfume . . .

which, even now, wafted across the desk and filled his head with impossible fantasies.

She paled so drastically at his unprovoked attack that the only color in her face was the dark emerald of her eyes. "I was just—"

"Curious?"

"Concerned."

"That's a first." He yanked open the lap drawer, took out his deposit check and tossed it onto the desk between them.

"What's a first?" Completely perplexed now, she didn't even look to see if it was made out in the amount they'd agreed upon before putting it in her purse.

He gave her the once-over, his eyes finally lighting on her onyx loveknot earrings. "A high-maintenance chick like you concerning herself with a lowlife delinquent like Frankie."

"High-maintenance *chick?!*" she repeated, her voice rising in pitch and volume until the last word had a righteously indignant ring that echoed off the ceiling and walls.

Jack lunged to his feet, sending the swivel chair spinning backward like a crazed top, and shot around the desk. To her credit, Maureen held her ground as he strode toward her, not stopping until he practically had her pinned between the hard wood and his hard frame. Until the front of his body was just inches from brushing the front of hers.

"Can't take 'em dancing because"—he let his glance slide down to her feet, which looked sexy as hell in those black slingback heels—"they're afraid they'll turn their ankle. Can't take 'em on a picnic because"—now his gaze flicked to the slight gap where her dress crossed over her breasts—"they're afraid they'll get sweaty." The blood pounded in his ears, his groin, as his eyes followed the slender column of her throat up to her wide, mobile mouth. "Can't kiss 'em because they're afraid they'll smear their lipstick."

Having gone this far, he decided to go for broke. He reached out and fingered a titian curl, finding the texture as rich as the color. "Can't make love to 'em because they're afraid they'll muss their hair."

Maureen couldn't move. Not without bumping into the wall of solid muscle that was Jack. She couldn't catch her breath, either. Not without inhaling the warm, spicy scent he emanated. Her mind knew that nothing had happened just now, but her body wasn't buying it. Her legs felt unsteady, her head foggy. And everything in between was pulsing with exquisite awareness of the man who'd erupted like a volcano with no provocation on her part.

"You're—" Her voice cracked. She cleared her throat and started again. "You're wrong about me."

His eyes pierced her like two icicles. "Am I?"

"I care," she insisted. "About Frankie, about—"

The door came flying open, cutting her off, and Duck announced his arrival with a gravelly, "We've got a problem, people."

Jack spun toward the trainer and retorted through gritted teeth, "You can say that again."

Maureen, grateful for the reprieve, peeked around his broad shoulder. "What's the matter?"

"Frankie's girlfriend, Tammy." Duck put a gnarled hand on the shoulder of the frightened-looking teenager standing next to him. Her hair was a malljammer's dream, long and blond and moussed to the max, but her heavily applied makeup would have given a Maybelline executive nightmares. She wore a virginal white crop-top, and enough metal on her jeans to set off every detector from here to the airport. "She's pregnant."

"He *promised* he'd pull out!" Tammy wailed, two enormous tears rolling out of her blue eyes and down her cheeks.

"Oh, Christ," Jack groaned, clapping both hands to his head and shaking it in disbelief.

"Poor baby," Maureen murmured, setting her purse on the desk and pushing him out of her way so she could go comfort the girl.

"I just hope it's not twins," Duck remarked, his logic escaping everyone but him.

"M . . . my stepdad is g . . . going to kill m . . . me," Tammy stammered through her tears.

"Surely not," Maureen soothed, taking the sobbing girl into her arms without even stopping to think about what she was doing.

"You don't know him." Tammy collapsed completely, burrowing her blond head against that sympathetic shoulder. "He's mean."

Maureen instinctively tightened her hold on the girl, whose terror had set such a tender hook. "Where's your mother?"

"Sh . . . she's a . . . afraid of him too."

Rocking the girl in her arms, rubbing her palm up and down her shuddering back and repeatedly crooning, "Shh, shh," Maureen felt tears forming in her own eyes. She had no experience with children or teenagers. All she had to go on was good intentions and memories of her parents consoling her thusly in her own moments of crisis.

She looked at Jack over Tammy's head, and their gazes locked. Two perspectives changed for the better during the timeless seconds of that shared stare. He realized she was right and he was wrong, that she really did care, while she came to a more profound understanding of life's injustices and his deep commitment to rectifying them.

Tammy eventually calmed down and raised her head. She sniffled and blinked and swallowed. Then, seeing the soggy smears that her mascara and tears had made on Maureen's shoulder, she moaned, "I've ruined your dress."

"It's cotton, it'll wash," Maureen reassured her. She reached in her pocket for a tissue and felt the torn half of the five-dollar bill she'd placed there earlier. Was there no end to the risky passages around here? she wondered as she wiped the girl's lower eyelids with her thumbs.

"I need to wash my face." Tammy stepped back, apparently realizing she'd just confided in a complete stranger. Her eyes were as puffy as they were wary as she looked around the office for a place to freshen up.

Maureen pointed her in the direction of the bathroom. She waited until the door was closed and the water was running full blast before turning back to Jack. "What now?"

He forked his fingers through his hair and shook his head in a symphony of frustration. "Beats the hell out of me."

"I used to date a woman who had twins." Duck cast another non sequitur into this sea of confusion, only to reel in Maureen and Jack's baffled expressions. "Their birthdays came on the same day," he explained with a shrug. "I damn near went broke buying 'em presents."

Tammy came out of the bathroom, her face scrubbed clean but her broken heart still clouding her blue eyes. "I guess I'll go try and find Frankie."

"Wait." Maureen grasped her shoulders and held them gently. "Please. We need to talk."

Jack glanced down at his watch, then up at Duck.

The trainer took the hint and headed for the door. "I'll be downstairs if you need me."

Tammy offered only token resistance as Maureen led her to the chair she had declined earlier and tried to smooth down her stiffly moussed hair. "Are you sure you're pregnant?"

The girl nodded listlessly. "I bought one of those home test kits."

"They're not always accurate, you know."

"Plus, I've missed two periods."

Maureen couldn't have looked at Jack just then had her life depended on it. She'd had intimate discussions like this with her women friends, of course. Numerous times.

But never with a man. Not even with her ex-fiancé . . . which, she realized now, was the main reason she hadn't married him.

Jack's next statement only added to her discomfort. "You said earlier that Frankie promised he'd pull out."

"He did."

"Why wasn't he using a condom?" Jack distributed them free to the boys in the diversionary program, no questions asked, so he knew Frankie should have had at least one in his possession.

"It broke."

"Then why didn't you stop?"

Tammy's spirit returned in spades. She tossed her head back and fixed Jack with a level stare. "It was too late."

Maureen put her own embarrassment on hold for the moment and placed a calming hand on the rebellious girl's shoulder. "Is there anyone besides your parents you can talk to—a teacher, a priest or a minister, a relative?"

"I just want to talk to Frankie!" Tammy's lower lip trembled like a damaged angel's as she tried not to cry again.

"So do I," Jack grated out.

"Have you considered your alternatives yet?"

The girl glanced at Maureen with apprehensive eyes. "You mean abortion or adoption?"

"Exactly."

"Abortion is murder!" Tammy declared with the vehemence of the very young. Then she crossed her arms over her still-flat stomach and shook her head. "And I could never, ever give Frankie's baby up for adoption!"

That said, the girl leaped to her feet and, before either one of the adults could make a move to stop her, tore out the door and down the stairs.

"Damn that Frankie!" Jack punched his open palm with his fist, sending biceps and triceps and pecs into play. "He knows better than this."

Maureen diverted her eyes from the rippling display of

muscle beneath his white shirt to his face. "Tammy's as much at fault as he is."

"They can't even take care of themselves, and now they've got a baby on the way."

"Children having children," she agreed sadly.

Recalling the American Pietà of a pregnant Tammy in Maureen's arms, Jack realized an apology was in order. "I'm sorry I accused you of not caring."

"I don't think I really knew how much I did," she said, and felt genuine pain at the admission.

"As for the other things I said—"

"I misjudged you too."

His lean cheeks dimpled disarmingly. "You did, didn't you?"

She had the grace to blush. "And for that, I apologize."

Relieved to have that behind them, Jack placed his hands on taut, trouser-clad hips and blew out a long breath. "I do okay with the boys—I can relate to them. But the girl threw me."

"I just hope this isn't another case of Frankie following in your footsteps." The words were out of Maureen's mouth before she could give them much thought.

His jaw firmed and his eyes narrowed menacingly. "Meaning?"

She met his glower without flinching. "Last Monday you said he reminded you of yourself at that age."

"So?"

"So, did you ever get a girl pregnant?"

He tilted his head arrogantly to one side. "I always asked if they were protected."

She bristled at his chauvinistic attitude. "Placing the burden on them, right?"

The *whomp-whomp-whomp* of someone hitting the heavy bag on the balcony level heralded yet another skirmish in the age-old battle of the sexes.

Jack broke rank with the Iron John brotherhood then,

not wanting them to part as enemies, and extended his hand as a peace offering. "Truce?"

Maureen relaxed her feminist stance somewhat and shook it, only to feel heat sizzle up her arm when his strong fingers swallowed hers. "Truce."

A grin lifted one corner of his lips as he released her hand. "Your freckles show up when you're mad."

She wrinkled her nose in reply. "Maybe your sarcastic comments bring them rallying to the fore."

He gave her a "Who, me?" look that would have made Miss Piggy green with envy, and their shared laughter almost drowned out the din of the punching bag that was being pummeled.

Curiosity got the best of her then. "May I ask you a question?"

"Fire away."

"When do you work?"

Mischief sparked in his eyes. "You mean why don't I sit in an office from nine to five like the other lawyers you know?"

That was exactly what she'd meant, but hearing him say it aloud made her realize how tactless she'd sounded. "Forget I—"

"No, I'm glad you asked."

"Why is that?"

His expression turned serious again. "Because most people don't understand how the juvenile justice system works."

She sensed his unspoken "or don't care," and rushed to assure him, "I'd really like to try and understand it."

Jack skipped the legalese in favor of a simple explanation. "The purpose of the system is twofold: First, to protect juveniles in neglect or abuse situations—"

"Like Jamal?"

He nodded. "And second, to protect the public from juveniles who are considered either delinquents, which means they've actually committed a crime, or status offenders, which means they've done something for which they wouldn't be prosecuted if they were adults."

Maureen shook her head. "I don't get that last part."

"Status offenders?"

Now she nodded.

"They're the kids who won't go to school or who break the city's curfew law, for example."

"And that's where you come in?" she surmised.

"If their families can't or won't hire an attorney, the judge appoints one to represent them."

The shouts and laughter suddenly resounding from the gym announced the boys' arrival. Anxious to see if Frankie had by some miracle returned to the fold, Jack walked to the window overlooking the main floor. Maureen followed, of her own accord this time, and resumed her line of questioning.

"Where's your office located?"

No blond head joined the group milling about Duck, which honed his answer to guillotine sharpness. "At 25th and Holmes, around the corner from the Juvenile Justice Center."

She was surprised to discover that she too was disappointed at not seeing Frankie. "What firm are you with?"

"There are a lot of good attorneys who choose not to join firms, you know," he mocked none-too-gently.

"I was just wondering who would cover for you while you're in training," she replied defensively.

Jack realized he was being too hard on her and softened his tone. "I share a secretary with a couple of other lawyers who specialize in juvenile advocacy, but people are as likely to call me here or at home as there."

"Frankie's caseworker, for instance?"

His shrug could have been a yes or a no, but it was definitely an attention-getter. "Essentially I'm on call twenty-four hours a day."

Tearing her gaze away from the distracting sight of his muscular shoulders, Maureen looked up at his frowning face. "Like a doctor."

A faint smile alleviated the harsh line of his mouth. "Except I don't get Thursdays off to play golf."

"You just box every afternoon instead." Her sparkling eyes dared him to argue with her specious reasoning.

His grin widened engagingly. "I guess that's my cue to head on down to the locker room and change clothes."

She got her purse off the desk, wanting to talk to Duck about the scrapbook. "You're really worried about Frankie, aren't you?"

Jack made an after-you gesture. "His caseworker wants to put him in detention for pulling this disappearing act."

"He might be afraid of facing Tammy's stepfather," Maureen pointed out as she preceded him out the door.

He fell into step beside her with a heavy sigh. "I'll start tracking him down tonight, and then we'll know for sure."

She couldn't resist smiling up at him impishly. "Maybe you'll find him in one of *your* old hiding places."

"Women," he grumbled in a teasing voice.

"Men," she muttered in that same vein.

They bumped shoulders on the bottom step, not entirely by accident, then grinned at each other as they turned the corner and entered the gym.

Jack gripped her arm, his callused thumb coming to rest against the soft, bare skin of her inner elbow. "Let me introduce you to the boys."

Maureen made no attempt to pull away from his commanding grasp, though the sparks igniting her nerve endings warned her not to let this go too far. "I'd like that."

"Ovary, Bovary—a Madame's a Madame," Duck was saying to Deron when they walked up behind Jamal and Tony, who were silently observing the showdown at the door.

But Deron wasn't buying the trainer's reasoning. And

neither, apparently, had his literature teacher. He shook his test paper under Duck's nose and demanded, "Then why did she mark it wrong?"

Jack jumped into the fray with what he considered a reasonable solution to the problem. "Maybe you should just read your assignment pages from now on instead of relying on Duck for all the answers."

"Yeah," Duck seconded, giving his waistband an emphatic yank. "You're never gonna learn anything if you don't read."

"That goes for all three of you," Jack added, his voice gruffer than normal with his annoyance over Frankie's continuing absence.

Jamal, Tony and Deron acknowledged his stern words with sheepish nods.

After they finished turning in their schoolwork but before they went down to the locker room to change out of their street clothes, Jack introduced Maureen to them as the woman from whom he was going to buy the gym. He made no mention of the fact that she was Sully's daughter, partly because it would have required an explanation that he was neither prepared nor entitled to give and partly because he wasn't sure how she would react if he did.

Maureen shook each of the teenagers' hands, then reached into her black straw bucket purse and pulled out a white bakery sack.

"What's in there?" Jack asked.

"Cookies."

"Cookies?"

She'd bought them on impulse at a drive-through bakery on her way to the gym. Unable to decide between peanut-butter and chocolate-chip, she'd had the clerk sack up four of each. Gauging by his frown, however, she gathered she'd made another stupid mistake.

"I thought the boys might like an after-school snack," she explained with a helpful shrug.

They eyed Jack uncertainly.

"I usually don't allow them to eat sweets. Slows them down too much." A smile tugged at his lips as he did something really rare and broke one of his own rules. "But I think we can make an exception this time."

"Yesssss!" the boys chorused as they grabbed for the bag.

Maureen watched in dismay as they tore open the sack and crammed the cookies into their mouths. Crumbs flew in every direction as they argued over who got to break Frankie's two cookies into three pieces, then who got the biggest pieces when the deed was done. Finally satisfied with the split, they raced each other to the locker room.

"Any news about Frankie?" Jack asked Duck.

"Jamal said he wasn't at school again today."

"I'll go by the women's shelter and talk to his mother this evening," he said as he turned to follow the boys. "But right now, I've got to get ready to go into the ring."

A ribbon of sensation spiraled through Maureen's middle as she watched Jack walk away. He moved with the precision and power of a well-oiled machine. The steely strength of his limbs was obvious, from the sight of his tanned arms in their white rolled-up sleeves to the length of his trousered legs and the light, alert steps of his wing-tipped feet.

Forcing her eyes away from his tapering back and trim buttocks, she shifted her attention to Duck. "Did you ever find the scrapbook?"

"I haven't had time to look for it yet," he said, lowering his gaze to the homework papers in his hand.

"I'd be glad to help you," she volunteered.

He glanced up at her uneasily. "Today?"

She smiled ruefully down at her skirt and heels. "I'm not exactly dressed for it today."

"Tomorrow's better for me, anyway," he said, and she could have sworn he sounded relieved.

"I'll wear something casual."

"We'll start in the locker room."

She frowned. "I thought you said last Monday that you'd already looked there."

His expression faltered briefly before he regained his composure. "I meant the furnace room."

"Fine," she agreed, and wondered why she suddenly had the feeling that he was giving her the run-around.

"Well," Duck declared as the boys came tearing out the door and into the gym, "back to work."

Since she had Jack's deposit check safely tucked away, Maureen had no real reason to stay. There was a stack of design jobs waiting to be completed back at the shop, not to mention the phone calls she probably had to return. Yet she was reluctant to leave. She glanced at her watch and saw it was only three-thirty. Then, trying to appease her all-work-no-play conscience, she flipped a mental coin. Heads, she'd stay till four. Tails, she'd leave now.

Heads won.

When he came up out of the locker room, Jack was surprised to find Maureen standing ringside. Not that he'd thought she'd take his money and run. It was just that when she was here last week she'd given him the impression she found the fight game distasteful. A violent sport perpetrated by violent men. But somewhere along the line she'd apparently changed her mind, because there she was, drawn to the action like the proverbial moth to the flame.

"Couldn't tear yourself away from the old palace of malice, huh?" he teased as he walked up beside her.

She answered his smile with a saucy one of her own. "Call it protecting my investment."

"In case I can't come up with the rest of the money to buy the gym, you mean?"

Maureen stared up into his taut face and said exactly what he needed to hear. "*Until* you come up with the rest of it."

Just as her memory had replaced his anger last week, so

Jack found that her optimism filled him with confidence now. His eyes softened as they looked into hers. "We should know for sure by the end of the week."

"Why do you say that?"

"After I called you on Friday, I issued challenges to the current heavyweight champion and the two top contenders."

She crossed her fingers. "Here's hoping all three of them say yes."

"You trying to get me punchdrunk, lady?" he said with mock severity.

They laughed together as the boys raced by, finishing their warm-ups with a series of wind sprints. Then Duck ambled over to begin wrapping Jack's hands before he gloved them. Maureen, watching him wind first the gauze and then the tape around those strong brown wrists and between the long square-tipped fingers, sensed that the ritual was truly a labor of love.

"When are you planning to fight?" she asked.

Jack made a fist and hit Duck's upraised palm. "Saturday, August fourteenth."

Maureen was surprised, to say the least. "I thought you said it took a minimum of two months to put on a fight."

"That I did."

"Well, the fourteenth is only seven weeks from this coming Saturday."

"It's also the only night we can get into the Main Arena at Municipal Auditorium," he said with a grim smile as Duck slid his sparring glove onto his left hand and laced it up.

"You're cutting it pretty close, aren't you?"

"We've already started our training schedule."

"You're training *here*?"

"Poor people have poor ways."

She caught his less-than-subtle rebuke and quickly

changed the subject. "Are you nervous about fighting professionally again?"

He jammed his right hand into the other glove, almost causing Duck to lose hold of it. "Comeback's the name of the game."

Maureen noted the touch of asperity in his voice, the ticking of the vein at his temple, and decided it was time to back off. "I'll see you tomorrow."

Jack looked at her blankly. "You're not leaving?"

"I need to get back to the shop."

He realized he was to blame for chasing her away and cursed under his breath. "I'm sorry I acted like such an asshole."

"You didn't."

"Yes, I did."

She slackened her defensive posture somewhat. "You win."

His lips split in a devastating smile. "I like to win."

"Then you'd better get into that ring and start practicing."

"Only if you promise you'll stay around a while longer."

"I really shouldn't."

"Call it protecting your investment," he said, using her earlier statement to his own advantage.

She lowered her eyes to her watch, saw it was a quarter to four, then lifted them to his face. "Fifteen minutes—no more, no less."

"Good." He grinned triumphantly before turning to go into the ring.

No, bad, she mentally corrected as she feasted on the beauty of his back, the tanned skin and contoured muscles that she suddenly longed to touch with her fingertips . . . her lips. She was flirting with disaster. Becoming emotionally involved with both the man and his mission to save the gym. The smart thing to do would be to turn and run as fast and far as her legs would carry her. Forget she'd ever met Jack or the boys or Tammy or—

"You comin'?" Duck asked in his cement-mixer voice.

Maureen didn't hesitate another second when she saw that the balding trainer had saved a spot for her beside him, right up against the ring. She smiled the smile of one who knows she's doomed and took the final step that sealed her fate. "Of course."

ROUND 5

"Yo, Mo."

"Hi, Rocstar." Maureen handed him the torn half of a five-dollar bill, noting as she did that he'd lost one of his followers since yesterday. Eager to start looking for the scrapbook, she didn't comment on the fact. She just said, "See you later," and breezed on into the gym.

As she'd promised Duck, she'd dressed casually today. Her natural-colored, silk noil romper had solved the what-to-wear dilemma. An elasticized straw belt encircled her slender waist, and her strappy taupe sandals put a new spring in her step. In deference to the heat and the storm-warning humidity she had pulled her red hair back into a neat chignon, but its severity was compromised by the wavy tendrils that had escaped to lie on her neck and to form a soft brush of bangs over her forehead.

Maureen sailed down the hall and through the doorway, drinking in the sights and sounds and smells that were becoming as familiar to her as home. It was still too early for the boys to be there, and she really didn't expect to see Jack for another hour or so yet. Duck, on the other hand, was ready and waiting for her.

He grinned in greeting. "Well, aren't you the picture of summer come early."

She eyed his jaunty avocado jumpsuit with a smile. "You look pretty sporty yourself."

The mutual admiration society moved toward the furnace room.

"We have to cut through the locker room to get there," Duck explained as he held the door open for her.

Maureen preceded him down the steel stairs, into a netherworld of rusted lockers, splintered benches and the mingled smells of sweat and liniment and mold. There was only one shower for all the guys, she noted, and with its cracked tiles and missing grout, it was the perfect breeding ground for athlete's foot. She dared not look at the urinals.

"This is deplorable," she declared with a sweep of her hand.

"The boys swab it down once a week," Duck said defensively.

"In this heat, it needs to be done every day."

"Jack tries his best to keep things ship-shape, but there's a limit to what one man can do."

There was a limit to what Maureen could stomach too. "Why doesn't he hire a cleaning crew?"

"Do you know how much that costs?"

"It would be worth every penny."

"By the time he supplies the boys with shoes and—"

Her brow lifted, cutting him off. "Jack buys their shoes?"

"Their clothes too, if their parents can't afford 'em."

Maureen realized she'd asked for that one. She swallowed, ashamed she'd even pursued this line of questioning. But she wasn't ready to let it drop just yet. "Where does he get the money?"

"Some he saved from boxing, though that's running low." Duck pulled a well-chewed cigar stub from the chest pocket of his jumpsuit and clamped it between his teeth. "The rest he gets from practicing law."

What went unsaid seemed to echo off the locker room walls. Jack was risking both life and limb so he could buy the gym from her. And that, more than anything she'd heard thus far, filled Maureen with a terrible guilt.

She picked up a pair of trunks someone had left lying on the floor, folded them neatly and placed them on the bench. "Has he heard from any of the three boxers he challenged?"

"Two of 'em—the heavyweight champ included—turned him down today."

· A sigh of relief lifted her shoulders. "Did they give a reason?"

"The champion doesn't stand to gain anything, even if he wins, and the contender could lose his ranking if Jack beats him."

"So that leaves only one."

" 'Poison' Ivy Stephens."

Maureen smiled in spite of herself. " 'Poison' being his ring name?"

Duck's milky blue eyes glittered with humor. "You catch on real quick."

She sobered then, her face turning worried. "How do you think Mr. Stephens will answer the challenge?"

"He'll probably accept."

"You sound pretty certain of that."

"Ivy's always wanted another shot at Jack."

"They've fought before?"

A ghost of a grin flickered behind Duck's unlit cigar. "Jack's the only fighter who ever beat him."

"So it would, in essence, be a grudge match?"

"They make for the best fights."

Maureen's heart drummed a heavy dirge as she glanced down at her clenched hands. "You mean the bloodiest, don't you?"

"Boxing isn't about who does the most hurting," he replied gruffly. "It's about who shows the most heart. Who has the brains and the legs and the wind to go the distance."

"But in the end," she said, not entirely convinced by his argument, "someone still gets hurt."

"A fighter who controls his fear, instead of letting it control him, doesn't worry about the pain."

"Fear?"

"The athlete's best friend or worst foe." At her inquiring look, he explained. "See, everyone's afraid of something—"

"I'm not." The instant the denial left her mouth, Maureen knew it was a lie.

So, apparently, did Duck. "Sure you are. You just haven't figured out what it is you're afraid of yet."

Oh, but she had. She was terrified of her reactions to Jack. One look from his dark eyes, and her heartbeat escalated; one word in his deep voice, and her breathing accelerated; one touch of his deft hand, and her body clamored for more. He made her feel as if she'd never really lived or laughed or loved before. And what frightened her most was the realization that she hadn't.

Maureen gave Duck a searching look. "Is Jack afraid of fighting again?"

"Of course."

"But he's going to do it for the money," she said, her own culpability ringing shrilly through her conscience.

"And for vindication," he added.

She was completely mystified. "What exactly are you trying to tell me?"

Duck did an about-face on her, essentially telling her that the subject was closed, and crossed to the furnace room door. "We'd better get busy if we want to find the scrapbook."

Maureen followed him down another flight of stairs, past a steam-powered monstrosity that was on summer sabbatical, and toward some boxes stacked along the far stone wall.

"Here." Duck produced two wooden folding chairs,

which he dusted off with the handkerchief he took from his back pocket.

"Thanks." Maureen sat, her emotional barometer soaring as they dug into the treasure trove.

Alas, Sully's scrapbook proved elusive once again.

But, oh, the memories they found . . . Photographs, some framed and some loose, some in black and white and some in color. All of them fascinating.

"Who's Joe Louis?" Maureen held up an autographed picture for Duck's perusal.

"The 'Brown Bomber'—heavyweight champ and the first black fighter to win the respect of the white press and white public."

"Rocky Marciano?"

"Took the title with a short right with thirty seconds gone in the thirteenth round."

Utterly captivated by his store of knowledge, she sorted through the stack on her lap until she came up with another one. "Jose Torres?"

"Silver medalist for Puerto Rico in the '56 Olympics, and former light-heavyweight champion of the world."

She added the three signed pictures to the growing "keeper" pile she planned to carry upstairs. "These should be hanging in the gym where the boys can see them."

"Good idea."

Picking up a black-and-white photo of a man who looked vaguely familiar to her, Maureen gave her partner in time travel a playful side glance. "Is this who I think it is?"

Duck peered at it in the dim light from the overhead bulb. "Yours truly, after I got out of the Army and before I decided I had a better future as a trainer than a boxer."

She smiled at his zoot suit, with its dramatically flared lapels and double-pleated pants. "You were quite the natty dresser, even then."

"I've still got that suit, believe it or not."

Maureen didn't doubt it for a moment. She added his

likeness to the pile between their chairs, then reached back into the box. Her heart melted inside her chest when she realized she was looking at the young Jack Ryan.

Judging by his *Saturday Night Fever* sideburns, the picture had been taken in the early seventies. He was sporting a black eye and a swollen jaw that made her ache for him. Despite his battered face, he proudly displayed a gold medal and a diamond-studded trophy for the camera.

"Gee, I wonder what da other guy looked like." Her attempt at humor sounded terribly lame, thanks to the lump in her throat.

Duck, seeming to sense her distress, gave her something to smile about. "That was the night he won the Golden Gloves."

She studied his bare shoulders and wiry physique, the harbinger of his prime physical condition today. "Did Sully buy his shoes and clothes?"

"Until he turned pro and was making his own money."

Instead of the bitterness she'd felt when Jack had told her about the remedial reading program, Maureen found herself hoping that Sully had bought him good shoes, with leather soles and strong laces, and decent wearing apparel. It was the least he deserved. And the most she could wish for him at this late date.

She set his picture aside for safekeeping and picked up the last one in the box. It was a framed photo of a smiling trio. A tide of emotions washed over her when she recognized the man in the middle as Sully.

With longing fingers, Maureen traced the planes of the face she only faintly remembered. There, in living color, were the green eyes and red hair that she had inherited from him. By blood, they'd been father and daughter; by the stroke of a pen, strangers.

"He was a handsome man," she said with a catch in her voice.

"A real ladykiller," Duck agreed on a laugh. Then, at her

startled expression, he hastened to add, "Before he was married to Slim, of course."

"Slim?"

"Your mother's nickname."

Maureen suddenly saw Laura—like a hologram—in a whole new light. A young, golden-haired wife awaiting her husband's arrival. Smiling as she cooked his dinner. Humming as she bathed his daughter and dressed her for Daddy's homecoming.

"She really loved him."

Duck nodded. "He thought the sun rose and set in her."

"They were happy."

"For a while."

Shadowed half-memories filled in some of the blanks. An anxious Laura watching the clock. Teary-eyed as she turned off the stove. Openly weeping as she fed her only child and put her to bed with the promise she'd see Daddy tomorrow.

"She wanted a traditional marriage." Maureen spoke pedantically, to hide the pain.

"He warned her from the day they met that a fightin' man works nights."

"Maybe love is deaf as well as blind."

Duck made her laugh when he cupped a liver-spotted hand around his ear and said, "Huh?"

The thunder of teenage feet, reverberating down from the gym, told them that their time was up for today. They rose and, by tacit agreement, divided the keeper pile between them. Then, their arms as loaded as their minds, they climbed the stairs.

"Where could the scrapbook be?" She felt the need, now more than ever, to find the missing link.

"We'll look in the attic next time," he said as they neared the door that led to the gym.

Had Sully wanted a boy instead of a girl? Maureen wondered as they entered the all-male world he'd created.

Someone to carry on his name, as well as his work? The questions, so long repressed, filled her with such a sharp regret that she tasted it as bile on her tongue.

She told herself not to be ridiculous, that she was reaching for an explanation where none probably existed. But, like the demons Pandora had released, doubts continued to plague her. Would her father have been as quick to sign away his son as he had been his daughter?

Maureen was so lost in thought that she didn't see Jack until she bumped into him. Or, more accurately, *off* of him. Disconcertingly, her eyes were on a level with his broad chest, bisected now by a red silk power tie.

Her heart tripped over itself as she lifted her gaze to his handsome face and said, "Excuse me."

"You've got cobwebs in your hair." He plucked one from the top of her head and she felt a too-familiar tingle of response all the way down to her toes.

"We've been in the furnace room," she explained, aware that she must look a mess.

But to Jack, she looked refreshingly artless, with those stray tendrils dancing about her cheeks and that smudge of dirt on her nose. He took the pictures from her arms and set them on an empty chair. "So I see."

She watched him automatically loosen the knot in his tie and free his confining collar button. "You look hot."

He partially lowered one eyelid as he assessed her long, bare legs. "So do you."

Laughter followed their simultaneous realization that, with him in a tailored navy suit and crisp white shirt and her in the take-it-easy romper and casual sandals, they were dressed in exactly the opposite manner as the day they'd met.

The boys, still in their street clothes, were playing an impromptu game of catch with the medicine ball while they waited for Duck to collect their homework. Problem was, they weren't playing by the rules.

Maureen winced when Tony slammed the huge orb into Jamal's stomach. "Have you located Frankie?"

"Not yet." Jack frowned as Deron was bowled over like a tenpin by the ball.

"What about Tammy?"

"She seems to be laying low too."

Wanting him to know that she shared both his frustration and his worry over the missing teenagers, she laid a hand on his arm. "Maybe they found each other."

He glanced down at her fingers, slender and pale against his navy sleeve, then up at the face that haunted him night and day. "Maybe they did."

The look they shared was so compelling that their rough-and-tumble surroundings temporarily ceased to exist.

Duck remedied that when he hollered, "Hey, is there a circus in town?"

"No," Jamal said as he dropped the ball with a *bang*.

"Why?" Tony and Deron queried in a cackling chorus.

"'Cause there's sure a lotta clowns around here."

The chastised boys straggled back to the door to present him with their homework papers.

"Never a dull moment," Jack muttered as Duck doled out five extra push-ups apiece with the locker room keys.

"Oh . . . wait!" Maureen, suddenly remembering why her shoulder bag felt so heavy, opened it and started pulling out peaches. "After my housecall out east this morning, I stopped by the farm and picked and washed these."

"What farm?"

"My father's."

Jack shook his head in confusion. "I thought your father was a banker."

"He was, before he retired."

"So where did he get a farm?"

"He grew up there." Maureen passed out the sun-ripened fruit she'd brought the boys in lieu of sweets.

"That's funny."

"What?"

"I always figured him for an 'old money' kind of guy." He gave one of those nonchalant shrugs that she'd grown to expect from him. "You know, Pem-Day from kindergarten through high school, then on to Wharton or Harvard, and back to good ol' K.C. to take over the family banking business."

"Wrong on all counts," she said as she took the last two peaches from her large purse. "His parents died of old age when he was still fairly young, which means he was probably a change-of-life baby. And he worked his way through college as a teller in the bank he eventually went on to run."

Duck, finding himself the recipient of one of those peaches, got rid of the cigar stub so he could properly enjoy his windfall while he reviewed the boys' homework papers.

Finally Maureen turned to Jack. "And one for you."

Was this how Eve had tempted Adam? he wondered. Had she gazed up at him with guileless green eyes and moistly parted lips as she offered him a taste of the forbidden fruit? Had his mouth watered for a sample of hers, his senses hummed with the sight and the sound and the scent of her before he'd taken the fall?

He accepted the peach with a husky, "Thanks."

Maureen, watching his strong white teeth sink into the soft, orange-red flesh, suddenly knew a hunger such as she'd never experienced before. Her blood swam hot with it. And when his tongue licked the succulent drops of juice from his lips, something deep inside her melted like a frozen pool in the first spring thaw.

"Wanna bite?"

She barely had enough air to ask, "What?"

His eyes remained pointedly on her mouth as he extended his peach and repeated the offer. "Wanna bite?"

"No . . . thanks." Get a grip, she told herself, and gestured toward the street door. "I have some more in my car."

"Speaking of cars, how much are you paying Roc 'n' the hoods to guard yours?"

"What difference does it make, as long as they're earning their money honestly?"

"The difference," he said through clenched teeth, "is that not everybody around here can afford to bribe them."

"Then my suggestion," she countered sweetly, "is that you turn the empty lot next door into a *parking* lot."

As much as Jack hated to admit it, she had him there. He smiled a gracious surrender. "Wish I'd thought of that myself."

Maureen had the good manners not to gloat.

He polished off his peach and tossed the pit in the trash. "What are you going to do with all those pictures you dragged up here?"

She diverted her gaze from his mouth, which glistened with juice. "If it's all right with you, I'd like to hang them in the gym."

"You're the owner."

"Not for long."

The boys came up out of the locker room then and launched into their warm-up routines—counting out for Duck and everyone else within earshot the extra push-ups they'd been assigned.

"Duty calls." But Jack found himself strangely reluctant to answer it just yet—a dangerous sign for a man in training. He looked at Maureen and shifted from one foot to the other. "You going to be around for a while?"

She glanced at the pictures she'd carted upstairs. "If I can find a hammer and some nails."

"Great!" He felt his confidence flood back and wondered why the hell it mattered so much that she'd consented to stay. "I'll see you in a few minutes then."

Their eyes connected, and her mouth curved into a soft

smile. "I'll look for the tools while you're changing clothes."

He thumbed toward the stairs. "In the office closet."

She nodded her thanks. "I'll find them."

"I'm going up there anyway," Duck said as, homework papers in hand, he stood and started in that direction. "I'll bring 'em down to you."

While Jack got ready to go in the ring, Maureen made a gallery of sorts for the pictures she'd brought up from the furnace room.

"Looks nice," he said when he saw the artful arrangement she'd created on the bare expanse of wall between the street and locker room doors.

"The Wall of Fame," Maureen joked.

Wall of Shame was more like it, Jack thought, as he studied the picture of himself. She'd made it the centerpiece of the circular grouping, and he couldn't believe how cocky he'd been back then. Back before—

"I'm hoping to unearth some more pictures in the attic."

"The attic?"

"We're going up there next to look for the scrapbook."

Jack weighed the wisdom of telling her she was being led on a wild Duck chase against the very real possibility he might not see her again if he did. He changed the subject. "Well, I'd better get warmed up."

Maureen shifted her attention from the victorious boy in the picture to the flesh-and-blood man at her side. Just looking at him, feeling his raw energy, sent excitement rippling up her spine like chain lightning. "Good luck, Champ."

"You gonna fight or flap your jaws all day?" Duck demanded around the cigar he was chewing on again.

Jack shot him a black look, and then stomped over to have his hands taped and gloved. The muscles in his back and shoulders felt as tight as steel bands when he started shadowboxing. Gradually, though, by forcing himself to concentrate on what he had to do in order to save the gym, he worked up enough of a sweat to relieve their stiffness.

"Snap it out . . . drive in," Duck shouted.

Drawn as much by her growing fascination with the art of boxing as with the boxer, Maureen drifted toward the ring. Muscles slid long and smooth in his arms and shoulders as he feinted left and hooked right. Perspiration rolled off him like the river of time while he moved backward and forward and in a circle, laying a foundation for the battle of his life.

"Off your heels . . . you're not in dancin' class."

"Aren't you being a little harsh on him?" Maureen asked as she watched Jack respond to Duck's orders as fast as he could issue them.

"You ain't seen nothin' yet," he replied, then hollered into the ring, "Pick it up . . . c'mon, c'mon . . ."

The boys and the wanna-be's crowded around, adding their two cents' worth to Duck's commands.

"Harder!"

"Faster!"

Maureen, hearing Jack gasping for breath, could hardly catch her own. It was so hot in the gym, she didn't see how he could stand it. She was wringing wet, and all she was doing was watching!

"Left . . ."

"Right . . ."

"Time," Duck called.

And none too soon for Jack. He leaned over and braced his gloved hands on his knees, wanting nothing more than to fall flat on his face on the canvas. Then he saw Maureen standing ringside and straightened, knowing he could do this for the rest of his life if it meant she was there for him.

"That was wonderful!" she exclaimed.

Duck took the cigar out of his mouth. "You want to try it?"

Her eyes flew to his. "Me?"

"Of course, you'd have to get in shape first."

"What's wrong with my shape?" she demanded, propping her hands on her slender hips.

"Well, you're a little on the skinny side." He punctuated his statement with stabbing motions of his stogie.

"Skinny?!" Maureen repeated stridently. "Just because I'm not built like a lady wrestler—"

"I think Duck means you don't have any muscles to speak of," Jack interpreted from inside the ropes.

Sensing the challenge in his statement, she looked up at him. Then she threw down a gauntlet of her own. "I'll bet I could develop muscles if I tried."

"It takes time."

"I've got time."

"Seven weeks and three days," Duck chimed in portentously.

Maureen bit her lip, uncertainty gnawing at her mind. "What exactly would I have to do?"

"Go on a diet," Duck said.

"Get a blood test," Jack added.

"What kind of diet?" She tackled the easy part first.

The trainer shrugged. "Salads, fruits, lean—"

"No problem—I eat that way, as it is."

"And lots of carbohydrates," Jack put in.

"Carbohydrates?"

"Pancakes, pasta and potatoes."

She made a face. "I'll look like a blimp!"

He laughed off her protest. "You'll burn it up if you're working out."

"Why the blood test?" She hated to sound like a whiner, but she hated needles even worse.

"Boxing's a contact sport," he explained. "Even the refs wear rubber gloves."

That made her a little squeamish, to say the least.

"No test, no training."

And no truth. Her heart gave a small spasm, like a caged

bird that longed to fly. Maybe this would set them both free, she thought, and nodded decisively. "I'll do it—on two conditions."

Recalling Sully's propensity for imposing conditions, Jack had trouble holding a grin in check. "Let's hear 'em."

"One"—she looked at the boys—"you clean up the locker room and keep it that way."

"What do you say, guys?"

They grimaced, then nodded in unison.

Jack turned twinkling eyes back to Maureen. "And the other condition?"

She pulled out the extra peanut-butter cookie she'd bought yesterday and transferred to the side pocket of her shoulder bag when she'd changed purses this morning. "I start my diet tomorrow."

"Aren't you feeling well, dear?"

"I'm fine." Maureen glanced at her mother, sitting across the linen-covered table from her. "Why?"

"You've hardly touched your dinner."

"To tell you the truth, I'm still full from breakfast and lunch." She set down her fork and gave up all pretense of eating the chicken breast smothered in butter and cream.

"Those must have been some meals," Paul observed from the head of the table as he reached for his wineglass.

"Microwave pancakes and orange juice this morning, then a salad and angel-hair pasta at noon." After she'd left the gym yesterday, Maureen had stopped at the grocery store. Then, true to her word, she'd started her diet today. Had she remembered her parents' invitation for this evening, however, she would have delayed another twenty-four hours.

"And that Band-Aid . . ." Laura blotted her lips with her napkin, worriedly eyeing the crook of her daughter's elbow. "Have you been to the doctor?"

Maureen's heart plummeted as she looked down at the small round patch her physician's nurse had placed there after drawing blood. She'd meant to remove it when she returned to the shop this afternoon. But then she'd gotten busy with a design job, and the damn thing had slipped her mind.

"Just a routine checkup." She caught her father's eye and realized she wasn't fooling him one bit.

Paul had been afraid it would come to this, but he understood what motivated Maureen. She felt incomplete, not knowing anything about the man whose genes she shared, and she yearned to find her roots. It was as simple, and yet as complicated, as that.

The chilled Chablis trickled down his throat as he fortified himself for the inevitable explosion.

Outside, thunder boomed, rattling the satin-clad windows as the storm that had been brewing all week finally broke. Inside, the Art Deco chandelier, original to the house, dimmed for a few ominous seconds.

Laura sat bolt upright, as if struck by lightning, and laid down her napkin. Her teal blue eyes, so warm with concern only a moment ago, iced over when she met her daughter's guilty ones. "This has something to do with the gym, doesn't it?"

"Yes." Maureen couldn't believe she said it so calmly. "I'm going into training."

Stunned, Laura reared back. "Training?"

"With Jack Ryan."

"Oh, my God."

"Please, Mom . . ." Maureen reached across the table, seeking a bond, but all she got for her effort was air.

Laura stood and, with one hand fisted tightly between her breasts and the fingertips of the other pressed to her pounding temples, started for the arched doorway that led to the staircase. "I refuse to have this conversation."

Torn between his wife's distress and his daughter's woe,

Paul rose and tried to mediate a truce. "Won't you at least listen to what—"

But Laura, terrified that history was repeating itself, wouldn't even hear her husband out. "You encouraged her to get involved with those people—you listen to her!"

"I'm sorry, Dad." Maureen dropped her head into her hand as the slamming of her parents' bedroom door echoed back down to the dining room.

"Don't be." Paul rounded the table, stopping behind her chair to rub her slumping shoulders. "You knew this wouldn't be easy when you began."

"But I hate driving this wedge between you and Mom."

"We've been through worse and we're still together."

She heard the pain in his voice and knew he was referring to Laura's trouble carrying another pregnancy to term. "Did you ever wish I was a boy?"

His hands fell still on her shoulders but his answer came in a comforting rush. "What—and miss learning how to braid my little girl's hair?"

Maureen laughed, remembering the lopsided pigtails she'd worn the entire week her mother had spent in the hospital following her second miscarriage. And how badly her head had hurt when Laura combed them out on coming home. "My hair was a rat's nest!"

"So I was informed," Paul replied wryly.

"I'm serious, Dad," she said, sobering. "Didn't you ever wish you had somebody to go fishing with?"

"We went fishing once," he reminded her.

"All we caught were colds," she recalled with a smile.

"Your mother still doesn't know I bought those trout we brought home."

"And you honestly don't regret not having a son to carry on the family name?"

"What is it you call your shop?"

"Bryant's"—tears blurred her vision—"Interiors."

"So," he said, his own eyes glistening, "if you think Sully gave you up simply because you're a girl—"

"I don't know what to think anymore," she admitted.

Rain pelted the windows, mimicking the sudden urgency that deluged Paul to tell her that birth mothers sometimes surrendered boys too.

Maureen raised her head and stared at her troubled reflection in the gilt-griffoned mirror on the opposite wall. "I don't even know what it is I'm looking for when I go down to the gym."

"Yourself." If there was one thing he could tell her for certain, it was that.

Her eyes met her father's in the mirror. "Yes, but . . ." She swiveled in her chair and frowned up at him. "How did you know?"

Paul smiled down at her, love and pride for the woman he had raised supplanting his own sense of loss. "Call it a lucky guess."

She stood, feeling as if she finally had at least part of the answer, and put her arms around the man who had cherished her and protected her from the moment she had entered his life. "What am I going to do, Dad?"

He held her close, wanting her to know he was in her corner all the way, and whispered the encouraging words she needed to hear into her hair. "You're going to keep looking, of course."

ROUND 6

Two days of rain and a ton of design work had kept Maureen cooped up at the shop. But a cloudless sky and the all-clear from her doctor early this afternoon had her driving north and east to share her news.

She hadn't really been worried about her blood test. A fumbling college fling and a monogamous engagement did not a risk-taker make. But in these days, when fatal diseases could lie dormant for years, it never hurt to be sure.

The sun touched the saw-toothed skyline with gold as she merged left, onto the downtown loop that would take her to Independence Avenue.

No one had answered the phone when she'd called the gym, and she hadn't remembered until she'd hung up that it was closed on Saturdays. Sundays too. What the heck, Maureen thought after looking up Jack's home number and then impetuously jotting down his address, she'd just go tell him in person.

Only now, as she turned off the avenue and onto Maple Boulevard, was she beginning to worry about what she was going to say to him.

"I don't have AIDS," seemed a mite crass, while "I'm clean!" made it sound as if she'd been overly concerned about the outcome. Maybe a simple "See you Monday" would be the best way to couch it.

Maureen's anxiety took a back seat to her awe when she realized Jack's neighborhood was not only a mixed bag, architecturally, but it was the epitome of urban renewal. Revitalized stone and stucco "shirtwaists," named for early twentieth-century ladies' white blouses and dark skirts, rubbed elbows with authentically restored Victorians. New sidewalks, shaded by hundred-year oaks, made it safe for the children of young families moving in to ride their bikes.

She was doubly impressed when she parked in the driveway to the side of his home—a three-story, gray-blue Queen Anne with lighter-colored fish-scale shingles and a white wooden porch swing that inspired fantasies of lazy summer evenings spent watching the world go by.

Maureen let herself in through a wrought-iron gate, climbed two steps to the covered porch and depressed the bell. Not thirty seconds after she heard it chime inside, a barefoot Jack, wearing faded jeans and no shirt, pulled open the door. He seemed surprised to see her standing on his threshold, but quickly recovered his equanimity.

"Hi," was all he said, but it was enough to scatter her emotions like a bevy of birds.

One hand fluttered to her throat as she returned his greeting. "Hi."

"Don't tell me," he said with an ironic smile, "you just happened to be in the neighborhood—"

"Actually," she admitted, her face catching fire when she met his amused gaze, "I came looking for you."

"Look all you want," he invited in a throaty drawl.

That she'd already taken in everything from his bare, hair-dusted toes, to the soft denim molded to his shape and defining his sex, to the small, dark nipples on his naked chest only deepened her blush.

She let go of her pent-up breath on a rushing gust. "I got the results of my blood test back."

"And?" he prompted, his sparkling eyes belying the seriousness of the topic.

"I'm clean." Maureen realized what she'd said and could have chewed through her tongue. She raised her hands helplessly. "I mean—"

"I know what you mean," Jack assured her, his grin widening as he stepped aside. "Would you like to come in?"

She heard the muffled voices emanating from an open upstairs window then and shook her head. "I'm obviously interrupting—"

"I'm just watching films."

"Old films?" She envisioned classics such as Bergman and Bogart or Hepburn and Tracy.

"Fight films."

Her eyes locked with his.

"It seems we both have something to celebrate," he said in a tone that was anything but festive.

Fear shot an arrow through her chest. "Oh?"

" 'Poison' Ivy Stephens accepted my challenge yesterday."

Maureen felt heartsick as her gaze flicked from the scar above his eyebrow to his bent nose. She'd pushed him into going back into the ring, left him no choice but to fight for the gym and the diversionary program, and now she wanted to beg him not to do it. But she sensed, without knowing why, that he needed this match as much for himself as for the boys.

"Well," she finally managed, "I guess congratulations are in order all around."

Jack watched the play of emotions on her tiger lily face and wished he'd kept his big mouth shut. He was still pinching himself over finding her on his doorstep, the embodiment of his dreams in a sundress the color of a frosted mint julep, simple gold earrings and jeweled sandals. Just looking at her made him feel like a winner again, and he wanted to savor the sweet taste of victory a little while longer.

"I guess they are," he agreed in a raspy voice as he drew her across the threshold and into an all-wood foyer that was breathtaking.

"This is red oak!" she exclaimed.

"Would you believe the previous owners painted it brown?"

She made a face at the thought and ran her palm over the smooth surface. "It feels like satin now."

Pleasure danced in his eyes at her compliment. "First thing I did when I moved in was strip and refinish it."

"How long have you lived here?"

"A little over ten years."

"It must have cost you a fortune to renovate it!"

"And you're wondering where I got the money?"

"Well . . ." Abashed, Maureen smiled at him. "You have to admit that a Queen Anne house hardly fits your image."

"You forget that I'm an attorney as well as a fighter." Truth was, he had trouble remembering it himself at times. Blame it on Sully's brainwashing or his own intrinsic mind-set, but his law degree aside, Jack still tended to think of himself as a fighter first and an attorney second.

She shook her head. "I didn't forget—"

"Besides," he said, giving the habitual shrug that turned her brain to syrup, "I did most of the work myself."

Her expert eye landed on the mission oak library table against the hall wall, and she breathed, "Is that a Stickley Brothers?"

"According to the name that's burned into the bottom of the drawer," he confirmed.

"May I?" she asked, touching it reverently.

"Be my guest." Watching her slender fingers caress the quartersawn white oak, he felt his body quicken with desire. He wanted. Lord, how he wanted. But he deliberately took one step back to put a little more distance between them.

She knelt, pulled open the drawer and poked her head beneath it to study its authentic imprint. "This is a collector's item, you know."

He caught a whiff of her expensive scent when she stood and shut the drawer. "I got it at a garage sale for twenty-five dollars."

"Remind me to go treasure hunting with you sometime."

"Name the day."

She turned to find his eyes on her. "Any more antiques hidden away in here?"

He did not look away. "See for yourself."

Given the state of the gym, she fully expected the house to be a mess. But as he led her past a staircase with the original spindles and newel posts and into the Spartan-clean living room, she realized he was as much of a perfectionist in his personal life as she.

Maureen lifted her gaze to study the ten-foot walnut ceiling he'd also stripped, and Jack found himself studying the curve of her creamy throat, the thrust of her breasts against the scooped cotton bodice.

"It's beautiful."

"I'll say."

The husky timbre of his voice turned her head, and the dark fires in his eyes as they roamed back up to her face sparked a purely feminine flare of response in the pit of her stomach.

She strove for that famous cool and came up with a tepid, "I'm talking about the house."

His smile flashed white in his sun-bronzed face. "Would you like a tour?"

"I'd love a tour."

Jack had decorated simply, sponging the walls of the living room and dining room, as well as the wooden blinds at the windows, with silvery-white paint. An angled fireplace created a cozy niche, plants thrived in odd places, and several Bernard Martin wildlife oils added splashes of color. The oak floors were polished to a soft patina, and the furniture was a masculine mixture of old and new.

For the center of the kitchen, instead of building an island, he'd bought a stainless-steel restaurant cart. Cooking utensils sprouted from wide-mouthed Mason jars, and copper pots and a cutting board shaped like a pig hung from a wrought-iron rack. A two-foot "border" of grapevines, attached to the wall with a staple gun, was both offbeat and interesting. Conveniently, he'd converted the unused utility porch into a half-bath.

"How about some fruit juice?" he asked before they started upstairs.

"Sounds good."

"Grab some glasses—first cabinet to the right of the sink."

Maureen did as he instructed. Then stood back in utter amazement when Jack pulled a juicer from beneath the gray-tiled counter and plucked apples and bananas from a basket atop it. In minutes, and with a minimum of fuss, he'd made them each a glass of fresh, frothy juice.

"To a clean blood test," he toasted.

"And a clean fight," she saluted.

Their gazes linked as their glasses clinked.

Warm sunlight, spilling in through the open window above the sink, struck a match to Maureen's unbound hair when she took a tentative sip of the concoction. Another kind of heat spread through Jack's middle, poured through his veins, as her pink tongue darted out to lick a drop from her glossy lips.

"Delicious," she pronounced.

"I'll bet," he replied gruffly, and promptly drained his juice in one long swallow.

Her insides quivered at the sight of his stern mouth upon the rim, his strong fingers wrapped around the fragile glass. Quickly, before he caught her staring at him, she drank her juice and set her glass in the sink.

"Onward and upward," he said then, leading her back to the foyer and up the stairs.

Pale steel-gray carpet muffled their steps, but the voices Maureen had heard earlier grew louder as they approached the second floor. Jack ducked into a room that served as his den and faced the street, hit the "eject" button on the VCR and turned off the television. From the doorway she watched the two boxers on the screen fade to black, and her stomach twisted painfully.

"Was that one of your professional fights?"

He nodded brusquely as he put the tape in its cardboard container and set it atop the entertainment center.

"Did you win?"

"By a knockout." He grabbed a cotton shirt the color of smoke off the glass doorknob and shrugged into it.

She tried again, thinking this was like pulling teeth. "Which round?"

"Third." Jack blew out an aggravated breath as he finished buttoning his shirt and stepped into a pair of Topsiders. "What is this, 'Twenty Questions'?"

Maureen saw his lips harden into that familiar line of bitterness and tabled her curiosity for the time being. "One more question."

"What?" he all but growled at her.

"Shall we continue the tour?"

His eyes warmed, and she could feel the heat radiating off him. "Follow me."

She did just that, pausing only to peek into the original bathroom with its clawfoot tub and black-and-white tile floor before trailing him down the hall to the master bedroom.

The creamy walls not only had a cool and soothing effect, they served as the perfect backdrop for a king-size brass bed covered with a toile comforter. White duck hung from black dowels, curtaining the windows and filtering the sunlight, while a buffed cork floor added its own mellow, leatherlike shine to the room. A massive Pennsylvania chest of drawers held a stack of books, a collection of empty cobalt bottles, and a ceramic dish brimming with keys and change.

"Not a trophy or a medal in sight." She caught his eye in the oval Irish mirror framed with silver gilding and Waterford glass beads that hung over the chest.

"I packed them away years ago," he replied tersely.

She got the message and moved on. In the adjacent bath, panels of sandblasted glass provided privacy while bringing in sunlight to perform ablutions by. Brass rings filled with fluffy towels lent a nostalgic touch to the otherwise modern facility. There was an oversized shower with a clear glass door, deep double basins, a private commode and a tub big enough for two.

That latter thought set her nerves on edge. As did the spicy scent of his soap permeating her nostrils. She averted her eyes from his personal grooming articles—the old-fashioned shaving mug and brush, the blue toothbrush in a brass rack, the tortoiseshell hairbrush on the marble countertop—and beat a hasty retreat.

"Nice job." She noticed he'd tucked in his shirt when she rejoined him in the bedroom.

"I lost the third bedroom on this floor when I remodeled, but I wanted a walk-in closet and master bath."

"That's the problem with these old houses—plenty of bedrooms, but not enough closets and bathrooms."

He chuckled. "People back then didn't wear nearly as many clothes as we do now."

"They needed bathrooms, though."

"Maybe they had better control."

She threw him a disparaging look across the bed. "I'll bet the first lady of this house had a constant bladder infection."

He thrust his hands in the back pockets of his jeans and frowned skeptically. "Why do you say that?"

"She would have had to have climbed those stairs."

"So would her husband."

"Three steps ahead of her," she said pointedly. "And after him came the children who probably couldn't wait."

He got her drift, of course, but was enjoying needling her too much to stop. "Meaning?"

"The woman is always the last to go."

"I wouldn't know about that."

"That," she said emphatically, "is because you're a man."

"And you," he returned softly, "are a woman."

Their eyes met in a conflagration of reaction across the king-size bed, and they both realized that they'd better get out of there . . . fast.

Maureen was the first to look, then move away. "What's upstairs?"

Jack followed her into the hall. "I'm saving that for sunset."

"Sunset?" Coming to a halt, she glanced at her watch. "But that's a good five hours from now."

He grinned and started down the stairs. "I guess we'll just have to come up with something to do in the meantime."

"Something to do?" Thoroughly confused now, she hurried to catch up with him.

On the bottom step, he looked back at her with dark eyes agleam. "Polly want a cracker?"

Realizing he was poking fun at her for parroting him, she laughed. "It's not part of her diet."

The front door stood open, admitting into the red oak foyer the shouts of children playing with school's-out fervor in the vest-pocket park across the street.

A bird sang in the oak tree outside as they turned, standing shoulder to shoulder, to watch.

He forgot Sully's oft-repeated advice that a fightin' man had no business getting married, and pictured a redheaded girl asking her daddy to push her on the swing. She felt her biological clock ticking for the first time ever as she visualized a brown-eyed boy showing off his newest skateboarding trick to his heart-in-her-throat mom.

A neighbor's car backfired, breaking the spell, and they turned back to each other.

Jack watched Maureen brush a loose strand of hair off her face and was shaken by how completely she'd gotten under his skin. She was like an itch he couldn't quite locate, a hunger he couldn't satisfy, a thirst he couldn't quench. Every instinct warned him to shake her hand, thank her for stopping by and send her back uptown where she belonged.

He reached for her hand. Beyond all reason then, he held it and said the first thing that came into his head. "Would you like to go to the City Market with me?"

In the last few months, Maureen had dined in the Starlight Room atop the Kansas City Club, at Trader Vic's in Crown Center, and at the Raphael on the Plaza. She'd also attended a play at the Midland Theater and a benefit performance of the Missouri Ballet. And if that wasn't enough to exhaust her, she'd recently donated an entire weekend— not to mention her professional expertise—to a Women in Business seminar.

But she hadn't been to the City Market in years.

Like many Kansas Citians, Maureen often vowed to buy her fresh fruits and vegetables at the regional farmer's market. When Saturday rolled around, however, she was usually too stressed out to even think about making the long drive and fighting the large crowds. So she would opt for convenience and do her grocery shopping closer to home.

"Where should I park?" She'd circled the Square twice

and now was essentially stalled at Fifth and Grand, heading north and trying to decide whether to turn right or left. They'd taken her car because it was already out, and his was in the garage behind his house.

"Do you mind walking?" Jack draped his left arm across the back of the leather seat, her hair tickling the fingers of his hand, and peered out the Mercedes's windshield.

"How far?"

"A couple of blocks."

Maureen breathed a sigh of relief. "Point the way."

He thumbed to the right, and she turned as soon as she got the green light. At the stop sign he directed her to turn right again, then left, and she found herself taking a driving tour of Little Italy, as the North End of the city was commonly called.

"This is like a self-contained village," she commented as she cruised by small homes with front-yard shrines to the Madonna and clapboard stores advertising pepperoni and prosciutto in their glass windows.

"From the baptismal font to the bier," he said when they passed a church and a funeral parlor within two short blocks of each other.

"Can we do this?" Maureen asked after he instructed her to park in the asphalt lot next to Jennie's Restaurant.

Jack shot her a sly grin from the passenger seat. "You afraid you'll get towed away by the police?"

"It's a possibility."

"I'll talk to Tom."

She tipped her head inquiringly. "Who's Tom?"

"The owner." He reached over and rubbed a knuckle softly against her cheek, sending little crackles of excitement surging up her spine.

"You're sure he won't mind?" Her voice sounded strange —as if she'd just burned a hole in her throat.

"Knowing Tom," he said thickly, "he'll exact some kind of payment."

"Like what?"

"Dinner for two."

She batted her lashes—something she *never* did. "Are you asking, Jack Ryan?"

An audacious gleam lit his eyes. "I most certainly am, Maureen Bryant."

"I'd be delighted."

"I'll make our reservation."

She waited outside, in the shade of a vine-covered lattice that gave the redbrick restaurant the look of a *trattoria*, while he went inside to inform the owner that they'd parked in his lot and would be back for dinner in a couple of hours.

That settled, they took the City Market by storm.

It was one of the most sensory experiences Maureen had ever had. Jack hailed most of the vendors by name, asking after their health and their families, as they strolled from stall to stall. For the better part of an hour, they did nothing but pinch fresh fruit, pet live animals and sniff the lush variety of flowers for sale.

"This is fun," she said as she paid for a cantaloupe whose pungent fruitiness told her what she'd be eating for breakfast the next few mornings.

He purchased one too. "I shop here almost every Saturday."

"I always swear I'm going to come down to the market." She smiled ruefully when they reached the end of one aisle and started up another. "And then I never do."

"You're making up for it now," he pointed out as he presented her with one perfect pink tulip that was somehow more beautiful than a dozen bouquets of roses combined.

Was she ever! Maureen got tears in her eyes when she took a taste of the horseradish Jack bought from an apple-cheeked woman who swore she'd grown and grated it just for him. Then she got a lump in her throat when he gently consoled a lost boy of five until he could be reunited with his frantic parents. And when they got separated for a few moments in the midst of the bargain hunters, she easily found him standing head and shoulders above the crowd.

They spent another hour traveling down the path of time at the Arabia Steamboat Museum. In 1856 the huge side-wheeler had hit a snag in the Missouri River. All the passengers on board had swum safely to shore, but the ship had sunk to the muddy bottom with its 220 tons of supplies for frontier towns along the river and had lain there until its excavation by a local salvage team in 1988.

A videotape explaining the history primed them for the tour that followed. Maureen was fascinated by the collection of textiles and tinware that had been preserved, while Jack was more interested in the hardware and medicine bottle displays. They walked away sharing childhood stories of digging for buried treasure—one with a silver spoon, one with plain old pot metal—in their own back yards.

Dinner at a corner table for two at Jennie's topped off their outing. A candle in a straw-wrapped chianti flask, dribbled with melted wax and sitting atop the red-and-white checked tablecloth, created an intimate atmosphere. Wine was out, since they were both in training, so they conversed over glasses of sparkling water.

"John Patrick Ryan." Maureen took great delight in repeating his full name after she'd finally coaxed it out of him. "Since you're Irish, I'm assuming you're also Catholic."

"Lapsed." Too late, Jack caught himself and wondered why he was telling her these things. He knew better. She wasn't his kind. Nothing could come of it.

"You don't believe in God, or do you just have a problem with organized religion in general?"

"It's hard to believe in a Higher Power when your old man is beating the hell out of you or your mother."

Candlelight was reflected in her green eyes as she

reached across the table and laid a compassionate hand over his. "It must have been a horrible experience for a child."

"I survived it." He was conscious of the play of light and shadow across her face, and of the absence of any rings on the delicate fingers atop his own deadly ones.

"You did more than survive—you broke the cycle."

He remembered a crumpled body on the canvas and, with a short, self-derisive laugh, removed his hand from beneath hers. "Don't bet the ranch on it."

"I've seen you with the boys," she reminded him saucily.

The humorous glint in his eyes belied his grim warning. "I repeat, don't bet the ranch on it."

Maureen laughed, the throaty sound of it working on his senses, then picked up her salad fork after the waitress set down their individual servings of sliced beefsteak tomatoes seasoned in olive oil, lemon juice and fresh basil.

Jack relaxed his guard a little more over homemade cheese ravioli and sesame-encrusted bread still warm from the oven. "I take it from everything you've said that the recession's been good for business."

She nodded as she dabbed at her lips with her napkin. "A lot of people can't afford to move, so they're staying in their homes and redecorating."

"Tell me about your most memorable job." Later, he realized, he would rue letting curiosity get the better of him. But right now he wanted to know all there was to know about the beautiful woman sitting across the table from him.

Between bites of the delectable pasta, she recounted the story of the divorcing couple who'd commissioned her to divide the home they both loved too much to leave into a "his" and "hers" duplex.

"Sounds like something out of *War of the Roses*.

"Actually, it was very civilized. He took the first floor, she took the second, and they shared the foyer."

"No hanging from the chandelier?" The seductive tone of his voice told her he wasn't talking about the mutually destructive act that ended the movie he'd just mentioned.

"Not in public." Leaning toward him flirtatiously—a bold move for her—she whispered, "But what they did in private was their own affair."

He couldn't help noticing the shadowy cleft between her breasts before she sat back. Immediately aroused, he lifted his eyes to her face and asked her another question. But while she was answering, he was mentally placing his lips in that velvet valley and pressing them against the precious flesh on each side of it.

The fight didn't come up for discussion until cappuccino was served in demitasse cups. Jack told her that Duck and "Poison" Ivy's manager, having agreed on the financial split, were now working on a pay-per-view deal with a cable sports network. Maureen told him how upset Laura was and how understanding Paul had been about her going into training with him.

He said to give her mother some time to adjust to the idea.

She said that was essentially what her father had counseled.

What went *un*said was that time was their worst enemy. The fight was exactly seven weeks away, and he would need every spare moment of the next forty-nine days to get into tip-top shape. Which meant that tonight might be all they would ever have . . .

"You ready to go?" he finally asked.

She sighed with repletion. "Anytime."

He paid their bill, then slid an arm around her slender waist and drew her to his side. She dangled the keys to her precious Mercedes in front of his face and asked if he'd like to drive. The westering sun threw their merged shadows across the asphalt lot as they ambled to the car.

Jack rolled down the windows, letting in the evening

breeze and the *shush* of the tires on the street while he drove the two miles east to his house. Maureen rested her head against the leather seat, twirling the tulip stem between her fingers and covertly watching the tightening of muscles beneath the leg of his blue jeans as he braked at a stoplight.

Neither of them moved to get out of the car when he pulled into his driveway and turned off the engine. The scent of mock orange wafted through the open window as she reminded herself they were doomed from the start. Nesting calls of birds filled the air while he tried valiantly to summon the discipline to send her on her way.

"Thanks for a wonderful day," she said in a soft voice, wishing it needn't end but knowing it must.

His eyes were as tactile as the brush of his fingers as he handed her keys back. "It's not over yet."

She sat up straight. "Oh, that's right—"

"The third floor," he reminded her.

A breeze so soft it might have been a lover's sigh rustled the leaves in the old oak tree as they shut the front door behind them. They eyed each other wordlessly in the shadowed foyer, then turned by tacit agreement to climb the plushly carpeted stairs. No voices from the past marred the perfect stillness when they reached the second floor and started toward the third.

"A sunroom!" she cried with delight when he opened the door.

"Sun*set* room," he corrected, switching on the light dimmer.

Call it what he would, it was a nature lover's dream come true. A wall of windows, facing west and wearing a valance of rolled shades, brought the outdoors in. Unbleached muslin upholstery on the massive sofa and birchbark lampshades added a rustic touch, as did the sisal rugs and rattan chairs arranged in conversational groupings.

"Oh, Jack . . ." Maureen breathed her awe as she gravitated toward the windows that afforded such a splendid view of the downtown skyline. "Look."

He did just that, taking in the subtle sway of her hips as he followed closely on her heels. "I come up here almost every evening to watch the sun go down."

Ol' Sol was making a gaudy exit now, waving good-bye with gold and vermilion-tipped fingers. No sooner had it slipped behind the horizon, leaving a void in the darkening heavens, than the prismatic-glassed Kansas City Power & Light Building's automated lighting system took up part of the slack. Other towers donned crowns of diamond-white or ruby-red, and the two rivers that met at the city's feet— the meandering Kaw and the mighty Missouri—reflected their jewel-like brilliance.

She gave up trying to count the stars winking on at an even one hundred. "I've never seen anything like it."

He couldn't take his eyes off the pure lines of her profile. "Neither have I."

Glancing down at her watch, she saw it was time to go. *Past* time, she thought, her breath fluttering in her throat when she turned to find his gaze steady on her face. She swallowed, trying to form the words to thank him once again and take her leave, but he beat her to the punch.

"Would you like a drink?"

"I'm in training, remember?"

Jack knew there'd be hell to pay when it was time to run in the morning, yet hastened to clarify. "Around here, 'drink' means juice or water."

Maureen realized she should decline so he could get his rest, but couldn't keep herself from saying, "Water with a twist of lime, if you have it."

"One water with lime, coming right up." He crossed to the corner bar and reached into the built-in refrigerator.

"This must have been a ballroom at one time."

"Why do you say that?"

"Oh, the parquet floor and the lack of walls." Too restless to sit, she laid her purse on the bar and wandered over to the stereo system.

"Turn on the radio," he suggested.

"Any particular station?"

"WHB."

She grinned. "You like the oldies too, huh?"

He set her glass on the bar as "Johnny Angel" came on the air. "It's the only music worth listening to."

"I'll drink to that." She did, mouthing the words to the song between sips of her lime-refreshed water.

"Here's a coaster."

"Thanks." She placed it on a twig table beside a rattan chair, but remained standing.

He held up an unopened can of peanuts. "Want some?"

"I'm stuffed as a cannoli," she groaned playfully.

They engaged in small talk while he wrapped the unused portion of lime in cellophane and wiped off the cutting board—this one shaped like a paddle.

Maureen watched his hands, captivated by the sight of his long fingers making short work of the clean-up. Finally realizing what she was doing, she moved her eyes back to his face.

Jack saw the flush on her cheeks as he cut around the bar, and wished he was responsible for it. He crossed to where she was standing just as the slowly evocative "Since I Fell for You" came on.

"May I have this dance?" he asked with mock formality.

She laughed, unable to keep a straight face as she answered, "Yes, you may."

The joking stopped the instant she stepped into his arms. Their eyes made sizzling contact when their bodies did. They both knew that dancing was merely an excuse to hold each other at long last.

Eschewing the traditional waltz position, he slipped his arms around her waist and drew her so close she could feel his searing heat through their clothes. Obligingly she raised her hands to his broad shoulders. Their eyes never wavered from each other's face as they swayed in smooth, sensuous harmony.

One song drifted into another, and still they clung together, their bodies melded more by their growing desire than by those golden oldies.

They found their own thrill during "Blueberry Hill." He brought one hand up from her waist and increased the pressure on her back until her firm breasts were flattened against his chest. She felt herself tremble with a passion no man had ever brought to the surface before.

"You grew up real nice." His voice was pitched low and provocatively challenging.

"I'm glad you approve," she murmured softly, the smallest of smiles curving her lips.

Jack looked down into her liquid green eyes and knew that he was going to kiss her. There were a hundred reasons he shouldn't, but they all escaped him as he slid his hands into the red-gold abundance of her hair and tilted her head back.

Maureen felt the wildness within herself for the first time ever as he tipped her face up with utmost tenderness and slanted his mouth over hers. She realized then that she'd been waiting a lifetime for a man who was strong enough to be gentle.

It was folly of the highest caliber, this kiss, yet thoughts of right or wrong, yes or no did not exist. For now there was only the soft tangling of breath, the moist coupling of lips, the sweet tango of tongues. And when he finally lifted his head, they saw in one another's gaze that it was much too short to satisfy either of them for long.

"I've been thinking about this since the first day you walked into the gym," he admitted raggedly.

She looked up into the bottomless darkness of his eyes and could no more lie than she could fly. "Me, too."

His right hand slipped to her ribs, his left cupped her

hip, bringing her firmly against his arousal. "God, you feel good."

"So do you," she whispered, running her fingers along the corded muscles at the back of his neck.

When his thumb stirred, caressing the underswell of her breast, she gasped for breath. Experimentally he let the hard pad climb that soft mound of flesh until it reached the peak, tautly belled beneath her cotton bodice. She moaned at the stimulating circular motion he made, but not in protest.

"This'll never work," he said hoarsely.

She swallowed hard. "I know."

"You'll be gone as soon as you get your money."

"You'll be busy with the boys after you fight."

Jack nuzzled her throat, her earlobe, her temple, leaving hot spots in his wake. "So, what do you think?"

Maureen inhaled his spicy masculine scent and tilted her head invitingly. "I think I'd like another kiss."

He gathered her close, only too glad to grant her request, and came back for more. She welcomed the pressure of his mouth with parted lips, then whimpered with passion when his tongue sought its counterpart. They tasted and tested and trembled, striking the kind of powerful physical chords that resonate long after a kiss has ended.

And end it must. Now, he told himself, before he went down for the count at her lily-white hands. As if he needed a further reminder that they came from two entirely different worlds, Billy Joel blasted him from the radio with "Uptown Girl."

Jack pulled back and gripped Maureen's shoulders, keeping her at arm's length. There were roses in her cheeks and clouds of confusion in her eyes as she looked up at him for an explanation of his abrupt withdrawal. He debated the wisdom of what he was about to do for several tense seconds before he dropped his hands and let her have it with a deliberate cruelty that sickened him.

"Sorry," he drawled in a tone that said he was anything but, "you're a little too rich for this poor boy's blood."

"I . . ." She swallowed heavily and touched her still-throbbing mouth with one finger. "I don't understand."

"Then I'll make it easy for you."

"Please do."

He gestured scornfully at the softly playing radio. "You're from the silk stocking district. I'm from the streets."

She grew angry in her own right then. "Do you honestly think I judge a person's worth by where they're from?"

"I think Laura does."

"What's my mother got to do with us?"

His eyes flashed like antic strobes. "I saw how she left Sully. He was a broken man when she was finished with him. And good, bad, or indifferent, we're all products of our environment, baby."

"Don't call me baby, you—you dumb jock!" The second she hurled the epithet at him, she would have given heaven and earth to snatch it back.

Jack flinched, confirming she'd hit her target, but continued ruthlessly, "So just as my father is part of who I am, your mother is very much a part of who you are."

Maureen was every inch Laura's daughter as she lifted her chin a fraction higher and turned on her heels. She deeply regretted the name she'd called him, but he'd never know it. And she'd be damned if she would apologize for what was essentially an accident of birth!

The fading refrain of "Uptown Girl" nicked her nerves like knives when she crossed to the bar to retrieve her purse before walking to the door.

"I'll get my car out of the garage and follow you home," he offered curtly, knowing he'd feel responsible if anything happened to her on the road.

"I found my way down here without your help," she declined as she reached for the doorknob. "I'm sure I can find the way back to my white bread world without it too."

ROUND 7

June melted into the firecracker swelter of July, and the two people who stood to gain the most from the upcoming fight turned a cold shoulder to each other in the gym.

Perspiration dampened Maureen's sweatband and her sleek black catsuit, but she continued to work on her form in front of the wall-length mirror, trying to remember to keep her arm stiff as she blocked imaginary punches. In the ring behind her, his naked bronze back an all-too-familiar reflection by now, Jack began boxing his own invisible opponent.

Maureen assumed a fighting stance, temporarily forgetting the antipathy between herself and Jack and focusing instead on shooting out those jabs until the little shocks in her shoulders told her they were straight and true.

Left . . . right. She'd finished her warm-up exercises today with energy to spare. Left . . . right. She found it amazing that these punching movements came so naturally to her after just two weeks of practicing them. Left . . . right. She failed to notice her reflection growing hazy as she recalled her first day in training . . .

"Come up real slow," Duck had told her that Monday.

Lying with her hands linked under her head and her toes pointed, Maureen had come up inch by trembling inch,

trying to keep her back and her legs straight and her heels
on the mat as she did his version of a sit-up.

"Now over," he said in that rock-crusher voice.

She felt the long muscles in her thighs pulling and the
muscles in her lower back tearing when she folded over
until her face and knees were almost touching and the
blood was flooding her head.

"Hold it."

What was she trying to prove? she wondered as, shoulders quivering and stomach muscles tightening painfully,
she fought to hold the position. Putting herself through
hell in order to be near a man who—

"Now up and back down."

Her entire body shuddering with the strain, Maureen
slowly lowered the back of her head to the mat and closed
her eyes in disgust. What a wuss! One sit-up and she was
hot and sweaty and ready to throw in the towel.

She'd pulled her hair up in a ponytail and changed into a
lilac Lycra unitard, matching socks and white cross-training
shoes. What she should have put on, she decided as she
opened her eyes to stare at the peeling plaster ceiling, were
prison stripes or a POW uniform. Because something told
her training was going to be pure torture.

"Twenty of those oughtta do it for today," Duck said.

"Twenty?" came the protest from Camille.

"You wanna get in shape or not?"

"In shape, yes; in traction, no."

"It's only pain."

"That's easy for *you* to say," she grumbled.

"I've been there," he reminded her gruffly.

Maureen drew several deep breaths, realizing what incredible self-discipline it took for Jack to exercise like this
every day. She also realized that she wasn't here just to win
his approval, but wanted to find out some things for and
about herself. On that thought, she resolved to finish what
she'd started.

The second sit-up was harder than the first, and the third was harder still. But by the fourth, her muscles were warming and weren't struggling against each other. She did twenty of the damn things before she flopped back on the mat, exhausted.

"You ready to reverse 'em?" Duck asked.

"I'm ready for a nap," she answered.

"Too bad."

She complied with a groan when he told her to roll over, onto her stomach, and arch her back like a cobra. The pain was excruciating, and she gave serious consideration to asking him why he didn't just shoot her and be done with it.

"In boxing, the stomach is more important than the chin," he explained.

"How . . . so?" she panted.

"A china-chinned boxer can never strengthen his jaw."

"China . . . meaning . . . glass?"

"Like mine, right," he said without a vestige of self-pity in his voice. "Hit the chin and you might break it or you might break your hand. But hit the belly and you kill the head."

"Just the opposite . . . of cutting off . . . the head of the snake?"

He bobbed his balding head in reply. "Feel Jack's stomach sometime—it's hard as a rock."

Maureen was grateful she was lying face down when Jack's name came up. Otherwise, Duck would have seen the tears of frustration that sprang to her eyes and the hot color that scorched her cheeks. This way she had an opportunity to compose herself before she lifted her head.

"I'll do that," she murmured. Then, determined to put her misery out of her mind, she arched her back again. What she couldn't oust, however, was the memory of Saturday night.

Sunday was her day off. Unless she had a pressing professional deadline, she usually went to noon Mass and then did something for her own personal enjoyment, like meeting a friend for brunch or taking in a new exhibit at the Nelson-Atkins Museum. Yesterday, though, she'd holed up at home, turning on her answering machine and trying to figure out what had gone wrong with something that had felt so wonderfully right.

Jack had wanted her. Maureen knew that as well as she knew a Manet from a Monet. And she had wanted him. More than she'd ever wanted before. But judging from the way he'd reacted to that damn song, he didn't believe they could bridge the differences in their backgrounds. Either that, or he saw her as another Laura. A woman who would love him and leave him and never look back.

After completing twenty reverse sit-ups, she laid her cheek against the mat and blew a stray, perspiration-soaked strand of hair out of her eyes. She ached all over. Not just from exertion, either, but with the need to convince that big palooka she was in for the long haul.

"Time to run in place," Duck said then.

An appropriate metaphor, Maureen thought wryly as she rolled over and got to her feet. Jack had been jumping rope when she arrived at the gym, and had returned her cautious "hello" with a cool nod. By the time she'd changed her clothes in the locker room and come upstairs, he'd moved into the ring.

He was still there, half-naked and all business as he shadowboxed with his back to her. She couldn't help wondering what he would do if she climbed in there with him, put up her dukes and demanded a showdown. The idea was so ridiculous, she felt laughter fizzling in her throat.

Duck burst the bubbles with an impatient, "You gonna run or you gonna stand there gawking at Jack?"

Two can play this game, Maureen thought as she turned her back on the man in the ring and began running in place.

"Reach up with your hands."

She punched her fists into the air. "Like this?"

"Like this." Duck demonstrated, opening and closing his hands. "Pretend you're picking flowers."

Maureen had never had a dance teacher put anything half that nicely. "This is fun."

"Tell me that when you're finished."

When she was finished, she wanted to tell him to take a flying leap off the Broadway Bridge. But first she had to douse the fire in her lungs. She grabbed the plastic water bottle she'd picked up at the convenience store on her way to the gym and took a long pull on the straw sticking through the top.

"Yo, Mo!" Jamal yelled as he came in the street door.

"Lookin' bad," Tony said, which made her feel good.

"So does the locker room." Maureen had gone down there not knowing what to expect, and had been pleasantly surprised to find that it had been scrubbed from top to bottom. The benches and the lockers had boasted fresh paint and the shower had sported new tiles. Even the urinals—when she'd dared a peek—had worn a sparkle.

"Jack sanded down the benches and the lockers and regrouted the shower on Thursday," Deron told her. "Then Duck ordered in a couple of pizzas on Friday and we all stayed late painting and cleaning up."

"Well, you did a wonderful job." She took another draw on the straw while the boys handed in their homework papers, then called after them when they started down the stairs, "There's peaches in my gym bag!"

Their *woof-woof-woofs* of acknowledgment echoed up from the locker room.

"What's next?" she asked Duck, really getting into the swing of things now.

"Footwork."

Her legs still felt like the linguini she'd had for lunch, but she wasn't about to complain. "What do I have to do?"

"You have to lay the foundation for a strong house—a

house that the Big Bad Wolf can't huff and puff and blow down."

Maureen bit back a smile as she stole a glance at Jack. He didn't have inordinately big eyes or teeth, but the simile wasn't all that inaccurate. She set her water bottle back down and nodded at Duck.

"Okay," she said. "Let's start building me a strong house."

Mercilessly, he put her through her paces. "Backward . . . forward . . . in a circle now."

Her feet did just what he told them to, and pretty soon she was dancing smoothly around the perimeter of the invisible ring he'd drawn on the floor. No matter how hard she concentrated, though, her hands and arms wouldn't cooperate. And she refused to believe that her "bosom"— as Duck so quaintly referred to her breasts—was pushing them out of position!

"You look like a chicken trying to fly," he'd commented as she'd struggled to coordinate her upper and lower body movements.

She'd finally gotten the hang of it, though it had taken her two full weeks to do so. At the same time her feet glided across the floor, her head stayed down, protected, and her hands remained guardedly up. She'd thrown herself into the routine every day since then—even practicing in front of the mirror at home over the weekends—beginning to feel a strange sense of power and a bone-deep pride in a physical ability she'd never really tapped before.

Now, closing one eye and peering over her extended left fist, Maureen smiled triumphantly at her own reflection in the mirror. As the boys would say, she looked *bad*. Slowly, then, she swiveled from the hips and set her sights on Jack's naked back as he climbed out of the ring and headed for the stairs that led to the balcony level.

If he could go the distance, then by damn so could she!

• • •

"Hired your sparring partners."

"Great. Who'd you get?"

Duck chewed his cigar from one side of his mouth to the other before he answered. "Beetlejuice Jones and Ray Howard."

Jack recognized the names and nodded his approval. "When can they start?"

"Monday the nineteenth."

Finished pounding on the peanut bag, Jack walked to the other side of the balcony to begin working on the heavy one. "I'll spar with the boys till then."

"And don't forget," Duck reminded him, "you promised Maureen a shot too."

Jack's jaw clenched down as hard as the gloved fist he drove into the bag. "I've changed my mind."

"She'll be disappointed to hear that."

A low, rippling laugh belonging to the lady under discussion drifted up from the main floor of the gym. The sound of it played on Jack's senses, and his mouth twisted with a hard humor. He'd come up here to get away from the sight of her lissome body in that black catsuit, and damned if she hadn't found a way to follow him!

Funny, how his taste in women had changed. He used to prefer them a little flashier and a lot fleshier. Especially on top. But recent and frequent exposure to those elegant gams had turned him into a full-fledged leg man.

"Maybe Beetlejuice will take her on," Duck said now.

"Don't even think it," Jack warned him tightly.

"He'd go easy on her."

"He gets paid to hit, not to pull his punches." And if any sonofabitch harmed so much as one hair on her head . . .

Duck scratched his balding dome. "Speaking of punches, the sports reporters'll probably be getting their licks in soon."

"You sent out the press releases." Jack's voice deepened to a forceful pitch, almost as forceful as the jab-right-cross combination he threw at the bag.

"Just remember, it wasn't your fault."

"Cold comfort for his widow and son."

Another warm, melodic laugh, unmistakably Maureen's, set Jack's teeth on edge. His temper, too. What was she trying to prove, hanging around this low-class joint, anyway? Why didn't she just go do her high-society thing and leave him the hell alone?

"You told her yet?" Duck asked then.

"No." That was something else that was eating at him. He could have broken it to her gently at Jennie's Restaurant, when she'd made that remark about his breaking the cycle, but he'd come back with that glib rejoinder instead. Now he was stuck with having lied to her by omission.

"She's bound to find out."

"I know," he fired back.

"And she deserves to hear it from you first," Duck added pointedly before he turned on his heel and headed for the door that led down to the gym.

Fighting his own frustration now, Jack buried his fist in the bag. The fire was there, burning deep in his belly. So was the fear. It was a volatile mix that would have to be carefully stoked over the next four and a half weeks, until he virtually exploded against "Poison" Ivy Stephens.

In the meantime, what was he supposed to do about the fire that was raging *below* his belt?

"This gym's not big enough for the three of us!"

Maureen, wearing a hot pink leotard over wave-print capri pants today, dropped her hands and spun away from the mirror to look at Duck.

Jack followed suit, stopping flat in the middle of his

footwork to glare down at the trainer from his lofty position in the ring.

"Get outta here!" Duck, standing halfway between them, threw his thumbs over his shoulders in a gesture of disgust. "The both of you!"

Maureen found her voice first. "You mean leave?"

"That's exactly what I mean."

Jack thrust out his jaw and demanded indignantly, "Why?"

"'Cause this silent treatment the two of you are giving each other is drivin' me crazy, that's why!" He waved a hand toward the street door. "And if that's not enough to shame you, think o' the sample you're settin' for the boys."

Their eyes met over his head. Maureen saw the remorse in Jack's, he the regret in hers, and each found forgiveness for the terrible things they'd said to each other two weeks ago. Their visual apologies exchanged, they made their verbal ones to Duck.

"I'm sorry."

"Me too."

"Does this mean you're speaking to each other again?" he asked cautiously.

They nodded in unison.

"Good, you can go running together tomorrow afternoon."

"Running?" Maureen hadn't counted on having to do that.

"Since when do I run in the afternoon?" Jack demanded.

The trainer's bushy gray brows raised like drawbridges over his pale blue eyes. With Sully gone, he was doing double duty, honing Jack's boxing skills and handling the business end of things. Apparently he'd decided this was the right time to press his managerial advantage.

"Since I told you to," he said in no uncertain terms.

All his life, it seemed, Jack had watched fighters and managers in their corners between rounds. The manager would talk and the fighter would nod his head. He never shook it; he never said no to the manager.

Neither had Jack. Until this moment. "But—"

"But nothin'!" Duck barked, looking at each of them in turn. "Just do it."

"You really want to do this?"

"What choice do I have?"

Jack, finished limbering up, put on his sweatband and frowned down at Maureen. He wasn't angry with her, but he was still expecting her to cry "uncle" at the first chance. Yet there she stood, ready to run in a pair of pastel peach jogging shorts that made her legs look longer than a stretch limo and a matching jersey crop-top that exposed a strip of white skin and enflamed his imagination to boot.

"You could plead cramps." He tossed her the suggestion in a smugly sexist tone.

Maureen heard his call to arms and placed her hands on her hips. "Wimp out, you mean."

"I didn't—"

"Yes, you did."

The gleam in Jack's brown eyes as they connected with her flashing green ones thrust Maureen's pulse into full throttle. Not that her sensory system needed the extra boost. To the contrary, only a female corpse could have failed to respond to the masculine energy he radiated. Or managed to ignore the fact that he looked like poured copper, all smooth skin and sculpted muscle, in those brief white jogging shorts.

"You're right," he finally admitted, not even bothering to mask his chagrin. "That was a low blow."

A smile she hadn't any hope of catching spread across her face. "To tell you the truth, I almost didn't come today."

He quirked an eyebrow. "Oh, yeah?"

"But not because I've got cramps," she quickly clarified.

"Then why?"

"Because I'm falling behind at work."

"That's not the only place you're falling behind, lady," he said with a challenging grin before he wheeled away from her and headed for the street door.

She stood immobile, staring speechlessly at his broad, brown back. Then, muttering a distinctly *un*ladylike curse under her breath, she took off after him.

The heat punched like a fist when Maureen hit the pavement. She caught sight of Jack, already halfway to the corner, and she almost said to hell with it. But if she quit now, before she even started, she would negate all the good she'd done in the gym. And besides, the person she really needed to prove herself to was . . . herself.

"Go, Mo!" Rocstar lifted the vicious-looking scythe in his hand like a medieval standard of victory as she put the pedal to the mettle of her willpower and sprinted toward the stoplight.

She waved at the gang leader, amazed at the progress he and his two remaining followers were making on the new parking lot next door to the gym. Miraculously, they'd jumped at the chance to earn some extra money clearing away the rocks and cutting the weeds. So now, in addition to guarding her Mercedes, the three of them had real jobs and a growing sense of self-respect.

A half mile from the gym, Jack glanced back over his shoulder. Sure enough, Maureen was still behind him. He'd set a fast pace—too fast for a beginner like her—but she'd managed to stay close. Leading her into Kessler Park, he realized his game plan was changing. Where before he'd wanted her out of his life, he now wondered how he'd get along without her when she left.

He slowed down to let her catch up with him. When she did, he took her hand, pointed to a tree at the top of the next hill and asked, "Think you can make it?"

"I'll . . . try," she answered through parched lips, praying she didn't let either one of them down.

Jack smiled that breath-stopping smile, and Maureen forgot for a moment that her feet hurt and her stomach was in a knot. Then they started to run together, and her burning muscles reminded her that training was serious business.

"Don't think about the pain," he cautioned, squeezing her hand to give her strength. "Block it out."

Easier said than done. A stitch knifed her side, and she was sure she was either going to pass out or throw up.

"Come on," he encouraged as if reading her mind, "it's only a little farther."

She heard their feet on the path, but somehow they didn't seem connected. Then she heard him saying in cadence with their slapping steps, "You can do it. It's the last round. You've got what it takes to go the distance," and it began to dawn on her that they were almost there. They really *could* go the distance.

"I . . . did . . . it!" she exulted when they reached the tree. She wanted to dance, to sing, to shout it to the world. But every muscle in her body ached and she could hardly catch her breath. So she contented herself with collapsing on the soft grass, throwing her arms back over her head and basking in this glorious sense of accomplishment.

But not for long.

"You've got to keep moving, sweetheart, or you'll cramp up." He used the endearment without a second thought as he reached down with those giant, gentle hands to draw her to her feet.

And it was there, in the shade of that leafy old tree, that the sun came up in Maureen's mind. That she realized she'd fallen in love with Jack Ryan. She relished the feeling as much as she rued it. For the one thing that history had taught her well was that it was futile to love a fightin' man.

"Let's walk." He took her hand and held on tight, won-

dering if he was somehow to blame for the way her beautiful face had gone from sunshine to shadow in the blink of
an eye.

"I'm sorry I slowed you down today," she apologized as
they started hiking toward the Concourse.

"You'll do better tomorrow," he assured her.

She tipped her head back. "Think so, huh?"

With the knuckles of his free hand, he brushed a way-
ward tendril of her sunburst hair away from her cheek. "I
know so."

On the Concourse, they paused to study the bronze
plaque erected in memory of John F. Kennedy. Though
Maureen had only been five and Jack eight, mere children
at the time, they both remembered clearly where they were
and what they were doing the day Camelot died.

"I'd just come home from morning kindergarten," she
recalled softly. "My mother was listening to the radio and I
was eating lunch when the news bulletin came on."

His eyes reflected the flame burning brightly in the
small torch. "I was sitting in the principal's office, waiting
to be punished for throwing spitballs."

"Mom started crying, then Dad called from the bank
and said he was coming right home."

"A teacher rushed in and told the principal the President
had been shot, and she burst into tears."

The *gong-gong-gong* of the ice cream truck's bell put an
end to their gloomy conversation.

Maureen shook off her melancholy and flashed a brilliant smile at Jack. "Want to split a Popsicle?"

He frowned and patted his empty pockets. "I didn't
bring any money."

"I did." She crouched down and pulled a dollar bill from
the jogger's wallet in her shoe.

"A woman of means," he said teasingly. "My favorite
kind."

She arched a brow as she stood. "I certainly never thought I'd hear you say that."

He smiled crookedly, but his eyes grew somber. "I never thought I'd say it, either."

They waved the ice cream truck to the curb and bought a banana Popsicle. After breaking it in two, they crossed the street to sit on one of the park benches near the gurgling fountain while they each ate their half. Birds chattered among themselves in the entwining tree branches that provided such welcome relief from the late-afternoon sun.

"This is where Sully proposed to your mother," Jack said between bites.

Maureen tucked one foot beneath her hip and turned to him in surprise. "How do you know that?"

"He told me."

"I can't believe it."

"What—that Sully proposed to your mother here?"

"That you know more about my parents' marriage than I do."

It was his turn to look surprised. "Didn't you and your mother ever discuss Sully?"

She gave him a get-serious glance. "He was the Berlin Wall of silence between us."

"I've got a news bulletin for you—the Berlin Wall came down a couple of years ago."

"Yes, but where Sully is concerned, my mother's made of steel, not stone."

"And you never took a blowtorch to the wall?"

"I was afraid to."

"Why?"

"One father had already signed me away . . ." A spasm of sadness crossed her face. "What was to keep the second one from doing the same?"

Jack said nothing in reply because there was nothing *to*

say. He simply slid his arm along the back of the bench and rested his hand on her shoulder in a show of support.

"Did Sully . . . ever talk about me?" Maureen asked casually, but he caught something in her voice, a carefulness, a groping as delicate as the lick of Popsicle she took.

"You'd better eat that fast or it's going to melt all over your hand," he warned her before answering her. "Yes, he talked about you. Bragged on you, in fact. And every time he got a new picture of you, he showed it all over the gym."

She bit into the banana-flavored treat, so cold against her teeth, and tasted relief. "So there really is a scrapbook."

"You doubted it?"

" 'Doubted' isn't the right word—"

"Well, rest assured, it exists."

She believed him as completely as she loved him.

They finished their Popsicle halves, rinsed their sticky hands and sweaty faces in the splashing fountain and started back to the gym. Heat rose off the sidewalk in shimmering waves, the sun beat down upon them with fiery fists, and no breeze stirred to cool the air. Neither of them even noticed, so delighted were they to be speaking to each other again.

"Any news about Frankie and Tammy?" Maureen asked.

Jack shook his head grimly. "Not a word."

"I don't see how they could just disappear like that."

"You forget, hide or get hit is how they grew up."

"I wish I could forget."

A rusted Ford Galaxie station wagon, loaded to the gills with used furniture, sped past. Rap music and raucous laughter blasted out of a boarded-up building. A little boy, all snips and snails and dirty blond rat-tail, practiced his soccer moves with an empty beer can in his postage stamp of a front yard.

"Has your mother given you any more trouble about spending so much time on the poor side of town?"

"I haven't seen her since the night I told her, but the last time I talked to her on the phone, she was full of dire predictions."

Jack grinned lopsidedly. "Let me guess. Somebody's going to mug you—"

Maureen laughed. "Or steal my car and sell it for scrap metal."

"And your father?" He slid his hand to the back of her neck, finding her skin damp with perspiration and as smooth as those pearls she'd been wearing the first day he'd seen her. "Is he still behind you?"

She nodded and, quite naturally, looped her arm about his waist. "He stopped by the shop yesterday and asked me all kinds of questions about training."

"What'd you tell him?"

"I showed him my muscles." She did an exaggerated bodybuilder's curl, proudly displaying the new definition in her arms and shoulders.

"Uh-oh. I've created a monster." He let his hand glide from the back of her neck to her gently rounded bicep. It was only a short trip from there to her firm breast, but in light of the fact they were on a public sidewalk in broad daylight he restrained himself from making the journey.

"Well, Dad was impressed." Keenly aware of the proximity of those long, strong fingers, now resting possessively on her shoulder, she felt a compulsion to keep talking. "And Donna—my secretary and soon to be my design assistant—said she wants to start working out too."

"Hey, Champ!" A middle-aged man stepped out of a small storefront, stopping them just a block from the gym. If the striped barber pole beside the door hadn't given his profession away, his stiff black pompadour and swooping handlebar mustache would have.

Jack removed his hand from Maureen's shoulder to shake the barber's proffered one. "What d'ya say, Danny?"

"Heard you're going back into the ring."

"You heard right."

"In August, huh?"

"The fourteenth."

"Ivy's got a mean right hook."

"Tell me about it."

Maureen pulled her arm from around Jack's waist and put some distance between them while Danny the barber did exactly that. Jack was the essence of patience as he listened to the other man's suggestions about how he could defend himself against "Poison" Ivy's punch. Eventually a customer came along, bringing the conversation to an end.

"Well, good luck," the barber said as he turned to go back into his shop.

"Thanks."

"And remember, if you need a trim before the big night, it's on the house."

Jack clapped him on his white-coated shoulder. "I may take you up on that."

"You've got some neighborhood grapevine around here," Maureen said when they'd resumed walking.

"Oh, yeah, we're regular California raisins."

"Seriously, how else would Danny have known you were going to fight when it hasn't been in the paper or on television?"

If fighters had premonitions, they would never get into the ring. So it wasn't some ominous notion that brought Jack to an abrupt standstill and caused him to look down at the sidewalk. Nor was it any kind of terrible gut feeling that had his insides tied up in knots. It was just the sudden knowledge that he couldn't perpetrate the lie any longer.

He smiled at the woman standing beside him. A woman who was grace under pressure personified. The only woman who'd ever given him a real run for his money.

She smiled back at him with perplexity when he gently took her shoulders in his hands and opened his mouth to break his long-held silence. "Maureen—"

"Yo, Champ!" Rocstar called. "You got some GQ dudes chillin' on the stoop."

Jack knew he'd been caught dead to rights when he saw the crowd of reporters in front of the gym. They smelled blood at the same time. Except for the television and still cameras, microphones and tape recorders, it might have been a school of sharks swimming toward him.

He felt cornered as they began circling him. Like he'd felt when he was only five and his old man had come after him with bared teeth and doubled fists, and he couldn't do anything to defend himself. Couldn't do anything but beg him to stop . . . please, stop!

Only this time, he'd painted himself into the corner.

And only the truth could get him out.

He tightened his grip and tried again. "Maureen, there's something I need—"

"We're coming to you live from Sullivan's Fight Gym," one of the reporters said into the unblinking eye of a camcorder.

"Is it true you're training here?" another one asked.

A photographer captured the picture that was to grace the front page of the newspaper's sports section the next morning—Jack's eyes narrowing in fury as yet a third reporter elbowed Maureen aside to get to him.

Fortunately, no one caught her expression when that same reporter thrust a remote microphone into his face and demanded, "How does it feel to be making a comeback after you killed a man in the ring?"

ROUND 8

"Books are accessories too."

"But where would they go?"

Maureen, seated behind the brass and glass desk in her elegantly appointed office, smiled and opened a manila folder to one of the sketches she'd made after a recent "walk-through" of her clients' home.

The sweaty Mo who'd been running with Jack Ryan in the park just yesterday was gone, along with her crop-top, shorts and cross-training shoes. Maureen Bryant, interior designer, had taken her place, complete with sleeked-back French roll, black short-sleeved coatdress with a scalloped neckline and tulip hemline, and spectator pumps. To look at her now, no one would ever guess that beneath her put-together exterior there lay a shattered heart.

"Let me show you where I think they should go," she said to the couple sitting across from her.

Sam Miller, a stockbroker, and his wife Libby, a commodities trader, were newlyweds in their late twenties. Not only had they accumulated a hodgepodge of personal possessions before their "merger," as Libby laughingly called it, but they had recently acquired a Dutch colonial house that needed a complete updating. The couple had taken an early lunch hour from their respective Board of Trade offices today to discuss putting the finishing touches on their starter home.

Decorating a first house was as exhilarating an experience as it was frightening, full of possibilities but also expensive pitfalls. Maureen was proud of the fact that she'd helped so many newly married couples like the Millers avoid some of the more costly mistakes while finding a "look" that suited both partners. All this without going over budget, either.

Now she turned the sketch so the couple could study it while she spoke. "Since the fireplace is the focal point of your living room, I suggest building shelves on either side of it for display purposes. Then we can mix Sam's history books with your collection of Staffordshire plates."

"What a wonderful idea!" Libby Miller enthused.

"How much would it cost?" her husband extemporized.

Maureen quoted him the figure she'd gotten from a carpenter she frequently used, then hastened to add, "You could do it yourself and save money, of course."

"I don't even own a hammer," Sam immediately admitted.

"What color would we paint the shelves?" his wife asked.

"Hunter green, to match the living room and dining room walls." Maureen had suggested dark walls with ample white touches to keep the medium-sized rooms from looking small. Pleated shades at the windows would guarantee privacy while letting in plenty of light.

"Plus, it would show off Sam's book jackets."

"And Libby's plates."

Maureen felt a pang of envy at the warm smile the couple shared. Call it an overreaction on her part—after all, Jack and she hadn't been to bed—but she'd been so out of it after that reporter had confronted him in front of the gym that she didn't even remember all the details of how she'd gotten home yesterday. Somehow, though, she'd managed to collect her clothes from the locker room, stumble to her car and make the drive. Then she'd spent a miserable night trying to absorb the shocking news that the man she'd fallen in love with had killed another man in the ring.

What was so awful about it, she'd finally decided, was that he *had* held her and kissed her and listened to her bare her soul about Sully. But he hadn't trusted her enough in return to share the deepest, darkest secret of his own soul. And that, more than anything, had fed her feelings of betrayal.

Libby leaned forward, bringing her back to the present. "What about carpeting?"

"Frankly," Maureen replied in her most businesslike manner, "I'd go with refinished floors in the living and dining rooms."

"That way, we could use my dhurrie rugs."

"Right."

Libby wrinkled her nose now. "But what are we going to do with Sam's ugly old club chairs?"

"Ugly?" He took obvious umbrage at her characterization. "I just got them broken in."

Maureen smoothed over the rough patch by pulling several swatches of material out of the file and laying them on the desk. "Slipcovers."

"Slipcovers?"

"Comfort and chic on the cheap."

"I like it," Libby said.

"Me too," Sam seconded.

"Now, as for the radiators . . ." Maureen reached for the sketch of radiator covers she'd made just as the door connecting her office with the reception area swung open.

"Pardon me," Donna said, "but Mr. Ryan's on the phone."

Maureen's entire system shut down at the mention of Jack's name. Her heart came to a thudding halt in her chest and her blood ceased to flow through her veins. But after the way he'd deliberately misled her, she'd be damned if she'd jump at his beck and call!

"Tell him I'm with clients and that I'll get back to him when I'm done," she clipped out.

Donna had obviously heard the news about Jack on television last night because she'd given Maureen herbal tea and a sympathetic look when she'd come downstairs this morning. They hadn't had a chance to discuss the tragic turn of events, however, because the Millers had shown up fifteen minutes early for their appointment. Now her pert face was painted with uncharacteristic distress at being caught in the middle.

"He said it's an emergency."

Maureen mentally reviewed the checklist of possibilities but she couldn't find a plausible reason for this "emergency" call. Still, she pasted on a smile for her clients' sake and asked them politely, "Would you excuse me for a moment?"

The Millers, busy studying all the sketches she'd laid before them, nodded their permission.

She could have used the phone on her desk, but she preferred to speak to him in private. As soon as she pulled the door closed behind her, she told Donna, "I'll take Mr. Ryan's call in the storeroom."

Maureen willed her hands to stop shaking and her voice to remain steady as she picked up the receiver. Try as she might, however, she couldn't control the love and the longing she felt when she finally said his name. "Hello, Jack."

"Tammy's in the hospital," he said without preamble.

"Wh—what happened?" she stammered.

"She snuck back into her house to get some clothes and her stepfather caught her and beat the hell out of her."

"Oh, Jack . . ." Maureen gripped the receiver with both hands, wishing she could reach through the line that linked them and put her arms around him. "Is she going to be all right?"

"She was unconscious when the police found her last night, but she's coming around now."

Her heart turned over in her breast at the thought of that poor pregnant—"The baby!"

Jack swallowed audibly. "She lost it."

Maureen was in danger of doing the same, but she blinked to keep the tears at bay. "Does Frankie know?"

"Apparently not."

"Where are you?"

"Truman Medical Center."

She told herself that she had enough problems of her own. Most of them related to the man on the other end of the phone. Yet she couldn't erase the mental picture of a battered teenaged girl lying in a hospital bed, her womb emptied not by personal choice but by pure cruelty.

"What can I do to help?" she asked wearily.

"Meet me for lunch and I'll tell you."

The Boulevard Grill's outdoor patio was the "in" place to be seen when lunching on the Plaza.

Jack had gotten there ahead of Maureen and just in time to grab one of the tables abutting the low brick wall overlooking the street. For all he noticed the view, he might have been back in a windowless cell. He did notice, however, that he wasn't the only man who turned his head when she arrived.

He stood, his steady gaze tracking her graceful walk across the crowded patio. She wore black, a color that played up the fiery gold of her hair and the pale chinoiserie of her skin. Enameled graphic earrings dangled at the delicate juncture of her jaw and neck. All told, she looked as if she'd been airbrushed with culture and confidence.

It was the faint break in her poise when their gazes met

that made him aware of just how painful this meeting was for her. Her eyes went teary, her mouth trembly, and she seemed in danger of falling apart right here in front of God and some of Giorgio Armani's best customers. Then she recovered, and her serene expression betrayed none of the shattered emotion he'd seen on her face yesterday, when that damned reporter had lowered the boom.

"I'm sorry I'm late," she said with commendable calm when she reached the table.

"I just got here myself." He pulled out her chair and waited for her to be seated before he resumed his.

They said nothing else for a moment, simply eyed each other warily across the round white table. One had a million questions whirling through her mind; the other hoped he had the answers. But this was neither the time nor the place to air their personal angst.

Maureen shook her head as she slid her napkin onto her lap. "I was tied-up with my clients till the last possible second. Then I couldn't find a parking place—"

"We're close enough to your office, I figured you'd walk." Jack opened the menu the waitress had set in front of him and stared at it sightlessly.

"Their Reuben sandwich is wonderful."

He did a double take. "What?"

She didn't miss a beat. "You know, corned beef and—"

"I know what a Reuben is." He closed the menu and leaned forward slightly, looking completely in tune with their trendy surroundings in a custom-tailored black and gray tic sportcoat, dove gray shirt and flawlessly knotted silk tie. "I just don't know what in the hell that's got to do with your driving instead of walking."

Maureen hated to admit, even to herself, just how nervous she'd been about seeing Jack again. All last night she'd vacillated between vowing she would hate him forever for keeping her in the dark about his past and swearing she loved him in spite of it. And now that she had him within arm's reach, she didn't know whether to slug him or hug him.

One thing she *did* know was that there had to be more to the story than so far met the eye. The man sitting across the table from her wasn't a wanton killer. Had there been a bookie standing by, she would have bet her life on that. As it was, she'd already wagered her heart.

"The reason I drove instead of walked," she finally said, "is because I have a house call at one-thirty and I didn't want to have to walk back up the hill to get my car in these damned high heels."

He smiled at that last. "Business is still booming, huh?"

She looked away, thinking there ought to be a law against his being able to disarm her with those dimples. "It seems the harder I work, the further behind I get."

"I know the feeling," he said ruefully.

Which brought them back to the original purpose of this meeting. But first they had to order lunch. He decided on the Reuben sandwich, she opted for a spinach salad, and they both asked for tea with lots of ice.

Maureen waited until their waitress had gone to get their drinks to ask, "How did Tammy take the news she'd lost her baby?"

"Better than I did, I'm afraid." Jack was still amazed at the anguish that had swept over him when he'd first heard the teenaged girl had miscarried.

Her sigh of remorse originated in her soul. "I wanted to cry when you told me."

"I wanted to tear her stepfather—" He realized what he was saying and made a tight seam of his lips.

"But you didn't," she reminded him. "And that's what separates you from that . . . monster."

"Are you sure about that?" His voice was quiet, slightly hoarse.

She felt his pain as deeply as she felt her own. "I'm positive."

Their eyes met. Held. Then parted company when their waitress set their iced tea in front of them and promised she'd be right back with their food.

He dammed a drop of the condensation that had already formed on his glass with a long, bronzed finger. "I hate that you didn't hear it from me."

She breathed in sharply, the memory of that awful moment still fresh in her mind. "Me too."

"I thought about telling you that night at Jennie's, then I started to yesterday, but—"

"Enjoy your lunch," the waitress said as she set his sandwich and her salad on the table.

"I got interrupted," he finished wryly.

They ate in silence for a moment, then she asked, "What's going to happen to Tammy's stepfather?"

"He posted bail this morning."

Maureen's salad was delicious, but she suddenly found she'd lost her appetite. "So he's out on the street again and she's in the hospital?"

"That's the way the system works."

"Well, in this instance, the system stinks."

Jack's sandwich was crunchy on the outside and chewy on the inside, but he realized he wasn't all that hungry either. "And in this instance, I have to agree with you."

"When does she get out of the hospital?"

"Day after tomorrow, if there're no complications."

"And where will she go from there?"

"Good question."

"She can't go home."

"Not while he's there."

"Where's her mother?"

"She's the one who brought him the bail money."

Maureen sat back, shocked. "How could she choose that fiend over her own flesh-and-blood?"

"I don't think it's a matter of choice."

"How can you say—"

"You heard Tammy the day she came to the gym," Jack reminded her. "He's mean and her mother's afraid."

"What about a foster home?" The thought of it sickened her, but where else could Tammy go?

"We're working on that, but most foster parents want babies or small children, not rebellious sixteen-year-old girls."

She warned herself to leave well enough alone. To eat her salad, say good-bye and let the system take care of Tammy. She picked up her fork, stabbed a spinach leaf and got the bite halfway to her mouth before setting it back down in the bowl.

"What will happen to her if they can't place her with a foster family?" she demanded.

He drained his tea and set the empty glass on the table, frustration filling his handsome face. "She'll probably wind up in a detention facility until she's eighteen or her stepfather's out of the house."

"But she didn't do anything wrong!"

"It's for her own protection."

Maureen suddenly felt as if the scales had dropped from her eyes. She knew now why Jack had called this meeting. He wanted her to take Tammy into her home and keep her safe. But it was a commitment she couldn't make. Not on the spur of the moment, anyway. And certainly not without giving it serious thought.

She couldn't meet his gaze, for fear of the expectation she'd find there, so she turned her head and stared over the low wall at her car, parked across the street from the Grill in the space she'd almost given up hope of finding until her second trip around the block.

A man who appeared to be in his mid-twenties, dressed in the plaid walking shorts and cotton knit pullover shirt that were practically *de rigueur* for a summer afternoon on the Plaza, was circling her Mercedes, obviously admiring its sleek lines.

Pride of ownership swelled inside her when he stopped, leaned down and peered at the leather interior through the driver's window. She wasn't a materialistic person, she truly wasn't, but she didn't see anything wrong with enjoying the fruits of her labor. Or with others enjoying them either.

"Are you going to offer or do I have to ask?" Jack's question brought Maureen's head around and her mind back to the problem of finding a haven for Tammy.

She gave the spinach salad another go, chewing without tasting and swallowing past the lump that had formed in her throat. What she was really doing was stalling for time. And she knew by the don't-hurry-on-my-account expression he'd adopted that he knew it.

"I—" She caught a familiar flash of silver from the corner of her eye then and glanced back toward the street just as that thief in chic clothing wheeled her car smoothly away from the curb. It took a few seconds for her to realize what was happening. When the fact finally registered, she still couldn't believe it.

Her beautiful Mercedes was being stolen!

From the Country Club Plaza!

Leaping to her feet, rattling dishes and overturning glasses in the process, she pointed her finger and screamed at the top of her lungs, "My car!"

Jack reacted immediately, jumping up from the table and over the wall. Maureen kicked off the pumps that were killing her feet, hiked up her skirt and followed his lead. He glanced back just as she hit the ground running. Then she caught up with him and they pursued her car together.

"Stop—"

"Thief!"

"I can't believe he actually stole my car!"

"I can't believe you didn't activate the burglar alarm."

"But we were on the Plaza." Maureen paused on the

passenger side of the '59 Pontiac Catalina convertible Jack had restored to mint condition. Its split metal grille stood out in shiny relief against its flame red body.

"Like the policeman said, crime is everywhere." He opened the door and helped her in, then closed it and cut around to the driver's side. "Even on that Valhalla of upwardly mobile values, the Country Club Plaza."

They'd just finished a three-hour marathon of fielding questions, filling out papers and waiting their turn with numerous other irate crime victims, most of them demanding immediate action from the city's overworked finest.

Now, Maureen wanted nothing more than to go home and take a long, hot shower. Then she wanted to climb into bed, pull the sheet over her head and hide from polite society until the turn of the century. Or later, she thought, grimacing when she got a glimpse of her reflection in the side mirror.

Her hair bore a strong resemblance to a bird's nest, her dress was missing the bottom two buttons, and her pantyhose were going in the trash as soon as she got out of them. As for her shoes, she should have thanked the waitress for holding on to them for her and then told her to keep them!

Jack tossed the sportcoat that would have to be cleaned before he could wear it again into the back seat. While he was at it, he divested himself of his tie, unbuttoned his collar button and rolled up his sleeves.

Comfortable now, he glanced her way and grinned. "Do you want me to put the top up?"

"Oh, right, so the wind won't muss my hair." If her reply sounded like sour grapes, it was.

His hair didn't look any worse for the chase. True, it was a little curlier than usual thanks to the heat and the humidity. But that only made her want to run her fingers through it to see if it felt as soft and springy as it seemed.

The last twenty-four hours—the worst twenty-four hours of her life—suddenly caught up with Maureen. It was a delayed reaction, she knew, and one she tried with every ounce of willpower she possessed to delay until she got home. She closed her eyes, fighting the tears, but she couldn't stop them.

Jack had already inserted the key in the ignition. But instead of turning the engine on, he reached across the seat and crushed her to him protectively, tucking her head beneath his chin and spanning her back with a wide hand. Then he held her, simply held her, and let her cry.

"I . . . I'm sorry," she sobbed against his neck, which smelled of soap and sweat and man.

He stroked her hair, which didn't look nearly as bad as she thought. "You've got a right to be upset."

"It's not just my car." Strangely enough, it was almost a relief not to have to worry about it anymore. "I can't stop thinking about T . . . Tammy."

"She'll be okay." He rubbed a soothing palm up and down her shuddering back. "After all, she's got us."

"And you." She thumped his muscular chest with her fist. "Damn you for not telling me!"

Jack tightened his embrace, figuring she deserved a hit. "I was afraid you'd hate me for what I'd done."

Maureen heard the emotion in his voice and was overwhelmed anew by her love for this man.

He continued to hold her even after her tears dried up, and she realized she'd never felt so safe as she did in his arms. They still needed to talk, of course. But not wanting to put him through more agony than she already had, she lifted her head and pulled away from him.

"Feel better now?"

She nodded, blinking to bring him into clearer focus, then fumbled ineffectually for a tissue in the purse their waitress had saved along with her shoes.

"Here," he said, raising up one hip to retrieve the folded white handkerchief from his back pocket.

"Thanks." She used it to wipe her eyes, removing most of her carefully applied makeup in the process, then blew her nose.

"Your freckles are showing," he teased.

She gave him a spare-me-the-details look. "Did you ever call Duck?"

"About an hour ago."

"What did you tell him?"

"That we went running together."

Maureen laughed and tucked his mascara-stained handkerchief in her purse so she could wash it. Jack grinned, put on the mirrored sunglasses he took off the dash and started the convertible's four-barrel engine. Then, with the sun shining on their faces and the wind whipping their hair, he drove her back to the shop.

"Are you going to be all right?" He frowned at the darkened windows fronting her duplex, uncomfortable with the idea of just dropping her off like this.

"I'm fine now. Really." She mustered a brave smile that only made her look vulnerable. And vulnerable, as he'd already discovered, she weakened him.

"I'll walk you to the door," he said, delaying the moment she would go her way and he his.

She delayed it a little longer when she looked up at him invitingly. "Would you like to come in?"

His shirt was still damp from her tears, her perfume had his nerve ends sizzling, and he had some serious explaining to do. All good reasons to say no. Right?

He took the key from her slender fingers and said, "Yes."

She stepped past him into the reception area, which was dim and cool and deserted.

Donna was gone for the day, but she'd left the answering machine on and a note for Maureen telling her she'd rescheduled that afternoon's house call for Tuesday of next week. Jack nosed around, sticking his head into her office and the storeroom, while she scanned through her messages and saved them to return tomorrow.

"Nice setup," he said when he rejoined her.

"Thank you."

Then he saw the computer and printer sitting on the credenza behind Donna's desk and whistled appreciatively. "Pretty sophisticated equipment, too."

"For all the good it's doing us," she said ruefully.

"What's the problem?"

"I bought it so we could make a master client list and update our billing system, among other things. But Donna and I have been so busy, we haven't had time to learn how to use it."

"I'll bet Tammy could teach you."

She blinked her surprise. "Tammy?"

Jack walked over and turned on the computer. After it *beeped* an all-clear, he typed in a code and watched the screen come up. "Believe it or not, she's a whiz on a computer."

"How did you do that?" she demanded, standing behind him now and staring in amazement.

Ask Tammy appeared in white letters on the sky-blue screen.

Maureen lifted her chin and met his challenging stare, refusing to give him an answer until she'd given it more thought. "I need to get out of these clothes."

He turned off the computer. "I'd be glad to run you home."

"I am home."

"I should've known."

"What's that supposed to mean?" She led him down the hall and unlocked the only door he'd missed earlier.

"Like father, like daughter," Jack said quietly when he saw the stairs that led to her living quarters.

Maureen stood dumbstruck for a moment, feeling another piece of the puzzle that was herself falling into place. She had, it seemed, inherited more than the gym from Sully. A part of her wanted to shout it to the world. Still another part wondered if she'd also inherited his inability to go the distance in a relationship.

"Well . . ." He broke the silence, thinking she probably needed some time to absorb this startling revelation. "Since I've seen you safely to your door—"

"I . . . Would you like to come up?" She realized she didn't want to be alone with her thoughts. Not just yet, anyway. What she didn't realize was what an appealing portrait she made.

Seconds passed while he studied her upturned face in the faint light spilling down the stairs and out that open door. He thought of the boys, for whom he was supposed to be setting an example, and searched for a polite refusal. But once a prisoner of the very system she'd condemned at lunch, he was now held captive by her alluring green eyes.

"After you," he said in a husky voice.

Upstairs, she excused herself so she could change her clothes. "Make yourself comfortable, and then I'll make us some tea."

Her living room reminded him of her—all classic lines, cool sophistication and simmering-below-the-surface sensuality. A soft apricot color warmed the stucco walls, *Out of Africa* organdy banded in gold billowed at the arched windows, and the Mediterranean-tiled floor gleamed warmly. Still, he couldn't shake the feeling that it was all for show.

Jack tried his damnedest to take her up on her invitation to get comfortable.

First he sat on one of the matching sofas, a full one hundred inches of plushly upholstered importance that should have fit a man of his size to a T. When it didn't, he switched to one of the plump club chairs angling away from the fireplace. Still no luck. Finally he gave up and stood up.

It struck him like a bolt from the blue then. No wonder he didn't feel like he was in someone's living room . . . No one really lived here. Every stick of furniture, every lamp, be it table or floor, every accessory, whether antique mirror or contemporary throw pillow, bore a—

"Ah, I can breathe again." Maureen padded out of her bedroom in her bare feet, an oversized purple tunic and floral print leggings. She'd washed her face, leaving it devoid of makeup, and brushed out her hair until it shone like a nimbus about her head. "Now, how about that tea I promised you?"

"Fine." Jack, still trying to make sense of what he'd just seen, pointed to the high, four-figure price tag dangling from the low, square leather ottoman that anchored the sofas. "I know a lot of kids today leave the price tags on their clothes, but I didn't realize the fad had spread to—"

"Oh, sometimes I use my apartment as a showroom— you know, to help a client visualize how a particular piece might work," she explained breezily. "Other times I just sell it to them right out of the room." She indicated the door she'd just exited. "If you need it, the bathroom's through there."

He nodded curtly and crossed to the door.

It didn't sink in until he'd finished washing up in her floral-scented bathroom and started to cut back across her bedroom. The room was peaceful and neat as a pin, with the walls and ceiling painted the same pale shade of yellow and shutters of woven grass cloth covering the windows. But once again, everything—even the lacy metal bed she slept in—had its price.

Why that should make him angry, he couldn't say. He only knew it did. And he let her know it the instant he joined her in her garden room of a kitchen. "What is it with you?"

"*We'll* get them," he corrected, his low growl rumbling deeply in his chest.

She gestured toward the nightstand, and he carried her across the room. "In the top drawer."

He bent down so she could open it. Then felt an enormous—and, yes, ridiculous—weight roll off his shoulders when she took out a brand-new box.

"Can't blame a girl for hoping," was all she said before breaking the seal with her thumbnail, lifting the lid and dumping the entire dozen on the bed.

Jack eyed the twelve foil packets lying in a heap upon her lightly striped comforter. "Don't get your hopes *too* high, lady."

Maureen smiled at the idea that there would be laughter even in their loving. "That's funny, I heard you were the Champ."

"Who'd you hear that from?" He let her feet slide to the floor, but kept his arms banded around her.

"Wouldn't you like to know?" she murmured, welcoming his hot, probing kiss with openmouthed ardor.

They clung together until they had to draw a breath or die. Then he reached for the hem of her tunic and whisked it over her head. She returned the favor, all but tearing the buttons from his shirt and pushing it off his shoulders. Her leggings and his pants formed a lover's knot at their feet.

"I dreamed of you like this." His eyes feasted upon the ivory teddy frothing over her firm breasts and flowing down to her long thighs. "All legs and lace."

Maureen made no pretense of being modest as she crossed her arms in front of her to lower the thin straps.

"No," Jack said, staying her hands. "Let me." Then with infinite care and kisses more intoxicating than summer wine, he dispensed with the fragile garment, leaving it in a pool at her feet and her as naked as he.

Flesh met flesh for the first time as she put her arms around his neck and he cupped her backside to pull her against his arousal. Mouths got reacquainted with a twining of tongues and nipping of teeth. Desire matched desire when he reached down to pick up one of the silver packets and she scattered the rest of them by drawing back the softly striped comforter.

They tumbled onto the bed, falling into the current of their mutual passion, and soon those pale yellow walls echoed their cries and their sighs as each learned the other's sweet spots . . . as well as some new ones of their own.

Her scent swam in his head as he explored the perfumed hollow behind her ear, tasted the elegant length of her throat, nuzzled the sensitive crook of her neck. Aroused by the quickened rate of her breathing, he let his mouth move lower.

A liquid gasp spilled from her lips when he drew on her nipples, first one and then the other, tugging and teasing them to taut peaks with a tenderness she'd never experienced before. Burning to touch him, too, she reversed their positions and wrapped her fingers around him, feeling him warm and throbbing against her palm.

He groaned a muffled curse and threw back his head in a spasm of delight, a stranger to himself, as she sculpted with her artist's hands that which made him male. Then he chanted her name—a sonnet, a lovesong—and knotted his fingers in her hair when she buried her face in the silky-crisp swirls on his chest and touched her tongue to the hard nubs of flesh she found there. Finally pushed to the limit of his control, he pulled her up and twisted her onto her back for another carnal kiss that lasted an eternity.

Little tingles swept upward in her spine when his fingers, sensitive to her needs, flickered down the delicate bow of her ribs to the narrow cleft between her thighs. He caressed her with a slow, sure touch, until the universe was reduced to the center of her body . . . until convulsions rippled through her limbs and she felt herself leaving the earth. Then, while she lay panting in this sensual paradise from which only he could release her, he levered up on his elbow and tore open the foil packet.

Just when he thought he knew all there was to know about her, she showed him something new.

"No," she said, staying his hands as he had earlier stayed hers. "Let me." And she reaffirmed that he was as magnificent below the belt as he was above, hot skin over hard steel, when she lovingly sheathed him.

"I want to fill you, Maureen," he whispered huskily as he moved over her and braced a palm on either side of her head. "With me."

"Love me, Jack." She meant in all ways and for always, but she knew better than to ask for that kind of commitment from this man.

Their eyes locked as he entered her, filling her so far beyond the physical bounds that she shivered with pleasure even as she arched her hips to accommodate his sure thrust.

"Yo, Mo," he ground out, smiling down into her face when he was fully embedded inside her.

She gazed up at him, green eyes soft and blood pounding through her. "Hey, Champ."

He rocked her slowly at first, prolonging the tempest that raged between them with deliberately long, deliciously sweet strokes. She fondled his back and cupped the solid curve of his buttocks, marveling at the smooth ripple of sinew beneath her hands. Then his mouth claimed hers and his tongue took up the same thrilling rhythm as their bodies.

Gradually, he escalated the tempo. Breathlessly, she matched it. Finally, they gave each other all they had to give.

Maureen came from a world of manners and money, while Jack had had to fight and scrape for every dime he'd ever made. Now, their bodies still joined and their breathing gradually slowing, he rolled them to their sides so they

were facing each other and took her to a world of their own
. . . a world where there were no uptown girls or downtown guys, only two sated people falling asleep in a gentle
afterglow.

Her bedside telephone called them back to the real
world.

Maureen had left her answering machine on but had
forgotten to turn the volume off. So it was her own taped
voice asking the caller to please leave a message at the
tone, rather than the ticklish chest hair of the man beside
her, that woke her.

It roused Jack, too. Lying with his arms wrapped tightly
around her and his chin propped on the top of her head, he
had to smile at the contrast between the passionate woman
he was still holding and the oh-so-polite one he was now
hearing.

But they broke apart and met each other's eyes in dismay when Duck responded to her gracious request with a
gravelly, "The police just arrested Frankie."

ROUND 9

They'd caught Frankie hiding under Tammy's hospital bed.

"So he put up a fight, huh?" Jack asked as he finished signing in at the main desk of the Juvenile Detention Center. According to the report he'd just received, the teenager had been completely out of control when the police brought him in. He'd swung wildly at anyone within arm's reach, actually connecting on a couple of them, and sworn repeatedly that he was going to kill Tammy's stepfather with his bare hands.

The night officer smiled ruefully as he rubbed his swollen jaw. "Let's just say he's got his right cross down pat."

Jack laughed for the first time since finally and reluctantly rising from Maureen's bed a half hour ago. "Maybe I'll bring him a pair of training gloves in the morning."

"Better bring the day officer a pair too—make it a fair fight." The other man noted the date and time next to Jack's signature, then sniffed the air between them. "You smell flowers?"

Caught off guard by the question, Jack almost told him it was soap, not flowers, that he smelled. Soap that he and Maureen had lathered over each other's bodies in the shower they'd shared before he'd taken his leave. He couldn't do that, of course, so he just shook his head no and changed the subject. "Where's Frankie?"

With a last suspicious sniff, the night officer set down his pen and said, "Follow me."

It was a familiar route for Jack, in more ways than one.

The dull thud of their soles on the tile floor as they walked down the darkened hall reminded him of late-night bedchecks with blinding white flashlights. The odor of grease that permeated the place prompted recollections of the three meals a day that never quite filled a growing boy's stomach. The thrift-shop vintage furniture in the visitor's lounge cued memories of a troubled adolescent waiting for the father who never came to see his son even once.

Frankie was slouching in an orange plastic chair with metal legs, paging through a well-thumbed copy of *Sports Illustrated* by the light of a lamp that was bolted to a rickety end table. He'd lost weight and his blond hair had grown shaggy in the month he'd been missing. Bruises were beginning to ring the bony wrists that had been manacled until he'd agreed to stop lashing out at everyone who came near him, and the tennis shoes that Jack had bought him before he disappeared were missing their laces.

When the teenager saw the man standing in the doorway, his face turned red. Still, he tossed the magazine negligently aside and let his lip curl in that tough-guy look he was so fond of wearing. Judging by the tears that formed in his blue eyes, though, it was strictly a defense mechanism.

"Ten minutes," the officer grunted before turning on his heel and heading back to the main desk.

"Gotta hand it to you, kid." Jack didn't cut Frankie any slack as he took the matching chair and crossed an ankle over his knee. "When you dig yourself into a hole, you dig yourself in deep."

Frankie's face flushed an even darker shade of red and his Adam's apple bobbed up and down, as if he were trying not to cry. His shaky emotional state aside, he replied belligerently, "You see what that bastard did to Tammy?"

Jack repeated the assurance he'd already given Maureen. "She's going to be okay."

"The baby's not."

"Maybe the baby's better off."

"You sonofa—!" Frankie lunged to his feet, fists poised for a fight. His beltless jeans slipped a notch as he took the two steps that closed the distance between their chairs. Then his pugnacious façade collapsed and he began to sob, his thin shoulders heaving as he flopped back down in his chair.

Jack was glad to see him cry, though he was sorry he'd had to make that cruel remark about the baby. But the more anger and sorrow and frustration Frankie got out of his system, the less chance it had of solidifying into the time bomb of hatred that existed deep inside every hardened criminal. He knew, because that same time bomb had ticked in him before Sully had helped him defuse it.

He reached for the handkerchief in his back pocket, then remembered he'd given it to Maureen hours earlier. At the rate he was mopping up other people's tears, he thought dryly, he was going to have to start packing a baker's dozen of the damn things.

"I'll go get you some Kleenex," he said, and stood.

"I'm all right," Frankie insisted, sniffing and backhanding his red-rimmed eyes. Then he sniffed again and wrinkled his nose. "You smell flowers?"

For the second time in five minutes, Jack shook his head no. As he sat, he also reminded himself to buy Maureen a bar of his own brand of soap to help eliminate some of these embarrassing questions. It never even occurred to him to question the wisdom of going back for more. Quite simply, he couldn't resist her.

Relatively composed now, the teenager rested his forearms on his knees. He worked his knuckles for a moment the way some people spin the cylinder of a gun, as if trying to keep something powerful just below the skin at bay.

Then he mumbled to the tile floor, "Saw you on the news the other night."

"You and everyone else in town."

"How'd it feel to kill a man?"

"Are you asking for your own information," Jack said slowly, "or are you just curious?"

Frankie's head came up as he caught the veiled reference to the threats he'd been making against Tammy's stepfather. Mixed emotions vied for supremacy on his tear-streaked face while he worked those knuckles, one by one. Finally he diverted his eyes to the floor again and shrugged. "Just curious, I guess."

"It felt like a part of me died with him," Jack answered honestly, wondering how he'd ever survived the soul-wrenching guilt and the constant self-recrimination. Understanding now that he'd done it a day at a time. Just like Frankie was going to have to survive detention.

"Was that why you hung up your gloves?"

Jack looked down at his hands, resting on the arms of that orange plastic chair, recalling how terrified he'd initially been of bruising Maureen's water-soft skin. He'd never seen anything more perfect, more elegant or fragile. And he'd never felt such total pliancy, such total trust as when her body had melted beneath his touch.

"Yeah, that was why I hung up my gloves."

"So why're you putting them back on?"

"Why do you think?" he asked, confident he already knew the answer to that.

But he was surprised when Frankie came back with, "To prove you can still fight?"

"That's part of it, I suppose." Now that he stopped to analyze it, Jack acknowledged that he had, in fact, put his pride on the line. If it was wrong to want to show the world that he hadn't lost his edge, that he still had the eye of the tiger, so be it. A man had to do what a man had to do.

The teenager scratched his shaggy head, his brow furrowing as he struggled to come up with the rest of the reason. "And to prove you're still alive?"

Out of the mouths of babes . . . Had he just taken one of Frankie's infamous right crosses on the chin, Jack couldn't have felt more stunned. For the last month, he'd been telling himself that he was going back into the ring strictly to save the gym. That he was all that stood between the diversionary program and disaster. And for the last month, he realized now, he'd only been partially right.

Because all his good intentions and noble purposes aside, the upcoming fight really boiled down to one thing: He had to confront that skull in the mirror—the ghost of his past—before he could be free to focus on the future. Before he could hang up his gloves for good and settle down at last with the woman he loved.

"Time's up," the juvenile officer said from the doorway.

Still reeling from the shock of Frankie's observations and his own reflections, Jack rose.

Frankie stood at the same time, eyes pleading and anxiety pinching features already too thin. "Sunday is visitor's day around here, if you, uh, want to come see me again."

As of tomorrow—correction, *today*, Jack thought as he glanced at the clock on the wall and saw it was after midnight—he had exactly four weeks to train for the last and most important fight of his life.

Even though he was in good shape for his age, thanks to the daily training regimen he'd maintained over the years, he couldn't afford to take anything for granted. Staying on his feet for twelve rounds would demand both stamina and fluidity. Especially in light of the fact that he'd be going toe to toe with a legitimate contender who just happened to consider their upcoming bout a grudge match.

But in the long run, which was really the most important? How Jack "The Irish Terror" Ryan looked against "Poison" Ivy Stephens? Or seeing that Frankie got through detention with as few problems as possible?

No contest there.

Jack put his hand on the teenager's gaunt shoulder and gave it a squeeze. "Tell you what—you do your time like a man, and I'll be here every Sunday from now on."

"I *told* you—"

"If you're going to eavesdrop, Laura, do it quietly."

"Thanks, Dad." Maureen relaxed her grip on the telephone receiver and hugged Jack's pillow a little tighter, inhaling the spicy male scent lingering in the soft cotton case. She'd called her father this morning to tell him about her car. Unfortunately her mother had overheard his end of the conversation and picked up the extension to put in her two cents' worth.

Paul didn't say, "You're welcome," but the warmth in his voice implied as much. "Would you like to borrow one of our cars until you've replaced yours?"

"I don't want *my* car being driven down to that horrible neighborhood." Laura resented that Paul was taking Maureen's side in this.

"Sounds like it'd be as safe there as anywhere," he tossed back dryly.

The three-way connection crackled with the tension that had been building for weeks between husband and wife.

But Maureen, basking in a morning-after glow so rosy it shamed the sunshine she'd opened the shutters to admit, refused to let her mother's digs dim her contentment.

"I appreciate the offer, Dad, but . . ." Her words trailed off as she yawned and stretched and glanced at the clock, surprised to see it was almost eleven. She'd phoned her insurance agent at home shortly after seven, figuring she'd paid enough in premiums over the years to more than compensate for waking him up. Then she'd spoken to Donna over the intercom at nine, filling her in on what had happened yesterday and telling her not to expect her until later today, if at all. "I've already made arrangements for a rental car."

"Are you still in bed, dear?" Laura's well-honed instincts had detected the slumberous note in her answer.

"Yes, as a matter of fact, I am." Maureen had fixed herself a steaming cup of raspberry tea—her favorite flavor—and brought it back to bed with her. It was the first time she'd ever done anything like this, but she didn't feel a bit guilty. A woman was entitled to some time alone to savor her remembrances of the man she loved.

Like mothers the world over, Laura immediately assumed the worst. "Are you ill?"

"No."

But Laura's dread billowed as diseases—some with acronyms instead of names—staged a protest rally in her mind. "Lord only knows what kind of germs you've been exposed to at that awful—"

"I'm fine, Mom." When the answering silence grew rife with skepticism, she added an insistent, "Honestly, Mom. I'm healthy as a horse."

"Then it must be the shock of having your car stolen," Laura concluded on a sigh of relief.

"Mmmh," Maureen replied noncommittally. She'd had a shock, all right. But it'd had nothing to do with losing her car and everything to do with discovering the joy of making love in Jack's arms. She let go of his pillow only long enough to run her hand over his side of the bed, empty since shortly after Duck's terse call telling them Frankie had been arrested.

"Did the police take you home?" Paul asked now.

"No. Fortunately, I was lunching with . . . a friend—"

"Who was that?" Laura had picked up on her hesitation and homed in on it as only a mother who thought it was past time for her daughter to settle down could home in.

On her end, Maureen could practically see Laura

flipping through her mental Rolodex of potential marriage partners. "No one you've met."

"Well, I beg your pardon." Laura's voice held a trace of pique at the obvious snub—until she remembered the picture and accompanying caption she'd chanced to notice in yesterday's newspaper. Then she took off the verbal gloves. "I certainly hope it wasn't that—that murderer you've been training with."

"Laura . . ." Paul said warningly.

"Not that it's any of your business, Mom, but, yes, it was Jack Ryan. And just for the record, he's one of the most caring, compassionate men I've ever met."

Laura emitted a soft, shocked gasp. Not once, from the day she'd been born, had Maureen spoken to her in such a rebellious manner. And thirty-five years old or not, she was going to hear about it. "Don't you dare use that tone with me."

"Then don't talk like that about someone you don't even know." Maureen closed her eyes and tilted back her head, striving for control. She'd always had a tendency to camouflage her feelings, so these quick, almost flippant retorts in Jack's defense surprised her too. But she just couldn't sit quietly by while her mother tore him down.

"I know he killed a man. And in or out of the ring, that makes him a murderer in my—"

"Stop it, Laura," Paul said in a voice that brooked no argument. "Now."

Again, the connection hummed with anger—mostly Laura's.

Maureen broke the heavy silence by saying, "I'll talk to you later, Dad."

"Let me know if you need anything," Paul replied before he hung up.

"I will. And thanks again."

"Maureen—"

"Good-bye, Mom." Maureen didn't give Laura a chance

to respond before gently replacing the receiver in its cradle. She didn't want to argue with anyone, least of all her mother, on what—despite all the hassle about her car— was the most glorious morning of her life. All she wanted to do was finish her now-cold tea and figure out where the woman who'd responded so wantonly to Jack had been hiding all these years.

She hadn't tried to stop him from leaving after Duck's call. She really hadn't. In view of the fact that their lunch had been so rudely interrupted and they'd never gotten around to dinner, she had even offered to fix him a sandwich to eat on his way to the Juvenile Detention Center.

But instead of jumping out of bed and into his clothes, as she'd expected him to, Jack had bent his head and kissed her until it felt like his life's breath flowed through her lungs and into her blood system. Until he was hard and she was dewy with renewed desire.

"What about Frankie?" she'd murmured against his lips.

His grin had been unrepentantly mischievous. "He's kept me waiting for damn near a month. It won't hurt him to cool his heels a little while longer."

And then . . . Maureen blushed anew at the memory of how Jack had scooped her gently off the bed and carried her into the bathroom. Whatever modesty she'd had left had gone down the shower drain, along with the soap bubbles he'd swirled over her body. The massaging action of his strong fingers had reignited the fires inside her, and his words had fanned the flames.

"I want you wet," he'd whispered hotly against her skin. "Here . . ." Using the tip of his tongue, he'd sipped water from her face and neck before moving his mouth lower, to bathe her breasts and lave her nipples until she gave a sultry moan. "And here . . ."

She'd had no thought of stopping him as he'd kissed his way down her stomach, pausing only to deflower her navel before nuzzling the red-gold curls that shielded her femininity. In truth, she'd had no thoughts at all. She'd simply braced her hands on his broad shoulders and shuddered against him as his exploring tongue charted new territory and sent untapped tributaries within her body flooding their banks.

When he'd risen through the mist, a perfect rendition of Poseidon, she'd reached shamelessly to return the pleasure. His pure animal groan had increased both her boldness and the amount of pressure she'd applied. She'd wanted him to scale the same dizzying heights where she'd soared earlier, but he would only let her take him half the way.

"I won't go without you," he'd declared hoarsely. Then he'd turned off the water and, without stopping to towel either her or himself dry, had carried her back to bed.

"Can I help?" she'd asked in a throaty voice when he'd laid her against the pillows and reached to pick up another one of those handy foil packets.

Jack had shaken his head, and there'd been a fine film of perspiration on his upper lip as he'd fought for control. "You even touch me, woman, and it'll be over before it's begun."

Maureen had taken his threat seriously enough to thread her fingers through the lacy metalwork of her headboard. Then to part her legs and purr, "Look, man, no hands."

Needless to say, he'd never gotten his sandwich.

"Here," was all Jack said to Maureen when she got to the gym that afternoon.

A frown pleated her forehead as she studied the yellow price tag he'd handed her. She recognized both its round shape and her own handwriting, of course, but she couldn't imagine what he was doing with it.

"Did Gordon Gekko ever sleep in the metal bed?"

Maureen looked up at him blankly. "*Who?*"

"That stockbroker you were engaged to."

"His name wasn't—"

Jack cupped his hand over her mouth, cutting her off. "I was just making a joke. Gordon Gekko. The guy in the movie *Wall Street*. Get it?"

No, she didn't get it. But he'd gone to such great pains to make whatever point he was trying to make, that she nodded her head yes.

He dropped his hand.

"His name was—"

"I don't give a damn what his name was," he interrupted tersely. "All right?"

She eyed him uncertainly, but agreed nonetheless. "All right."

"I just want to know if he ever slept—"

"Oh, he had a futon—"

Jack's hand came back. Harder, this time. "No details, please. Just a simple yes or no. Did he ever sleep in the metal bed where you and I—"

Maureen shook her head no.

"Good." He removed his hand again and indicated the price tag she still held. "Then add that to my bill."

"Your bill?"

"What I owe you for the gym."

Her perplexed expression demanded an explanation. "I don't understand."

"I'm buying you that bed."

"You're . . ." She stared at the price tag again, tears welling in her eyes, moved as much by the sentiment of his gift as by the magnitude.

He frowned when she lifted her tear-filled gaze to his. "What's wrong? You don't like that bed? You want a different one? What?"

Maureen swallowed hard, trying to find the words to tell him how much she loved that bed. How much she loved him. But it seemed she'd lost her voice, so she just twined her arms around his neck and, in full view of everyone in the gym, kissed him for all she was worth.

"Thank you," she whispered breathlessly when she finally pulled back.

"Thank *you*." Jack smiled, amazed anew at the hot-blooded passion that could spring from this cool, contained woman. Then he scowled when she took a slim rosewood pen out of her purse, drew a line through the price on the tag and wrote another number beneath it.

"What're you doing?" he demanded, unable to read upside down.

She showed him. "The least I can do is give you the bed at cost."

"That's more like it." He nodded his approval on seeing that the new price was twenty percent lower than the old one.

Maureen returned the pen along with the price tag to her purse before braving the question that she, too, needed to have answered. "How about your bed?"

Jack remembered the Camp Annies—groupies who'd haunted the locker room corridors after every fight, looking to add another notch to their garter belts. And the other women—some of whom, oddly enough, had been as attracted by the violent nature of the sport as by the virility of the man. "I bought new mattresses."

"When?"

"Almost a year ago."

"Well . . ." She smiled, more relieved than words could say. "I'd better get changed if we're going to run."

"How'd you get down here?" he asked as she picked up what appeared to be a new gym bag.

She'd had to buy shoes, too, because her other ones had been stolen along with her Mercedes. "My insurance company rented me a car."

"What kind?"

"A black Mustang convertible."

He eyed her windblown hair with a smile. "You left the top down, I see."

"And loved every minute of it." In fact, she'd felt like a moth emerging from a chrysalis.

Jack's grin widened as he walked her to the locker room door. He'd already changed into his jogging shorts and donned his sweatband. "What'd Rocstar say when you drove up?"

"He said, 'Some bucket.'" Maureen laughed. "At first I thought he'd said, 'Scum bucket,' and I figured he was talking about the guy who stole the Mercedes."

"He'll have you talking jive yet."

"I'm not doing too bad now."

He shook his head, but in agreement, as he reached to open the door for her. "No, you're not."

"See you in a few minutes," she promised before slipping down to the locker room.

They limbered up together, Jack in those brief white jogging shorts that made the most of his muscular build and Maureen in that sleek black catsuit that did incredible things for her legs and inflammatory things to his imagination.

"Race you to the Concourse," he challenged when they'd finished stretching and started for the street door.

"Oh, that's so childish." She laughed at his startled expression, then took off running with a shouted, "Eat my dust!"

He didn't, of course. But only because she slowed down for him. Or so she told herself when he caught up with her halfway to the corner.

Rocstar, working alone now, waved them on with the shovel he was using to spread gravel over the emerging parking lot that Jack had granted him the concession on. A white-haired woman in the redbrick rooming house across the street—the same woman who'd been afraid to come to Maureen's aid that first day—smiled down upon them from her second-story balcony. Danny the barber, his handlebar mustache bristling happily, tapped hello and good-bye on the plate-glass window when they jogged past his shop.

To look at them running shoulder to shoulder along the city sidewalks and crosswalks, no one would ever guess that they came from such disparate backgrounds. They were as perfectly matched as a pair of Irish thoroughbreds—long of leg and trim of torso, with sweat glistening on their faces and arms in the fierce afternoon sun.

In the park, they followed the hilly footpath to that leafy old tree where she'd silently acknowledged her love for him only two days before. He raised an eyebrow, tacitly asking her if she wanted to stop and rest, as they had then. She shook her head and they continued on until they reached the Concourse.

"Ready . . . for a . . . Popsicle?" she panted.

He whipped a dollar bill out of his pocket. "My treat."

They split a grape Popsicle today and then crossed the street to share the shaded bench beside the gurgling fountain where Sully had proposed and Laura had accepted lo those many years ago.

"So," Maureen said enticingly as she dropped her wooden stick in the trash and turned back to him, "what are you doing this evening?"

Jack read in her eyes an invitation that had his pulse soaring and his heart sinking. "I promised the boys a pizza and a movie."

Making a moue of disappointment, she stood. "Too bad."

He followed suit. "How about tomorrow night, instead?"

"I'm afraid I'm going to be busy tomorrow night." Reaching into the pool fed by the fountain, she scooped up a handful of water and let it dribble through her fingers.

"Doing what?" Watching a bead of perspiration river

down her throat, he realized she was the only woman he'd ever known who could make sweat look elegant.

Maureen wiped her wet palm on the thigh of her skin-tight catsuit, then looked him square in the face. "Getting Tammy settled in."

Jack planted his hands on his lean hips and stood slack-jawed for a long moment before finally asking, "What made you decide to take her home?"

"I'm not sure." She crossed her arms over her flat stomach. "I only know that I can't let her go into detention after losing her baby through no fault of her own."

"You know what this means, don't you?" He stepped forward, closing the distance between them, then laid his hands on her shoulders and drew her against him.

"No christening my new bed."

"Not for a while, anyway."

Maureen lifted her chin, and Jack's lips came down on hers, soft as a summer breeze. They left her sighing, "I just hope Tammy appreciates the sacrifice I'm making on her behalf."

Tammy had lost more than her baby.

Two patches of her beautiful blond hair had been shaved by the emergency room staff for the stitches they'd taken in her scalp. One of her front teeth had been badly chipped at the hands of her stepfather, and her face had the tissue-paper color that results from hemorrhage. Saddest of all, though, her survivor's spirit seemed to have been drained right out of her bruised blue eyes.

"Here we are." Maureen forced herself to speak cheerfully as she unlocked her front door. Still in shock over Tammy's appearance, she stepped aside and said gently, "Go on in."

The drive home from the hospital had been a silent one, with the woman suffering an agony of helplessness as she wove in and out of the Saturday afternoon traffic and the teenager sitting woodenly, all her worldly possessions in a brown paper grocery bag on her lap, in the passenger seat.

Now, Tammy looked neither right nor left as she preceded Maureen into the dimly lit office. Dressed in a pink halter top and a pair of blue jeans that were a little too baggy in both the seat and the stomach, she paused just inside the door as if awaiting further instructions.

"Well . . ." Carrying herself with a lot more confidence than she possessed inwardly, Maureen closed the door behind them and turned on the lights. "What do you think?"

Three bruises, each spaced a finger's width apart on Tammy's slender neck, showed up clearly as she turned her head and spoke for the first time since they'd pulled out of Truman Medical Center's parking lot. "I think I've changed my mind about staying with you."

"Oh?" Maureen came to a stop beside Donna's desk, surprised to find she felt more alarmed than relieved. She'd spent half the night wondering if she'd taken leave of her senses, offering to take in a sixteen-year-old girl whose history of physical abuse read like an Andrew Vachss novel. Instead, she was horrified at the prospect of her going back out onto the streets.

Tammy rolled the top of that brown paper bag a little tighter with hands that still bore IV tracks. "I can bunk with the friends Frankie and I were staying with till he gets out of detention."

"Where do these friends live?" Maureen asked in what she considered a perfectly reasonable tone.

"What do you care?" Tammy answered in a clipped voice that dared her to prove she did.

Maureen had heard those same words before, from Jack, and they hurt as much now as they had then. She understood the root causes for their mistrust, of course. What she didn't understand was why people automatically assumed that just because she had money, she didn't have a heart.

Rather than rise to her own defense—talk, after all, was terribly cheap—Maureen cast about for a plausible excuse to keep Tammy from bolting. Her eyes came to rest on the computer and printer, and, with a silent hosannah, she remembered the message Jack had typed on the sky-blue screen: *Ask Tammy.*

"Actually," she said with a casual wave of her hand, "I was counting on your teaching me how to use that thing while you're staying here."

Tammy's pale face lit up with a brief flare of interest when she saw the expensive equipment that had been sitting idle, yet she didn't let down her guard. "Any dweeb can use a computer."

"I hate to think what that makes Donna and me." Maureen prayed that her secretary-cum-design assistant would forgive her for slandering her so, but she sensed she was on the brink of a breakthrough.

"Who's Donna?"

"My secretary."

Tammy's eyes shot to hers, disbelieving. "You hired a secretary who can't use a computer?"

Maureen managed a credible expression of chagrin. "I guess I should've checked her out a little better, huh?"

"I guess so."

"I'd be glad to pay you."

That seemed to be a real enticement, because Tammy set the brown paper bag on Donna's desk and sat down at the computer. "How much?"

Maureen began to wonder just who was the boss and who the potential employee here as she searched for a fair figure. "Five dollars an hour."

"And what do I have to pay you?" Tammy asked as she turned on the computer, typed in a code and waited for the screen to come up.

"Pay me for what?"

"For rent."

Maureen was on the verge of saying, "Nothing," when she saw the way the girl was stiffening, squaring her shoulders, lifting her chin. She understood then. Tammy's pride was all she had left.

"I was figuring on five dollars an hour plus room and board," she said briskly, all business now. "After all, on-site computer lessons are expensive."

Tammy nodded as if to say the arrangement suited, then sidled her a glance and changed the subject completely. "Jack told me that Sully was your real father."

It took Maureen a few seconds to shift gears from finances to family. "Biologically speaking, yes, but when my mother got remarried—"

"Did your stepfather beat you?"

"Oh, no! Never."

Tammy turned and met Maureen's horrified gaze, squinting a little as if it hurt her to do so. "He just slapped your mother around, huh?"

Maureen shook her head, as sickened by Tammy's assumption that all men beat the women in their lives as she was by those terribly bruised eyes. "He never laid a hand on her, either."

"So," Tammy said, looking around her with the first real interest she'd shown in her surroundings, "where do you sleep?"

"Upstairs, in my apartment." Maureen used her last bargaining chip. "Would you like to see your room?"

"I'd have a room of my own?"

"Of course."

Tammy turned back to the computer and stared at the keyboard, her young profile a study in concentration.

Maureen stood there mutely, her mind whirling with the awesome responsibility she was preparing to assume. She knew nothing about the care and feeding of teenagers on a daily basis, but she was sure she couldn't do any worse of a job than what Tammy's parents had done. And she had a feeling that helping the girl would bring her one step closer to filling in the rest of the blanks.

"All right." Tammy looked up, a hint of wariness in those puffy blue eyes, as if she were afraid to believe Maureen really wanted her under her roof. "I'll stay. But just until you and Donna learn how to use the computer."

ROUND 10

"Hey, can you tell me—"

Maureen jumped at the sound of that strange voice and, clutching her partially open blouse over her breasts, spun away from the locker where she always hung her clothes.

A man she'd never seen before was standing in the bathroom doorway, his wet brown hair plastered to his head and a white towel wrapped precariously around his hips. No need to panic, she told herself. Just ask him who he is and what he—

But she felt as if her throat were closing up when he started walking toward her. Rape . . . murder . . . her mother's dire predictions echoed afresh in her mind. Abruptly then, she remembered Tammy's blue eyes—the week-old bruises that were beginning to fade, the laughter that occasionally lit them in the office or across the dinner table—and experienced a sudden rush of courage.

Squaring her shoulders and planting her feet in imitation of the stance she'd seen Jack take in the ring, she glared at the intruder and demanded, "Who are you? And what the hell are you doing down here?"

"My name is Bruce." The man stopped, looking at her as if she'd suddenly begun foaming at the mouth. "Bruce Webster. And I was just wondering where I could . . ." He raised his right hand and brandished an object in the shape of a gun.

Oh, God, he was going to shoot her! Maureen shut her eyes tightly, preparing for the agonizing pain of a bullet ripping through her body and picturing poor Tammy being locked up in detention after the funeral. Why hadn't she stopped to think more clearly before confronting this creep? She should have screamed first and asked—

"Plug in my blow dryer?"

Maureen opened her eyes, amazed that she was still alive. Anger canceled out fear when she saw that he did, indeed, hold an innocuous-looking blow dryer in his hand. "You frightened me to death with that thing!"

"Oh, hey, I'm sorry," he said in a nasally voice that grated her already frazzled nerves.

"That's all right." She was still trembling, but otherwise no worse for the scare. Giving him her back, she began buttoning up her blouse. "It's just that I'm usually the only one down here at this time of day."

"Well, if they're going to admit women," the man declared self-righteously, "the least they can do is partition off the dressing room."

"Locker room," she corrected through clenched teeth.

He harrumphed as if to say six of one, half dozen of the other. "So, how did you hear about the gym?"

"It's a long story."

"I read about it in the paper last week."

Maureen slipped her suit jacket back on, realizing that she was probably going to have to change her clothes up in the office from now on.

"And then after I saw that profile piece on Jack Ryan the other night—You know the one I'm talking about?"

She nodded and smiled as she recalled the interview and film footage that a local sportscaster—a former professional football player himself—had presented on the six o'clock news. Not only had Jack demonstrated a few of his training exercises for the camera, but he'd also gotten a chance to explain how the diversionary program worked. When all was said and done, it had given the viewing audience a behind-the-scenes glimpse at the sweet science of boxing and an eye-opening look at a viable alternative to simply detaining the growing number of juvenile delinquents.

The best thing to come from the broadcast, according to the ticket office at Municipal Auditorium the morning after it aired, was an increase in sales for fight night.

The worst, Maureen decided as she turned and set her gym bag on the bench, was this half-naked nerd who seemed determined to tell her the story of his recent conversion.

"After I turned off the TV, I got to thinking, hey, I'm tired of wimpy sports like tennis and golf. I want some real action." The man almost got it, too, when the tuck he'd made in the towel began to come undone. Grabbing it with his free hand, he didn't miss a beat in his adenoidal monologue. "Something to get the old adrenaline going. Know what I mean?"

Maureen, busy emptying her locker, didn't acknowledge his rhetorical question with even so much as a nod this time. She just stuffed a bottle of sun-block in with her extra socks.

"So," he droned on, "I called and talked to Goose—"

"Duck." She closed her gym bag with an emphatic *zzzip!*

"Oh, right. Anyway, he said he had his hands full, what with training 'The Irish Terror' for the fight and all. But he said he'd ask Beetlejuice—Can you believe some of these names?"

The woman who answered to "Mo" slammed her locker shut with a clang that echoed through the room. Then she picked up her gym bag and her purse, turned on her heel and marched toward the stairs.

"Hey, wait!" Both hands occupied, the man trailed her

as far as the bottom of the steps and stood there helplessly. "You never did tell me where I could plug in my blow dryer."

Maureen had a suggestion for him, but she was too much of a lady to make it.

"I want to hit something!"

"First we've got to tape your hands."

No, first Maureen would have to take the hand she'd clamped over her mouth away. She looked at Duck, horrified by what she'd just shouted, and shook her head. "I can't imagine what made me say that."

Well, that wasn't entirely true. For one thing, Jack and she hadn't been completely alone all week. Even when they ran together, they weren't really alone because someone was always stopping them to ask for his autograph or to give him advice on how to roll with "Poison" Ivy's punches. And for another, she was still upset by that jerk who'd caught her unawares in the locker room a little while ago. If he'd wanted to commit mayhem, she wasn't sure she could have fended him off.

"Okay." She extended her hands, thinking it was time she learned how to hit back. "Let's tape 'em."

Duck grinned behind his cigar and beckoned her over to the worktable, where he wrapped the gauze around her wrist and in between her fingers, doubling it over to protect her knuckles. Then the tape went on. When both hands were done, he had her make a fist and hit his upraised palms.

Lastly, like a rite of passage, he helped her put on the red leather training gloves. At first they felt like lead pillows on her hands. But after practicing her moves in front of the mirror for a while, she began to get used to the extra weight.

"Ready?" Duck asked, holding the ropes open for her.

"As ready as I'll ever be," Maureen answered, and climbed into the ring. She smiled as she bounced on the balls of her feet. It was the first time she'd been in there since the day she'd gone to Jamal's rescue, and she'd forgotten how springy the canvas was.

"Now fall back against the ropes to get the feel of it," Duck instructed.

As a little girl, Maureen had always refused to fall backward into anyone's arms. Even Paul's, come to think of it. She was sure a psychiatrist would have a field day with her early fears, but she didn't care. Because at that moment, she would have dived out of the ring headfirst if Duck had asked her to.

"Here goes," she said nervously. Then, keeping her legs straight, she let herself fall backward. It worked! She ricocheted off the ropes and, after an awkward half stumble, gained her feet.

"Try it again," Duck ordered.

Backward and forward she went—"A regular rope-a-dope," he commented at one point—until she was comfortable with the sensation.

"Now," Duck said, "hands up and head down."

Maureen assumed her fighting stance, ready to block a punch.

"You're wide open."

"For what?"

He showed her with a soft right to her chin.

"Ow!"

Next he pressed a nerve in her neck.

"*Ow!*" She understood, already.

They worked on her form until Duck was satisfied that she was ready to block a punch. And then he threw one, a slow but graceful left hook.

Maureen blocked it, all right. But she'd forgotten to keep her arm stiff, so her gloved fist flew into her forehead. Her sheepish eyes met the trainer's told-you-so ones.

"I know," she said ruefully. "It's only pain."

The next time, she kept her arm stiff and . . . hallelujah! . . . she did it. Someone had tried to hit her and she'd prevented it! Pretty soon, she was slapping away hooks and blocking punches like a pro, always remembering to get back into position.

"You learn fast," Duck said. "Just like Jack."

Maureen beamed, recognizing high praise when she heard it. She looked around, wanting to share her small triumph with the man she loved, but he was nowhere to be seen. Her smile faded and she found herself praying that nothing else bad had happened.

"Where is Jack?" she asked as casually as she could.

"Doing a promo for the cable TV people."

She let out a disgusted breath. "How's he supposed to train for the fight with the media hounding him night and day?"

Duck gestured toward the crowded gym. "Not to mention all these other hangers-on."

The trainer's remark reminded her of her original purpose for putting on the gloves. "I want to hit something."

"Come on." He held the ropes open to help her out of the ring and led her to the balcony level.

Maureen went to the heavy bag and whipped out a jab . . . from the shoulder, of course.

The bag barely moved.

"Again," Duck said. "And this time, give it everything you've got."

She fired a hard right, immediately followed by a left to the side.

The bag twisted. Slowly, to be sure. But the longer she hit it, the more it moved.

Maureen put all of her anger—at Sully, for abandoning her; at Laura, for shutting her out—into her punches. All of her frustration—with the system that had failed Tammy; with the fact she couldn't be alone with Jack—too.

Finally, she was exhausted. Duck wiped her face with a towel as she sat, cross-legged, on the floor. Her hands hurt and every muscle in her body ached . . . but she'd never felt better in her entire life.

"How does it look?"

"Very natural."

"It feels natural, too." Tammy, practicing her smile in front of Maureen's cheval mirror, ran her tongue over the temporary cap on her broken tooth for perhaps the hundredth time since she'd left the dentist's chair yesterday.

Her hair was starting to grow back where the stitches had been removed, and she'd styled it differently to hide the bristly spots. With her first paycheck, she'd splurged on new makeup that was a little softer-looking than the old. Then she'd just had to have the sleeveless denim minidress she was wearing now . . . oh, and those neat rainbow-colored clogs, too!

Smiling puckishly at the preening teenager's reflection, Maureen nudged her away from the mirror so she could finish getting ready for Sunday Mass. "My turn, Narcissus."

The bell at the front door of the shop pealed through the apartment.

"I'll get it," Tammy said, and bolted out of the bedroom.

"Call up on the intercom before you let anyone in," Maureen cautioned.

Downstairs, Jack was completely bowled over when the smiling teenager answered the door. He hadn't seen her since the day he'd visited her in the hospital. Then she'd been a terrorized mass of tubes and tears; now, except for the fact that her taste in clothing still ran to the funky, she looked like an entirely different girl. And for that he credited Maureen.

"Wow" was all he could think to say.

Her smile widened under his approval.

Jack noticed a change for the better there, too. "You had your tooth fixed."

"Maureen's having her dentist make me a permanent cap." Tammy couldn't resist running her tongue over the temporary one. Again. "Plus"—she pulled a pair of rhinestone-studded sunglasses from the breast pocket of her dress and put them on—"she bought me these, too."

"Lookin' good." Jack screwed up his face comically. "Or am I supposed to say, 'Lookin' bad'?"

They laughed together, the man and the girl who had every right in the world to fear his gender, and it was yet another healing moment for her.

Suddenly seeming to remember what had brought her here, Tammy removed the sunglasses and let her gaze fall to her feet. "How's Frankie?"

"Well," Jack said, a frown replacing his smile, "that's what I came to talk to you about."

"Who is it, Tammy?" Maureen demanded over the intercom by the front door.

Jack stepped past the teenager into the reception area and pushed the "talk" button. "I'll give you three guesses, and the first two don't count."

Upstairs, Maureen's heart did cartwheels in her chest. She took a deep breath, not wanting to come over as too excited, and said, "Good morning."

He thought of a dozen ways to reply to her throaty greeting, most of them too erotic for a teenager's ears, so he answered with a husky "Morning."

"What's wrong?" She realized she sounded like her mother now, automatically assuming the worst. But given all that had happened lately, what else could she think?

"Not a thing."

"Then what—"

"I want to borrow Tammy for a little while." He told her in as few words as possible about his promise to visit

Frankie every Sunday. "I just thought it'd be good for him to see how well she's doing."

"Awwright!"

As much as Maureen hated to put a damper on Tammy's enthusiasm, she had to. "We were just leaving to go to Mass."

"Aww Jeez."

"I've got a suggestion." Maureen wasn't sure how well it would be received, but there was certainly no harm in tossing it out. "Why don't you come with us, and then we'll go with you?"

Jack frowned down at the floor. He hadn't been inside a church for so long, he figured the walls would probably cave in on him. Then he looked over at Tammy, all fading bruises and flourishing hopes, and punched the "talk" button again.

"How soon do we leave?"

"I'll be right down."

Maureen gave silent thanks as she grabbed her purse and fairly flew down the stairs. She wore woven sandals today instead of high heels, and a button-front linen sundress that she'd left undone at the bottom for freedom of movement. Her only jewelry was a hinged sandalwood bracelet and large matching hoops in her ears.

Jack's eyes lazily tracked her from head to foot when she made her appearance, and every sensory receptor in her body went wild in response. Her eyes took a quick tour of their own, noting the trim cut of his olive slacks and the open-throated ivory polo shirt that accented his healthy summer tan. They looked their fill, and still it wasn't enough.

"No hat?" he asked when his gaze eventually returned to her hair, which she'd tied at her nape with a chiffon scarf.

"Not since the late Sixties."

He gave her a sheepish grin. "I told you it'd been a while."

She laid a reassuring hand on his arm. "I think He'll remember you."

They stared at each other for a moment, the emotions and desires that had been held too long in check on both sides bubbling just beneath the surface. Had they been alone—

"Let's go," Tammy urged the adults.

Maureen bit back a smile at the teenager's anxious tone and said, "Your convertible or mine?"

Jack did a double take. "Come again?"

"She bought the Mustang," Tammy informed him.

"Pretty sporty for a society decorator," he said teasingly.

"Pretty smart mouth for a dumb jock," she returned in kind.

"We're going to be late," Tammy reminded them impatiently.

Jack laughed. "Shall we flip a coin to see who drives?"

Maureen dug a quarter out of her purse. "Heads or tails?"

"Tails."

Tails it was, and the three of them piled into his Catalina. Tammy wanted to ride shotgun, so Maureen sat in the middle, between her and Jack. Not a bad place to be, she decided as he draped his right arm around her shoulders and steered the convertible with one hand as well as most drivers control their cars with two.

Noon Mass was always crowded with late sleepers and Saturday night revelers, but they managed to squeeze into a pew together. Maureen went in first, followed by Tammy, and Jack took the aisle seat. Standing, kneeling or sitting, they looked for all the world like a small family doing their Sunday duty.

Maureen's heart had never felt so full as when the three of them exchanged the Sign of the Peace. She turned and shook Tammy's hand, then reached for Jack's. Their palms met, hers so soft against his hard one, then he leaned across the teenager to press his lips to hers in a chaste display of affection that nonetheless left her tingling.

"There now, that wasn't so bad, was it?" she asked as they filed up the aisle after the last notes of the recessional hymn had faded away.

Not yet ready to admit to the fact he felt as if he'd come home, he quietly conceded, "They don't kneel quite as much as they used to."

In the parking lot, Paul was holding the passenger door of his Lincoln Towncar open for Laura. He tossed them a smile at the same time she gaped at them as if they were ghosts. Then she turned her back on the trio and climbed into the car.

Maureen saw the stunned reaction on her mother's face before she reached to wrench the door from Paul's hand and pull it closed. She stared at the tinted glass, her heart aching with pity for a woman so full of bitterness that she would cut herself off from her own daughter rather than bend.

Paul, too, wished his wife weren't so brittle, but he wasn't about to let her icy refusal to accept the choices Maureen had made keep him from following his heart's dictate. He crossed the lot, arms outstretched, and greeted her with his ritual hug.

"Hi, Dad." Maureen kissed his cheek, smelling his familiar crisp aftershave, before introducing him to Jack.

"Pleased to meet you, sir," Jack said as they shook hands.

"Same here." Looking from his daughter's glowing face to the fighter's gentle eyes, Paul realized that she had, indeed, met her match. And a damn fine match it was, he thought as he released the younger man's hand and turned to Tammy.

He'd met the teenager when he'd stopped by the design shop one day last week, on his way home from running errands. She'd been hard at work on the new billing system, having despaired of either Maureen or Donna ever finding the time to learn how to use the computer. Once he'd recovered from the shock of her bruises and broken tooth—and his anger at the stepfather who'd inflicted them—Paul had offered her a few pointers on how to set it up.

"Did you ever get the billing system figured out?" he asked her now.

She nodded and smiled. "The bills went out in Friday's mail."

Paul would have loved to stay and visit—or, better yet, invite the three of them out for a leisurely brunch—but he could feel Laura's eyes boring into his back from the front seat of the Towncar.

"Well," he said, proffering his hand to Jack again in farewell, "good luck on your upcoming fight."

"I hope you'll be there," Jack replied.

Paul had always been more interested in books and flowers than in football games and boxing matches. Now he surprised himself by saying, "Maybe I will."

"I'll see that you have ringside seats." Jack had been prepared to dislike the man who'd adopted Sully's daughter, but he discovered to his amazement that just the opposite was true.

After giving Maureen a hug, Paul reminded her, "If there's anything I can do to help, I'm as close as the phone."

Tammy, also the recipient of a hug, smiled at Maureen as Paul finally tore himself away from the trio. "You're really lucky, you know, to've had two fathers who love you?"

Maureen had never thought of it from that angle before. "You're right," she said, feeling a new and happy stinging in her eyes, "I have been lucky."

"Let's go, ladies." Jack put his arms around both of them, much the way Paul used to do with his two best girls, and the three of them headed for his car.

The Juvenile Detention Center, encircled by a high chain-link fence, sat in the shadow of the downtown skyline.

Going in, they had to follow the same procedures and route Jack had followed the other night. Maureen hated the dun-colored walls and speckled tile floors on sight. Tammy, on the other hand, was so eager to see Frankie that she didn't seem to notice the depressing decor.

A disbelieving smile spread across Frankie's thin face when he saw the three of them standing in the doorway of the visitor's lounge. Jack and Maureen hung back while Tammy took two hesitant steps forward. Then she began running, those rainbow-colored clogs clunking against the tile floor, across the room.

The instant his arms went around her, she burst into tears. "Oh, Frankie, our b . . . baby."

"We'll make another one," he soothed his sobbing girlfriend. Then glancing at the guardian adults across the room, he added, "When we're older."

"You were right," Jack said huskily as he observed the embracing teenagers.

Maureen swallowed hard and looked up at him with misty eyes. "Right about what?"

"They found each other."

"Who *are* all these people?"

"Nuisances, that's who."

Maureen set her gym bag on the floor, the noise created by a dozen new half-naked bodies skipping rope and running wind sprints pounding at her head. "How can Jack concentrate on his training routine with this going on around him?"

"He can't," Duck growled around his cigar. "Which means we're either going to have to make camp somewhere else or call off the fight."

In the ring, a slender man in headgear and gray satin trunks jabbed at his spindly shadow, while in front of the wall-length mirror Maureen had come to consider hers, a woman wearing orange leg warmers and an oversized pink sweatshirt practiced what looked to be ballet positions.

Ballet positions in a boxing gym, for God's sake!

Outside, it was just as crowded as it was inside. When Maureen had pulled her new black Mustang into the gravel lot where she'd begun parking last week, she'd been greeted by a gleaming fleet of Volvos, Mercedes and the occasional van. Fortunately, Rocstar had remembered to save her a space near the door or she would have been back on the streets.

"What can we do about it?" she asked Duck.

He shrugged and thumbed toward the sign he'd tacked to the street door. "I've started charging 'em locker fees— five dollars a week, payable in advance."

"Make it ten dollars."

"That's pretty steep."

Remembering all those expensive cars in the parking lot, she snorted indelicately. "Not for them."

"Well . . ." He reached up and ran a hand down the back of his balding head. "You're the owner."

That's right, she was—for the next two and a half weeks, anyway—and it was time she remembered it, too. "On second thought, make that twenty dollars a week."

Duck almost swallowed his cigar at the order. "Twenty?"

"Washing towels costs money," Maureen declared as she watched a blow-dried wanna-be wrap one around his neck, then spread another on the floor to use as an exercise mat.

"And they take forever to dry."

"Then limit them to one a day."

The trainer's expression turned dubious. "Most of 'em ask for extras when they get ready to shower and shampoo their hair."

The owner's expression turned defiant. "Well, then,

charge them a dollar for every towel they request after the first one."

A cloud of cigar smoke accompanied his next observation. "That's gonna make for a lot of paperwork."

"I'll ask Tammy to print out some logs," she decided. "Then we'll teach the boys how to keep them."

"Are we gonna pay 'em?"

"Heck, yes, we're creating an enterprise zone here."

"Damned if we aren't," Duck said on a note of amazement.

As she picked up her gym bag in preparation for changing clothes in the office, Maureen noticed the new lost and found box next to the street door. "Oh, and while you're at it, post a sign in the locker room saying NO SWEATY CLOTHES OVERNIGHT."

"What'll we do with the ones we've already collected?"

"If nobody's claimed them by the end of the day, donate them to the Salvation Army tomorrow."

Duck reached into the box and held up a large-cupped black lace bra. "Even this?"

"Especially that," Maureen said on a laugh before she headed for the stairs.

Pausing on the balcony level to watch a heftily-built man practicing body blows on the heavy bag, she came up with what she thought was her best idea yet.

Duck had spent almost his entire adult life in the gym, so why not ask him to design some kind of "after work" training program for all these would-be pugilists? Obviously there was a market for it, what with the big emphasis on fitness these days, and clients were only a couple of miles west—in the office buildings and executive suites that comprised the downtown skyline. And she knew from her own experience that sweating out one's stress in the ring beat fighting the traffic rush hands down any day of the week.

Jack would have to approve the plan, Maureen conceded as she climbed the last few stairs to the office. After all, it was going to be his gym in a couple of weeks. But considering that it would provide jobs for the boys as well as a boost for the neighborhood economy, she really couldn't see him rejecting it.

He probably would resist the renovations she had in mind, however. Paint for the walls, polish for the floors, and, eventually, separate locker rooms for men and women. But maybe she could show him on paper how the improvements would pay for themselves over time.

Deciding she'd draw up a rough draft after she'd changed her clothes and while it was all still fresh in her mind, she opened the office door.

"Sorry, honey, I saw him first."

Maureen stopped flat at the peep-voiced comment and gaped at the sight that greeted her. A twentysomething woman wearing a black thong leotard over flesh-colored tights was sitting on the edge of the desk. Her fluffy dandelion hair framed a heart-shaped face, her neckline was cut for maximum exposure, and her long legs were crossed in a torch singer's seductive pose.

Putting two and two together and getting 36-24-36, Maureen was tempted to ask her if she'd lost a black lace bra. Instead, she repeated the question that was beginning to sound like a broken record to her own ears. "Who are you?"

"All the fighters call me Barbie Doll."

"So . . . you're a friend of Jack's?"

"Not yet," the blonde admitted in her high-pitched voice, "but I have a feeling we're going to be real good friends before the night's over."

Maureen had heard of rock groupies, of course, but never in a million years could she have imagined there was such a creature as a *jock* groupie. A hard knot settled in her stomach as she closed the door. She didn't know which sickened her more—the athletes who used these women for fun and games or the women who allowed themselves to be treated like meaningless nighttime toys.

"I think you'd better go," she said as she set her gym bag in the middle of the desk.

Barbie Doll uncrossed her legs and propped her fists on her hips. "Says who?"

"Says the owner, that's who."

"You own this dump?"

Maureen nodded with no little satisfaction. "I sure do."

"That means you own Jack Ryan too, huh?"

"Right again."

"Lucky you," she said in her Bo Peep voice as she hopped off the desk. At the door, she paused and turned back. "Listen, I'm really sorry about trying to run you off."

"No hard feelings."

"I'll spread the word that Jack's spoken for, but"—the girl shrugged, almost lifting her breasts out of the leotard's low neckline—"that probably won't stop them."

"Them" meaning the groupies, Maureen realized. She went to the window overlooking the gym and watched the girl move toward the street door. The boys came in at the same moment she started out, and their adolescent eyeballs bulged when she brushed against each of them in turn as she took her leave.

It was just the jumpstart Maureen needed. Spinning on her heels, she stalked to the desk, picked up the telephone receiver and dialed her parents' number. Her prayers were answered when Paul answered on the second ring.

"Hi, Dad."

"Hi, darlin'."

After a brief exchange of amenities, she got to the point of her phone call. "Did you really mean it when you told me to let you know if I needed anything?"

"Of course."

It was a lot to ask, Maureen acknowledged, and she wouldn't blame her father one bit if he said no. Still, nothing ventured, nothing gained. "Could I borrow your farm for a couple of weeks?"

ROUND 11

It was a colorful motorcade, to say the least, that left the "Closed till August 16th" gym to make camp on Paul Bryant's farm two Saturdays before the fight.

Maureen, driving her new black Mustang convertible with Tammy riding shotgun, led the caravan east on I-70 and south on Lee's Summit Road. Jack sat behind the wheel of his flame red Catalina while from the passenger seat Duck, wearing a jaunty plaid cap to protect his balding head from sunburn, pointed out such interesting sights as the Truman Sports Complex to the boys in the back. Rocstar steered the shiny white '79 Cadillac Coupe de Ville he'd financed through the Loan arRanger after providing a fat downpayment from the proceeds of his parking lot. Sparring partners Beetlejuice and Ray Howard brought up the rear in two bright yellow U-Haul trucks that were bursting at the seams with all the equipment necessary for a two-week training camp.

Paul looked eager to get them going when he met them at the gate. Truth be told, he was as thrilled to be a part of his daughter's project as he was glad to see his parents' old farm put to such good use. He'd held on to it in hopes of living out his retirement years puttering in the garden and planting a few crops. But Laura loved the hustle and bustle of the city, and he loved her too much to even think of leaving her behind.

Dressed in the navy, crinkled nylon wind suit Maureen had bought him for Father's Day, he'd already opened and aired out the house. Summer sunlight through the windows had revealed the shredded newspaper nest left by the mice who'd wintered there. He'd swept it away under the smiling photographs of people dead and friends lost that hung upon the walls.

In the bedrooms, he'd shaken out blankets. In the kitchen, he'd checked out appliances. Now, in the heat of excitement, he played traffic cop.

"The cars go behind the house," he directed, "the trucks in front of the barn."

At the end of a quarter-mile drive—a drive that dropped through an open field where cattle used to pasture and a screening weald of ash and oak and hickory where a boy used to perch in the high branches and watch for the woman who never came back—stood the two-story field-stone farmhouse and the cluster of outbuildings that was their final destination.

Like ducks in a row, Maureen and Jack and Rocstar parked near the back door of the old homeplace. Across the way, Beetlejuice and Ray Howard backed up to the wide barn doors so they could unload the equipment after lunch. As soon as Paul pulled up in his car and everyone had piled out, Maureen made the introductions.

"You already know Jack and Tammy, of course."

"Good to see you again." Paul shook the fighter's hand and smiled at the teenager. "You too."

"Duck," she said then, turning to the trainer, "I'd like you to meet my father, Paul Bryant."

Much to her surprise, Paul hesitated just a heartbeat before extending his hand. "Duck."

Even more baffling was the way Duck's expression faltered before he grasped it. "Paul."

Maureen was positive the two men had never met, so she chalked up the awkward moment, which passed the instant they pumped hands, to the fact that one had been Sully's surrogate and the other his staunchest friend.

Following another round of shakes and "Pleased to meetchas" for and from Rocstar and the boys, Paul popped open the trunk of his Towncar and pulled out the big wicker basket that had accompanied the Bryant family on picnics for years.

"Anybody hungry?" he asked, hefting the basket high.

Ridiculous question, with five teenagers in tow.

Jack grabbed the blankets from the Towncar's trunk and told Tammy and the boys to spread them beneath the peach trees that used to keep Paul's mother in pie filling and, more recently, the boys in after-school snacks. Maureen passed out the sliced barbecue sandwiches her father had brought and—increasingly the mother hen—fresh veggies that she'd cut herself, while Duck distributed cold cans of cola. For dessert there were Black Diamond watermelon slices eaten out of hand; for entertainment, a seed spitting contest.

After they cleared away the picnic clutter, they unpacked the cars and set up housekeeping.

Maureen and Tammy, who would be staying in town until the day before the fight, put away twelve bags of groceries. Rocstar and the boys carried their sleeping bags and Duck's suitcase up to the second-floor bedrooms. Beetlejuice and Ray Howard would share the detached garage that had been turned into a studio apartment for some nameless hired hand, while Jack claimed the one-room guest cottage to the west of the house. Paul passed out sheets and towels and instructions on how to operate the water heater and the air conditioner.

Then the transformation from barn to boxing gym began.

Maureen and Tammy helped Rocstar and the boys unload the trucks. Jack and Duck, along with Beetlejuice and Ray Howard, tore down the old horse stalls that had been sitting empty for years and put up the boxing ring they'd dismantled the night before. Paul, who needed to leave by five o'clock in order to get ready for the dinner party that Laura and he were attending that evening, lent tools and a hand wherever and whenever he could.

Three hours later the metamorphosis was complete.

"Can you believe it?" Maureen stood with one arm linked through her father's, the other through her fighter's, in the doorway of the converted barn.

Paul shook his head in amazement. "It looks great."

"If you have to go into seclusion," Jack said, "this is the way to go."

Duck crossed his arms over his chest like a self-satisfied Buddha. "Now we're gonna see some action."

It really was remarkable, what they'd managed to accomplish in such a short amount of time. The ring stood beneath the center beam, from which a flood lamp dangled, while the heavy bags and the speed bags hung from alternating rafters along each side and between the windows. A massage table promised relaxing rewards after laborious workouts, and a gleaming metal scale awaited daily weigh-ins.

Jack's training schedule for the next two weeks was tacked to the door, and from the looks of it, he was going to be one busy guy. *Spartan* was the word that came to Maureen's mind as she studied the strict regimen he would be following from six in the morning until eleven at night. But if he wanted to win—

"It needs a name." Tony's declaration drew her attention.

Jamal snapped his fingers. "How about Bryant's Fight Gym?"

"It's a barn, not a gym," Deron said dismissively.

Tammy waved the wildflower she'd picked like a flag. "Daisyland."

Rocstar rolled his eyes, putting the kibosh on that.

"Barn Again," Maureen suggested, meaning it as a joke.

Jack's eyes glinted down into hers like dark, metallic sparks. "Not bad."

Paul nodded. "I like it."

Duck's gesture encompassed the lot of them. "And Lord knows, it's the truth."

"Barn Again" it became.

Like Sisyphus putting his shoulder to that boulder, Jack started up the long road back.

Training was the most brutal work a man could do, but this fight was his last hurrah. He was hungry for it. Almost as hungry for it as he was for the woman who answered to "Mo." Yet he couldn't even begin to contemplate satisfying his craving for her until he'd slaked his thirst for self-respect.

For years he'd been trying to outrun his guilt. The coroner's report stated that his opponent had died of a brain hemorrhage, the direct result of too many fights in too short a period of time, but Jack knew he was responsible. *He* was the one who'd been fighting with anger; *he* was the one who'd come out of the corner and seen his father's face there; *he* was the one who'd hit him as hard as he could.

And he'd been beating up on himself ever since.

Oh, true, he'd gone on to college and to law school at Sully's urging. Also true that he'd eschewed a big bucks legal practice in favor of fighting for the little guys. Still, he'd been emotionally *hors de combat*. Unable to make a commitment to one woman because he didn't know how to make it last. And unwilling to create a family only to find that the sins of a violent father had been visited upon the son.

But no more. He had religion now, so to speak, and he was going to go the distance come hell or "Poison" Ivy's mean right hook. Toward that end, he worked his butt off from morning till night for the next thirteen days.

Oddly enough, silence served as his six a.m. wake-up call. A city boy used to round-the-clock street racket, he would open his eyes at the crack of dawn, stack his hands behind his head and listen to the quiet that was broken only by occasional bird song. Then he'd roll out of bed and into his running clothes to leg it over hill and dale for forty-five minutes straight.

Drills on slipping punches consumed another full hour. Beetlejuice was not only an early riser, but he also had the longest reach of the two sparring partners. So Jack traded jabs with him until Duck showed up to rub him down with a rank but muscle-relaxing mixture of ammonia, camphor and alcohol that he brewed himself and swore was better than anything he could buy in the store.

Breakfast consisted of fruit juice and oatmeal and microwave pancakes, prepared by and shared with the boys.

Paul Bryant's parents, whose names were Ed and Ruth, had apparently hoped for a large family because the huge old needle-leg table in the dining room seated eight without extension. Jack often found himself staring at the picture of the smiling farm couple that hung on the wall. He looked for some resemblance between them and their only child, but try as he might, he couldn't find any.

Reviewing films was his least favorite part of the regimen. He was a different man now, fighting for entirely different reasons. But he'd obviously done something right because he'd won seventeen professional bouts in a row. So he set up his portable TV and VCR in the old-fashioned living room where Ed and Ruth and Paul Bryant had once gathered round the radio, to watch and to listen and to relearn some of his better techniques.

"Look at that right!" Tony exclaimed from the depths of an overstuffed club chair that had been the ultimate in comfort during the Great Depression.

Jamal sat forward on the horsehair sofa. "Like *Robocop 2*'s pile driver!"

"The other guy looks like Apollo Creed," Deron pointed out.

Rocstar hummed the theme from *Rocky II*.

Duck, full of good food and fresh air, snored along.

Stretching and hand strengthening drills ushered in the lunch hour.

August afternoons in Missouri were too hot for anything but cooling off with the boys in the creek. Then he worked up a sweat again during his evening sparring session with Ray Howard. His final reward was another rubdown from Duck.

Dinner, a salad and some sort of pasta dish, preceded a discussion of the next day's regimen.

Lights out at eleven brought a bullfrog lullabye from the nearby creek bank and dreams of a beautiful redhead sleeping in a metal bed clear across town.

They'd never spent the night together, but Jack invariably rolled to his side and reached to pull Maureen against his body. It was then, when he came up with empty arms, that he realized he was missing the most vital element of his life. And it was then that his confidence faded and his doubts bloomed in the darkness, vivid as fireflies.

He would drift back to sleep swearing he was going to call it quits come morning. But when the quiet woke him, he always rolled out of bed and went through the same damn regimen again. He jogged and he jabbed, he stretched and he strengthened, he watched and he worked on what he'd seen.

Because in his champion's heart, he knew this was his

last, best chance to show the boys that it was the effort, not the win, that made the man.

"Mmm—what's cooking?"

"Tacos."

Maureen smiled at Tammy as she entered the kitchen. Then almost had heart failure when she saw the mess the teenager had made. Oh, the bistro table was neatly set for two. But the stove was covered with hamburger crumbs and bits of chopped onion, the counter was littered with shreds of lettuce and curls of cheese, and the sink was loaded with utensils that had yet to make it into the dishwasher.

Usually they closed the shop at six, turned on the answering machine, and came upstairs to cook dinner together. This morning, though, Tammy had announced that she planned to leave a little early and fix the entire meal herself. She had something she wanted to talk about— something *really* important, she'd stressed, her blue eyes sparkling mysteriously—and she wanted everything to be perfect.

"Need any help?" Maureen asked now, thinking she would start at the sink and work her way backward.

The teenager shook her head so vigorously that some of the warm salsa she was carrying from the microwave to the table sloshed over the edge of the bowl and onto the floor. "All you have to do is sit down and eat."

Realizing that Tammy would be crushed by even one word of criticism after putting her heart and soul into preparing this feast, Maureen did exactly that. And discovered, three delicious tacos later, that messy was half the fun.

"Look at me!" she said, laughing as she dabbed at the front of her yellow cotton blouse with her napkin. "I'm covered with salsa."

"It'll come out in the wash."

"Maybe I should put it to soak now."

"Wait." Tammy's request stopped her before she could stand. "Please. I need to talk to you before Frankie calls tonight."

Seeing the beseeching expression on her face, Maureen remained in her chair. Ever since Frankie had been granted telephone privileges for good behavior, he called promptly at eight. "How's he doing?"

"Fine." Tammy propped her elbows on the table to lick salsa off her fingers. "He said Jack came to visit him Sunday night, after we were there, and that he's going to try and get tickets to the fight for the whole detention facility."

Just hearing Jack's name made Maureen's heart beat a lonely dirge in her breast. He'd been in training camp almost a week now, and she'd never dreamed she could miss him so much. Only the knowledge that they would be spending the final twenty-four hours before the bout together kept her from jumping into her car this very minute and driving out to the farm.

"That's great." Ignoring the teenager's breach of manners, she tilted her head inquiringly. "What was it you wanted to talk to me about?"

"Stay there," Tammy instructed, then leapt to her feet and dashed to her room. She came back carrying a sheaf of papers—computer printouts, from the looks of them. After haphazardly stacking their dishes off to the side, she laid them on the table so Maureen could page through them.

"Diagrams?"

"Of every room in this apartment."

"I thought they looked familiar." Maureen flipped back to the first page—a layout of her living room, complete with furniture. "Where did you get these, anyway?"

"I made them."

"When?"

Tammy shrugged nonchalantly, but her face was taut with tension. "I've been working on them for a couple of weeks now, in between sending out bills and making the master client list."

"What gave you the idea to do it?"

"I was watching you drawing diagrams on graph paper one day, and I got to wondering why you couldn't do it on a computer instead."

Maureen shook her head in amazement as she turned to the diagram of her bedroom. Again, complete with furniture. "How did you get such exact dimensions?"

"I measured the rooms first, and fed those measurements into the computer. Then I measured the furniture and put it in the proper rooms."

"You've even got the correct curve on the cheval mirror."

Tammy might have been speaking in Sanskrit as she explained how she'd entered the various shapes and sizes into the computer, but Maureen recognized a brilliant idea when she saw one.

"I'll call my attorney first thing in the morning," she declared when the teenager finally wound down.

"Your attorney?"

Maureen saw the flash of fear in Tammy's eyes and rushed to extinguish it. "I want to ask him to refer us to an attorney who specializes in patents for computer programs."

"Why?"

"Because you, my soon-to-be-very-rich young genius, may have just single-handedly revolutionized the entire industry of interior design."

Tammy smiled uncertainly. "You're jivin' me, right?"

Maureen shook her head to say she most certainly was not. "A program like this would free a designer to experiment. Let her take her creativity to the limit. Not to mention relieving the eyestrain that comes from working with graph paper."

"I can teach you to make one of those printouts in a day," Tammy said casually.

"That's not the point."

"What do you mean?"

"You've accomplished something really remarkable here." Maureen tapped the stack of papers with the tip of her nail for emphasis. "Something that would not only finance your college education, but would set you up—"

"I don't want to go to college," Tammy stated defiantly. "All I want to do is have Frankie's baby."

"Having a baby is an admirable goal." Maureen smiled wistfully, envisioning a little boy with Jack's dark eyes and devil-may-care grin. "But only if the circumstances are right for all concerned."

"We're going to get married first."

"I hope so."

Tammy's bruises had long since healed, but her blue eyes suddenly developed darkly haunted shadows. "My mother wasn't married when she had me."

Maureen wasn't surprised by the news. Girls who'd been born out of wedlock often repeated that same pattern themselves. She was, however, grateful for the opportunity it gave her to make her point without openly criticizing Tammy's mother.

"Pregnancy lasts for nine months." As she tiptoed through this minefield of reasoning, she couldn't help but think of Paul. Not only of the material advantages he'd given her, but of the way that he'd never made her feel less than completely loved because she wasn't his own flesh and blood. He'd always been there for her, and she knew without a doubt that he always would be. "Parenthood is a lifetime commitment."

"So what you're saying," Tammy replied thoughtfully, "is that I should get this patent and go to college so I won't be worried about money when I have my baby?"

"Not exactly."

"Then what?"

"You should apply for this patent so that both you and Frankie can take advantage of the opportunities the money from it will provide. Then after"—she swallowed the words "you've grown up" just in time—"you've completed your educations—"

"Maybe we can even go to the same college." Tammy's expression brightened at the thought, then almost immediately dimmed. "But what if someone else has already come up with a computer program like mine?"

"We'll know for sure after the attorney does a patent search," Maureen pointed out.

Tammy sighed forlornly then. "I don't know, it all sounds too good to be true."

"Why do you say that?"

"I'm afraid I'll make a mess of things," the teenager confessed. "Like I did with the baby."

Maureen wanted to tell her that it wasn't her fault she'd miscarried, but she didn't want to start playing the blame game. She glanced around her kitchen, which looked as if a small tornado had whirled through it, and smiled. Then she stood, beckoning Tammy to do the same, and began collecting their dirty dishes.

"If you make a mess," she said, "you clean it up."

Watching that old fight film of Jack's had been a horrible mistake, Maureen realized.

No sooner had Tammy and she arrived at the farm that morning than they'd been ensconced on the scratchy old living room sofa by the boys and subjected to an hour's worth of taped savagery that had made her sick to her stomach. For up until then, the fight had been little more than a faraway fantasy in her mind. More of a long-range goal than an immediate reality.

Maureen had known from the beginning that boxing was

a brutal sport, of course. The scar over Jack's eye and the bend in his nose were proof enough of that. And since the day the press had confronted them, she'd known men could get killed with one wrong punch in the right place. She just hadn't known that that preview of things to come would hit her in the emotional solar plexus like this.

Worse yet, she'd had the entire day to stew about what she'd seen. To worry about what was going to happen to him tomorrow night. An entire day in which he'd been too busy working on his game plan to give her anything more than a quick kiss when she'd gotten there and another peck before he'd turned in at ten-thirty.

Tammy and she were sharing the master bedroom that had belonged to her grandparents. It was situated on the first floor of the farmhouse and had its own bathroom, so there wouldn't be any embarrassing run-ins with Duck or Rocstar and the boys. The still-recovering teenager had fallen asleep the instant her head had hit the pillow, exhausted by a day of fun in the sun.

Lucky her.

Maureen had bathed and brushed her teeth and put on her meadow-green cotton nightshirt, all in preparation for bed. And all for naught. Because the instant she'd closed her eyes, she'd seen the fists flying and the faces bleeding and a man falling in painfully slow motion to the canvas.

And the crowd . . . She'd rolled onto her stomach and pulled her pillow over her head, but she couldn't drown out the loud yells and the low boos and, at the end, the deafening cheers. Not wanting to wake Tammy with her tossing and turning, she'd left the cool house and gone out on the back stoop to let the hot summer night wash over her.

The cicadas' high droning and the fireflies flitter-flashing . . . A white chocolate moon and a million winking stars . . . The loaminess of the nearby fields and the lingering sweetness of night-blooming jasmine . . .

She had soaked up the peace of it all like a sponge. Drunk it in through every pore. Then, thirsty for more, she'd wandered aimlessly around the farmyard for a while. North to south, east to . . .

Facing west, Maureen had picked out the pale blue silhouette of the one-room guest cottage where, judging by the darkened window, Jack lay in pre-fight slumber. The temptation to go pound on his door, to wake him and beg him to call off the fight, had been almost more than she could resist. But knowing it would take more than her losing her cool and laying her fears on his doorstep to stop him, she'd turned in the opposite direction and followed the recently beaten footpath to those wide wooden doors.

And now here she sat, on a folding chair in the starlit "Barn Again," wondering how she could keep him from going back into the ring tomorrow night.

The gym was the key. He was fighting to get the money to buy it from her, so if she wanted to put a stop to the proceedings, she had to give it to him. The question was, would his pride allow him to accept her gift of love?

Probably not. She surged to her feet in frustration and stalked over to the pear-shaped speed bag that hung idly, innocently, in the near darkness. Doubling up her bare fist, she hauled off and hit it as hard as she could, and heard the *rat-a-tat-tat* echo from the rafters.

He was so damned stubborn . . . She hit the bag with her other hand. Knowing she'd have bruises between her fingers by morning because she wasn't wearing gloves, but not really caring. Hearing again the machine-gun clatter, but not really listening.

"You rang?"

At the sound of that dear, deep voice, Maureen spun away from the speed bag and saw Jack standing in the wide, open doorway. The moonlight spilling in behind him kissed his curly hair and draped his naked shoulders, but left his face in darkness. Only the flash of white where she knew his beloved mouth to be told her he was smiling.

"I'm sorry." She grabbed the still-chattering bag, held it until it fell silent, then let go. "I didn't mean to wake you."

"I wasn't asleep."

"Oh . . . ?"

He turned and closed the door, shutting out the moonlight and throwing the bolt with a firm click. Then the whisper of his cotton jogging shorts against the hair-roughened skin of his strong thighs warned her that he was coming for her. "I *couldn't* sleep."

She stated the obvious. "Me, either."

And then those giant bare hands clasped her head and tilted it back with loving concern, and those gentle brown eyes picked up the silvery trail of tears down her cheeks. "You've been crying."

"I . . ." She hadn't realized, but when she flicked a corner of her mouth with her tongue, she tasted salt. "Yes. I've been crying."

"Why?"

"Because I'm afraid."

His expression went from tender to tormented in the wink of a star. "Of me?"

"No, my love." Her swift assurance erased the harshly drawn lines between his brows and on either side of his mouth. "Never *of* you. Only *for* you."

"I'll be all right."

But in her heart beat the unspoken questions: What if he wasn't? What if he was badly hurt? Or worse, what if he—

Maureen felt a fresh stinging of tears in her eyes as she pictured Jack falling, blood staining the canvas beneath him, while above his crumpled body "Poison" Ivy's gloved hand was raised in triumph.

He received her silently telegraphed worries and tried to

alleviate them. Touching his lips to her upturned brow, the tip of her nose, he vowed, "I promise."

She shivered despite his fervently voiced pledge. Trembled with the need to tell him that he didn't have to fight tomorrow night, after all. She opened her mouth to deliver the good news, and his tongue mistook it as an invitation to mate with hers.

Her thoughts, her words, her fears . . . His kiss scattered them to the winds of her long-denied desire. She moved against him, lifting her hands to clasp them behind his neck. He was hard and warm and here. And it was easy . . . oh, so easy to pretend that tomorrow might never come when his arms were banding her body and her breasts were pressed to his chest as they were now.

"Barn Again" was hardly a romantic setting.

Yet the old-fashioned spice of his soap and the fresh-picked floral of hers completely eradicated the reek of sweat and muscle-relaxant. The soughing of his breath and the quickening of hers totally drowned out the reverberations of the grunts and groans that had accompanied those twice-daily sparring sessions. And the silver starlight and springy canvas more than compensated for the lack of a softly glowing lamp and a metal bed.

"I love you." It mattered not who said it first, for the other immediately sang the second verse.

Kissing her again as if he couldn't get enough of her, Jack caught Maureen up with one arm under her knees and the other across her back. She chased his tongue with her questing one as he strode swiftly across the room, surely up the steps. And then, just as he had lifted her out of the ring the first day they met, he lifted her into it.

The ropes parted to admit him, her lips to accommodate him. Her nightshirt flew over her head and into the far corner. His jogging shorts, which he'd slipped on after his shower and before coming to see who was causing all that racket, landed in the opposite one.

No son of Ares had ever stood as splendidly naked as he, no daughter of Athena so flawlessly sculptured as she. They were a perfect match, born of the gods, and this was the moment for which they'd been waiting for weeks. So it was only fitting, only right, that they meet in the center ring.

For *this* was the main event, and each heeded the call to arms with a glad cry. She gasped as he rained hot, searing kisses on her mouth and throat, trailed fire across her cheek and up to her temple. He groaned when her fingers grasped the resilient length of him, seeking to return the tremulous pleasure he gave her.

When they fell to the canvas, they fell together, with mouths clinging, hands moving and hearts drumming a demand for more. There was no gentleness in him, and she wanted none, as he nipped at her bottom lip, her shoulder. She meted out a loving punishment of her own, sinking her teeth into a meaty bicep, and then begging his pardon with her laving tongue.

Her breasts, the hollow between her ribs, her belly . . . She buried her fingers in the springy moss of his curls when his head moved down between her thighs and his hot mouth branded her forever his. Then he climbed her body and claimed it, kissing her with her own sweet taste on his lips, and she wrapped her long, lithe legs around his back to draw him even farther into herself.

A duel to that little death that all lovers seek, it was. To the heart-stopping heights, where they ceased to breathe. And then over the top, where they were reborn in each other's arms.

"Comfortable?"

Maureen's sigh of contentment said it all.

Jack tilted his head to smile down at her, and the mattress springs of the platform bed he'd been sleeping alone in these past two weeks squeaked a mild protest. It had taken them a little while to recover from their first round of passion. Longer yet from their second.

Finally he'd carried her and their clothes to the guest cottage from the "Barn Again," not wanting to risk their getting caught in yet another compromising position in the center ring. And they had tried another one. One that had fulfilled her fantasy of being on top and his of seeing her there, enjoying the trip to paradise and taking him along for the ride.

Now they lay facing each other, his hand resting in the curve of her waist, her fingers playing in his chest hair, and their legs forming a King's X. It was still dark out, later than midnight but no telling how much later. The moon peeping through the window, however, provided all the light they needed.

She wished they could stay here forever, hidden away from the awful reality of the world and wrapped in the warm afterglow of their love, but she knew that was tilting at windmills.

"Why the frown?" he asked gently.

Maureen tensed up and started to move away, but Jack locked his arms across the small of her back. Unbeknownst to him, he'd given her an opening for a discussion about the gym. An opening she prefaced with what was in her heart.

"I love you," she sighed.

"Loving me is something to frown about?" he teased fondly.

She made a successful effort to relax her facial muscles. "I certainly hope not."

He could see by the look in her eyes that she was leading him somewhere else. "C'mon, out with it."

"I'm giving you the gym."

"What?" Surprised, he sucked in a short little breath and let her go.

"I'm giving you the gym," she repeated softly. "Which means . . ."

This was the hard part. The part where, if he was going to refuse her gift, she would have to spell out her fears for him. And the word they spelled was *coward*.

Jack propped himself up on his elbow, looked down on her face and prompted, "Which means what?"

Maureen drew in a deep breath and expelled it and her news on a soft rush. "You won't have to fight for it."

That was not what he wanted to hear, if his unsmiling eyes were any gauge of his mood. He lay down on his back, hands balled into fists at his sides, staring at the ceiling for a long, ponderous moment. When he finally spoke, his voice was as ragged as torn paper.

"I have to fight."

"No, you don't." She came up now, gathering her wits like wildflowers she could strew in his path. "Not if I give you the gym. And I *am* giving it to you. Free and clear. No stri—"

He cut her off with a quiet, "But I'm not just fighting for the gym, Maureen."

"Then what are you fighting for, Jack?" She drew up her knees and hugged them tightly, as if that would help her hold her tears at bay. "For blood?"

"Don't be ridiculous."

But remembering that fight film, she couldn't be anything else. She dropped her head and pressed her closed eyes to her kneecaps, trying to blot out those gruesome pictures. "For glory? For money? What?"

"For myself."

That brought her head up and around. It took a few seconds, though, for the black and yellow spots to fade and her eyes to focus in on his face. On the white slash of a scar above his left brow and the slight but discernible bend of his nose.

"Yourself?"

He called on Frankie's apt description. "To prove I'm still alive."

She shook her head in confusion. "But—"

"And for the boys. To show them that anything's possible if you're willing to work for it."

Her heart beat frenziedly in her breast. "What about us?"

He reached up and twined a lock of her hair around his finger, loving the way its subtle fire seemed to lick at his flesh. "If I don't fight, there is no us."

Maureen paled as though he had struck her, and tears—like tiny prisms in the moonlight—penciled her cheeks. Jack pulled her into his arms and drew her head down to the warm hollow of his shoulder. They lay there in silence and in sadness until, finally, he broke open the sealed door of his dark past.

"You know I killed a man in the ring."

She nodded mutely, so afraid of losing him in the same manner that she couldn't speak.

"What you don't know is how the guilt almost destroyed me."

"I know it caused you to hang up your gloves," she whispered, citing the newspaper accounts she'd read and the telecasts she'd watched.

"That's not the half of it," he scoffed softly against her hair. "He was a fighter on his way down the ladder and desperate for money. I was a fighter on his way up and equally desperate." He paused for a moment, recalling the events leading up to the fatal bout as if they'd happened yesterday. "Sully didn't want me to fight him. He said the guy had been knocked out twice in less than a month's time and that we were asking for trouble if we took him on. But"—he blew out a hard breath—"like I said, I was young and desperate and it looked like easy money, so Sully finally said yes."

Maureen listened quietly, not daring to interrupt, sensing that Jack was telling her things he'd never told anyone else in his life.

"The first round went fine," he continued. "We were both throwing punches, of course, but mostly we were just feeling each other out. I'd hit him a couple of times, but I hadn't really connected yet. Still, when the bell rang, he kind of—I don't know—staggered back to his corner.

"Sully saw that he was acting strange and asked the ref to check him out. After that, it was a vicious cycle. His handlers got mad at Sully and said he was afraid *his* fighter —me—had bitten off more than he could chew. So then Sully turned around and gave me hell until the bell that started the second round."

Jack tightened his hold on Maureen, wanting her as close to him as possible as he got to the part of the story that damn near did him in.

"He came out swinging at the bell, and he landed a couple of body blows that literally took my breath away. Well, that made me angry. And when I got angry with an opponent back then . . . I'd see my father's face, and I'd have to take him out before he took me out." The pain in his voice was almost more than she could bear. "Hurt or be hurt. Kill or be killed. So I threw a straight right to his chin, and his mouthpiece flew into the crowd."

He rubbed the hand he'd just spoken of down her back, then held it up where they could both see it. "The guy wasn't seeing or hearing a thing at that point. He was just standing there, like a puppet waiting for someone to pull his strings. But I was still angry. Still seeing my father's face." He balled his hand into a fist. "So I hit him again— harder—and he crumpled to the canvas."

Maureen bit her lip to keep herself from begging Jack to stop, oh, stop, knowing he needed to purge himself of the grief and the guilt.

"He started bleeding then. From his nose and his mouth. His eyes and his ears. So the ref shoved me into my corner and called for the ring doctor. Then he called the fight—I won on a TKO, a technical knockout—and they took him to the hospital."

His raised fist shook with remembered shame. "By the time I changed clothes and got to the hospital, he was dead. A brain hemorrhage, brought on by three knockouts in a little over one month. I was okay with it, or so I thought, until I met his wife—his widow by that time—and saw his baby boy in the emergency room corridor. Then I almost lost it.

"I'd killed a woman's husband and a boy's father. And for what? Money to buy a car, that's what. Revenge on my old man, that's what." His long, serrated sigh was like a knife in her heart. "After that, it wasn't my father's face I saw . . . it was *his* face. His skull, actually. It was in the mirror every morning. Reminding me I'd killed him."

Maureen swallowed back her tears and her fears long enough to say, "He shouldn't have been in the ring."

"I shouldn't have been there either," Jack said curtly. "I should've listened to Sully."

She almost didn't ask, but then she decided she had a right to know. "Do you still see his face?"

He dropped his hand to her hair and gently brushed it back from her forehead. Then he looked deeply into her eyes and said so sincerely she had no choice but to believe him, "All I see anymore is you."

Their tears mingled as their mouths met in a tender kiss. A healing kiss. Then she speeded up the healing process when she took hold of his right hand—the one he would have given to bring the other man back—and placed it, open, over her left breast.

Her heart beat against his palm. A poem of love and life. His hand massaged her breast. A ballad of battles won and battles lost. Two bodies merged and moved as one. A ballet as old as time.

"I love you, Maureen."

"Oh, Jack, I love you too!"

But she was still afraid of losing him. So when the loving was over and they lay spent, she kept her arms about him, thinking as she drifted off to sleep that if she held him tightly enough, he couldn't leave her.

ROUND 12

Maureen lost Jack at the crack of dawn on the day of the fight.

She didn't realize it until she rolled to her side and reached for him. Reluctantly she opened her eyes. Bright sunlight flooded the room as she saw to her sorrow that his side of the bed was empty.

He'd left her a note on his pillow. Small comfort, she thought as she picked it up and then sat up to read it. But better than nothing, perhaps.

Written on the back of an envelope in a bold hand that bespoke his strength of character, he said he loved her, first and last. He said he'd gone to the weigh-in at the arena and that he would be sleeping—storing up energy—the rest of the day. Said, too, that she could pick up her ringside ticket at the box office and that he would see her tonight, after the fight.

No! She crumpled the note in one hand and clamped the other over her mouth. He wouldn't see her after the fight because she wasn't going to it. She refused to sit in some ringside seat surrounded by thousands of blood-thirsty fans and watch him get beaten to a pulp by "Poison" Ivy Stephens's mean right hook.

Maureen looked around the one-room cottage, wanting to get out of here, and saw that Jack had left her something else—his white satin training robe, draped over the back of the small prayer bench that sat at an angle in the corner.

She didn't know what time it was because there was no clock. No bathroom, either, which was what moved her from the bed to the bench. She paused only long enough to pick her nightshirt off the floor, where he'd dropped it in the heat of passion, and pull it over her head.

Then she put on his white satin robe.

It was way too big for her. The shoulder seams drooped halfway to her elbows, the sleeves sagged past her finger-tips, and the hem hung down to her lower calves. She could have wound the sash around her waist twice and still had enough left to tie a big, fat bow.

Oh, but it smelled of him.

She slid her hands under the wide lapels and lifted them to her nose, drinking in the lingering aromas of spice and sweat and the man of her dreams. The man she'd lost at dawn's early light. She dropped her hands, letting the la-pels fall back over her breasts, and crossed to the door.

No crying, she swore, blinking rapidly to keep the tears at bay as she reached for the brass knob. No wailing, she vowed, sealing her trembling lips as she opened the door and stepped out onto the gingerbread porch. No gnashing of teeth, she promised, gritting hers as she followed the beaten-grass path back to the fieldstone farmhouse.

A bird called for its mate, humiliating to hear when her heart was breaking. The morning sun shone in blinding mockery of the midnight madness in her soul. A summer breeze kissed the crest of her cheek, a slap in her winter-set face.

Maureen came to an abrupt halt when she got to the back of the house and saw that her new black Mustang was the only car still parked there. She hadn't expected to see Jack's flame red Catalina, of course. But Rocstar's shiny white Cadillac and Beetlejuice and Ray Howard's bright yellow U-Haul trucks were gone too. Which meant that it was either very late or she was very much alone.

Then she remembered Tammy, whom she'd left sleeping in the master bedroom last night, and, picking up the hem of that white satin robe, dashed up the steps and into the house. Relief whispered through her when she saw that the teenager was still asleep, her blond head resting peacefully upon her pillow and her unblemished eyes shut tight. She saw, too, when she glanced at the bedside clock, that it was early yet—only half past seven.

First things first, Maureen decided, and hit for the adjoining bathroom. By eight she was showered and shampooed, blow-dried and dressed in sandals, shorts and one-pocket pullover shirt. Tammy, however, was still in dreamland.

Leaving the teenager to sleep—after all, it was Saturday and there was no special reason to wake up—she went to the kitchen to brew herself a cup of tea.

And found Duck's note sitting on the table.

Feeling a little bit like Dorothy at this point—only this was Missouri, not Kansas, and her dogs were named Bonnie and Clyde—Maureen picked it up and started deciphering Duck's hasty scrawl.

"Tell Tammy that Jack bought tickets for the boys in the detention faculty"—his misspelling of facility—"so Frankie will be at the fight tonight. And when you go to the gym today"—dammit, how had *he* known that she planned to clear her things out of the office?—"be sure and look on the desk."

Okay, so maybe they'd moved State Line a few miles east this morning and had forgotten to tell her about it.

Maureen dropped Duck's note on the table and followed the hardwood road back to the bedroom to wake Tammy.

"Frankie's going to be at the fight tonight" were the first words out of the teenager's mouth.

Dumbfounded, Maureen just gaped at her for a moment before asking, "How did you know?"

"I got up to go to the bathroom in the middle of the night," Tammy said around a wide yawn, "and—"

"Wound up in the kitchen looking for something to eat," Maureen interrupted, thinking of her skyrocketing grocery bill as much as the teenager's habit of raiding the refrigerator.

Tammy didn't ask where *she'd* been at the midnight hour, but her china blue eyes brimmed with questions. Questions that Maureen balked at answering at first. After all, she hadn't answered to anyone for her actions in years.

But then, knowing that she hadn't set a very good example for the girl, she sat down on the edge of the bed and said in a soft voice, "I love him."

"Are you going to marry him?"

Maureen shook her head with the same bittersweet realization her mother must have experienced thirty years ago. "He's a fightin' man, not a family man."

"He's got a family," Tammy shot back. Then she went on to elucidate. "He's got Duck and the boys and Rocstar and me and—"

"I'm speaking of a traditional family."

"*Is* there such a thing anymore?" Tammy asked with wisdom beyond her years.

Tears trembled on Maureen's lashes as she pounded her knee with her fist. "Yes, dammit, there is!"

"I sure don't know any."

"Mine . . . my parents and me."

"Oh, right," Tammy scoffed. "If traditional means rich—"

"Traditional meaning a mother and a father and . . ." Maureen's voice broke, but she got it out. "And children."

Tammy watched her struggling to keep her composure, then sat up in bed as if spring-loaded, her eyes going as round as silver dollars. "Oh, Jeez, *you're* not pregnant, are you?"

"No." Maureen had never preached to the teenager, but she grabbed the opportunity to make a point. "Jack and I both used precautions."

"Condoms?"

"And pills."

Tammy fixed her with a stare. "Well, I told Frankie we're not doing it again—condoms or no condoms—until I'm eighteen."

"What did he say to that?" Maureen wasn't sure she wanted to hear what he said, but she was obviously in the mood to talk.

"He said he respected my decision." Tammy looked utterly amazed as she repeated Frankie's words. "He said it was my body, and even though he might get zits or go blind before I turned eighteen—"

"Old wives' tales," Maureen interrupted with a laugh.

"Jeez, I hope so." Tammy shuddered. "He's got the best skin for a guy. Smooth . . . no pores. None!"

"He's got them, you just can't see them."

"I guess." The teenager flopped back down on the bed and threw her arms up over her head. "You know what I think?"

"What?"

"I think Jack's been talking to Frankie."

"About having sex?"

"And not having it."

Maureen nodded, remembering her own frustrations of the past month. Remembering, too, what a physical man Jack was and knowing it must almost have killed him not to be able to get his hands on her. She smiled. "I imagine so."

Tammy ducked her head, looking down her reclining body at her uptilted toes, and muttered shyly, "I guess I really put a cramp in you guys' style, huh?"

"No, you didn't."

"You sure?"

Maureen reached over and squeezed the teenager's hand, wanting her to know she didn't regret a single moment of the time they'd spent together. "I'm positive."

Tammy smiled and stretched, then sat up, obviously re-energized. "So what're we gonna do today?"

"I have to go down to the gym."

"And then?"

"I don't know." Maureen shrugged, at a loss as to what she would do after that. The shop was closed on Saturdays, but she was more behind than usual, what with all the folderol about the . . . "Work on some design plans, I suppose."

"What're you going to wear to the fight?"

"I'm not going to the fight."

Tammy blinked in disbelief. "But you've *gotta* go!"

Maureen set her jaw. "I won't go and watch Jack get—"

"It's his last fight. Forever! And everybody'll be there. Even Donna and—"

"Donna?!"

"And her husband and kids."

Maureen realized she should have known, after the way her now full-fledged design assistant had raved on the first week she'd met—

"If you love Jack, you'll go," Tammy stated categorically.

"If he loved me, he wouldn't—" Maureen broke off, refusing to wallow in self-pity. Or to play emotional blackmail with a teenager whose family history had probably turned her into an expert at the game. Abruptly she stood and said, "I'd better get moving if I'm going to work today, so why don't you get dressed and—"

"Drop me off at Donna's house on your way to the gym," Tammy said dully as she swung her legs over the side of the bed.

"Why?"

"So I can go to the fight with *her* family."

Maureen didn't have any trouble finding a parking place today in Rocstar's recently graveled lot. She pulled into her usual space near the door and cut the Mustang's V-8 engine with as decisive a flick of her wrist as she had cut the Mercedes's engine that first day she'd come to the gym. But that, she realized when she got out of her car and started down the sidewalk, was where the resemblance between her initial visit and this visit ended.

For the first time in weeks, she stopped and looked—*really* looked—at all the positive changes taking place in the neighborhood surrounding the gym, and saw reason for hope.

A pretty pink geranium in a plain clay pot sat on the second-floor balcony of the redbrick rooming house across the street. The white-haired woman responsible for placing it there came out with a watering can. Spotting her younger, redheaded sister standing below, she smiled and waved.

Maureen returned both before looking up the street.

No inebriated men—or inebriated women, for that matter—stumbled out the door of the corner bar these days, because the corner bar had closed down last month. A small, independent grocery store—a welcome addition in a neighborhood that had none—would be reopening the doors when the remodeling was done.

She turned to go into the gym, and stopped again when she saw two little girls turning a jump rope for a third one on the sidewalk that, just seven weeks ago, had seemed stripped of human habitation. Pigtails flapping, the one in the middle merely proved that little girls are the same no matter where they grow up as she repeated the "Fudge,

fudge, call the judge" rhyme that Maureen and her friends had singsonged in their greening years.

"Ma-ma's gonna have a ba-by." She just had to say it as she unlocked the door and went into the gym.

Those tigers' eyes followed her down the hall one last time. The warm, moist air in the gym enveloped her for a final hug. The balcony level's pungently masculine aromas would soon be mingling with feminine ones, but she'd never know how well the chemistry worked.

Because if she didn't go to the fight, she couldn't come back to the gym. That was a given in her mind. Proof positive that she lacked the courage to go the distance.

Maureen sighed resignedly as she opened the door to the office—once Sully's, then hers, soon to be Jack's—and stood there for a moment, trying to decide what to do first. Clear her toiletry items out of the bathroom medicine cabinet or her spare workout clothes and shoes out of the closet? Glancing at the desk and spotting a large, closed album sitting atop its scarred surface, she suddenly remembered Duck's message and crossed the room.

Sully's scrapbook.

Sundries and such flew out of her mind as she sank to the swivel chair and stared at the album for a few breathless seconds.

It wasn't made of leather, only a cheap imitation, but it was more precious to her than gold. Because it was the missing link. It contained the lost years and the long-overdue answers.

Maureen opened the album gingerly, as if afraid the cover might crumble in her hands. If she'd expected a letter from Sully with an explanation as to why he'd given her up for adoption, she was deeply disappointed. But since she hadn't known what to expect, she was merely grateful to have something to remember him by.

Her mother had a few pictures of her as a baby, but not

nearly as many as parents normally take of their first child. She'd always wondered why. Well, now she knew.

For here, in black-and-white, were a beaming mother and father and a drooling baby girl in a frilly dress and matching bib. The small family sat, the father's arm around the mother's shoulders, their daughter half on his lap, half on hers, on a park bench that baby grown recognized well. And the smiles on the parents' faces and the sparkle in their eyes told their progeny some thirty-five years later that she had been conceived in love.

A burning question, answered.

Daddy's little girl, her arms up over her head and her fingers tightly wrapped around his as she took her first steps for a laughing, applauding Mommy.

A missing link, found.

Ugh, her first birthday cake! Frosting smeared everywhere. Her mother wiping off one sticky hand, her father the other. And their smiles were still there.

A lost year, accounted for.

Color film came into the picture at that point, but the smiles began to fade. And then both they and the mother disappeared entirely.

Still the photos and newspaper clippings of a growing girl kept coming: playing tea party with her daddy and her dolls in this very office; prepubescent but stylish for dancing class in a green linen "musical dress" with rickrack, a musical scale and notes running across the front of her flat chest; a proudly beaming proprietor of her own interior design shop and—like father, like daughter—her home.

Interspersed with pictures of Maureen from baby daughter to belle of Miss Porter's Ballroom Dance School to designing woman were fight programs and clippings from sports columns. Maybe these were the letters Sully hadn't written to her. His way of telling her what he was doing while the world turned and the years went slowly by.

She closed the album, not knowing if she'd been looking

at it for minutes or hours. Not that it mattered. She had nowhere to go, nothing to do, no one at home.

Where had Duck found it? she wondered, running a loving.hand over the imitation leather cover. Had it ever really been missing? Or had he hidden it from her until he thought she was ready to see it?

Maureen sat back in Sully's old swivel chair, feeling almost whole. *Almost?* She sat up, startled by the thought. What else could she possibly want to know? What else did she need to know to make her feel complete? And who could she—

She jumped to her feet, heart beating fast, and grabbed both her purse and the scrapbook off the desk. Clothes and toilet articles and the work waiting at her shop were the last things on her mind as she tore out the office and down the stairs. Her sandaled feet slapped against the hardwood floor of the empty gym and the hot concrete of the sidewalk as she raced to her car.

Please, God, let him be home! Maureen prayed as she started the Mustang. Let him be there for me one more time! she pleaded as she spun the wheel and stepped on the gas, spraying gravel in her wake. Please, please, please . . . She drove fast but safely, going uptown to see the man she'd called Dad these last thirty years.

Paul was not only there for Maureen one more time, but he told her what she needed to know and took her where she needed to go to fill in the blanks at long last.

Calvary Cemetery was the final resting place for a great majority of the Catholic families in Kansas City. A low stone wall separated it from busy Troost Street, reducing the noise level considerably, while the wrought-iron gates stood open during daylight hours for those who wished to commune with the loved ones they'd lost. The gentle hills and grassy dales were impeccably manicured, the tall marble tombstones and flat bronze markers flawlessly maintained.

Maureen wondered, as Paul followed the winding drive, why and how he knew the way, but before she could ask he was braking the Towncar and pulling over near a plot she knew well.

She looked at him in surprise across the wide leather seat. "This is where your parents are buried."

Those long Modigliani lines of his face lifted in that familiar smile. "Sully too."

She realized then why and how he knew the way, and her heart was filled to overflowing with love for her father.

"Shall we get out and walk over there?" he suggested matter-of-factly.

Maureen opened the passenger door, while Paul climbed out of the driver's side. Arm in arm then, father and daughter climbed the little incline to the side-by-side graves where the grandparents she barely remembered were buried. They stood there a moment in silent respect.

Ed and Ruth Bryant, both born before the turn of the century and joined in Holy Matrimony shortly after the First World War, had matching bronze markers with permanent vases for the fresh flowers that the son who physically resembled neither one of them placed there every Memorial Day.

Maureen took a deep, bracing breath when they turned away and Paul pointed to the gentle mound that was still more dirt than grass, telling her that the person buried in the ground beneath it had died much too recently to have a headstone yet.

So this was where Sully lay.

Paul stood behind her while Maureen dropped to her bare knees beside his grave. She'd found him. Finally. Her throat tightened as she whispered a prayer for the repose of his soul. Then she said farewell for a while, thinking she would bring flowers later, and got to her feet.

"Are you all right?"

Maureen turned tear-filled eyes to her father's concerned ones and finally said it aloud. "You paid for Sully's funeral, didn't you?"

"He gave me a daughter," Paul replied quietly. "The least I could do was give him a decent burial."

"Oh, Daddy." She slid her arms around his waist and buried her face against his chest, crying for the man who'd relinquished her and the man who'd raised her.

Father and daughter stood in a loving embrace, his shirt blotting her tears and his body absorbing her shudders, until she was all cried out. She raised her head then, feeling a strange lightness as the last piece of herself fell into place, and released him. He experienced a flash of regret as she stepped back, but he let her go with a smile.

She was free now to move on with her life, Paul thought with paternal pride. Free to pursue her love for a man he happened to like very much. And that, he decided with no little sense of satisfaction, is what fathers—

"I'm afraid, Dad." Maureen said it softly, but the admission brought his silent musings to a screeching halt.

"Afraid of what, darlin'?"

"Of going to Jack's fight."

Paul stopped himself from saying, "But you *have* to go," and asked instead, "Why?"

"I'm afraid he'll get hurt."

"He'll recover."

"I'm . . ." Her voice dropped so low now, he had to strain to hear her. "Afraid he'll be killed."

Paul reached over and clasped her shoulders, giving them a gentle squeeze. "He has too much to live for."

Maureen smiled crookedly, but her eyes took on a dreamy glow. "I really did it this time, didn't I, Dad?"

"Did what, darlin'?"

"Fell in love with a fightin' man."

•   •   •

"I'm warning you, Laura. . . ."

Paul stood in the hall, on the wrong side of their locked bedroom door, gauging his chances of carrying out the threat he was about to make. He didn't have a violent bone in his long, lanky body, but looking at the solid mahogany barrier that separated him from his wife, he realized he might very well have a few broken ones before the day and after the deed was done. Still, as their daughter had recently taught him—no pain, no gain.

"If you don't unlock this door, I'm going to break it down."

The soft click of the lock being turned told Paul that Laura believed he was capable of doing exactly that. He entered the expansive master bedroom suite they'd shared for thirty years and looked around him as if he'd never seen it before. As if he might never see it again.

Plush cream carpet and blue and white silk window treatments offset the hand-painted wallpaper. A silk-shaded lamp cast a soft glow upon a chintz-covered Victorian chaise lounge. Mother-of-pearl inlaid the dressing table at which the woman he loved now sat, her stiffly-held back to the door.

"Why?" Laura wasn't just asking Paul why he'd taken Maureen to the cemetery, but that was the question he chose to answer at the moment.

"She had a right to know where Sully was buried."

"And I had a right to know that you paid for his funeral." She had only found out this afternoon, when Maureen and he had come back from the cemetery, and she had been locked in this room ever since.

He couldn't disagree with her because what she said was true. But he could try to explain why he'd done it. And he would, even knowing that what he was going to tell her might reduce him to nothing—less than nothing—in her eyes.

First, though, he wanted her to look at him. See him for himself. Not as the solid family man she'd been seeking in her second husband or the former bank president who'd provided so well for her all these years. He wanted her to see his face, wanted to see the reaction on hers, when he revealed his own long-held secret.

Paul crossed to the dressing table, not stopping until he stood directly behind his wife. His voice, when he finally spoke, was quiet but filled with determination. "Turn around, Laura."

Her icy eyes met his iron-willed ones in the tilted oval mirror. She stared at him, tight-lipped, for a moment before she exhaled an impatient breath and swiveled on the small tufted bench.

"Do you love me, Laura?"

"What kind of question—"

"I don't want an argument, I want an answer."

She bristled at this new note of command in his voice. "You're my husband, for heaven's sake!"

"That's a description, not an answer." He looked at her sadly. "What I want to know is, do you love *me*. Paul Bryant. The man."

"Of course I love you!" she snapped. "But I still don't see what that has to do with your paying for Sully's funeral without consulting me first."

"I'm going to tell you what one has to do with the other." Paul moved to the chaise and sat down on the edge of its curved seat, bringing him to eye level and within reaching distance of Laura. "But first, you have to promise that you won't interrupt me until I'm finished."

It began to dawn on her that he was about to say something she might not want to hear. But what? That he was ill? That he wanted a divorce? Either prospect struck terror in Laura's heart. Melted the ice in her eyes and made her

realize how much she really did love Paul Bryant, the man
. . . for better or for worse.

"I promise." She reached for his hand, bridging the painful gap that had existed between them these past seven
weeks.

Then she listened, without interruption or comment,
while he told her about the unmarried girl who'd helped
Ruth Bryant around the house and the hired hand who'd
worked with Ed Bryant in the fields. And about the girl
getting pregnant and the hired hand disappearing in the
middle of the night after hearing the news.

Paul's bereft smile when he admitted that he'd never
learned the hired hand's last name nearly broke Laura's
heart, but she only tightened her hold and waited wordlessly for him to continue.

Ed and Ruth Bryant, having given up hope of ever con-
ceiving a child, had offered to adopt the girl's baby and
raise it as their own. She had agreed and, shortly after
giving birth to an eight-pound boy, had legally surrendered
him to the farm couple and caught a westbound train.

Laura began to understand then why Paul had paid for
Sully's funeral. It was his way of laying the past to rest. Of
doing for Maureen's natural father what he'd never been
able to do for his own.

"I always knew I didn't look like either one of my parents," he said in conclusion. "But I didn't know I was
adopted—in those days, children were ashamed of being
adopted because it meant their real parents had 'sinned'
and they were the result of that sin—until one of my cous-
ins spilled the beans when I was eight."

She broke her silence to say consolingly, "That must
have been a terrible shock to you."

"I cried and called him a liar, then I ran home to my
mother as fast as I could." He coughed unnecessarily and
cleared his throat. "After she told me the truth, I was so
humiliated, I hid in my room the rest of the day."

"That's why you kept the farm, isn't it?" she said astutely.

"Foolishly, perhaps, I used to think my birth mother might come back for me."

"Is that why you wanted to retire there too?"

He shook his head no. "If she were still alive, which I doubt, she'd be in her eighties. I just have a sentimental attachment to the place, I suppose, and I hated to think about selling it to some developer who'd divide it up—"

"You could donate it to a children's charity with the understanding they'd use it as a summer camp," she suggested. "And, heaven knows, we could use the tax deduction."

He remembered an excited crew of inner-city boys pitching in to create "Barn Again," and knew exactly who he wanted to donate it to. "You may be on to something there."

"Paul . . ." Laura had never found it easy to apologize, but this apology was thirty years overdue. "I'm sorry I made you feel like you couldn't tell me before today."

"I was afraid you'd be ashamed of being married to me."

She *was* ashamed—of herself, not him. "Can you ever forgive me for behaving like such a snob?"

Reaching over, he framed her face between his hands and looked into her teal blue eyes. He didn't see the tiny lines that time had etched around them, and he prayed she didn't notice the small bags beneath his. Neither one of them was as young as they used to be, and not all of their plans had worked out as they'd hoped. But now, remembering the grace and the beauty and the color she'd brought into his life, the daughter she'd given him, he realized she was the best thing that had ever happened to that lonely little farm boy.

"I love you, Laura," he said at last and, leaning over, touched his lips to her forehead.

"I love you too, Paul." And this time she didn't have to

be pressured into saying the words, for they came from her heart.

Now came the hard part.

Paul took a deep breath, and then he took the plunge. "I promised Maureen—"

"No!" Sensing what he was about to say, Laura stiffened up on him again and tried to turn her head away.

But he was having none of that. She'd wanted a family man and, by George, she'd gotten one. Now he wanted his two favorite women to stop this foolish squabbling over that fightin' man.

Paul put a new twist on Laura's thirty-year-old argument, but it rang as true today as it had then. "If you love Maureen—really love her—you'll go to Jack Ryan's fight."

EPILOGUE

"Ladeeez . . . and gentlemen. The main event. A twelve-round nontitle rematch."

Maureen took a deep breath and lifted her chin when the ring announcer pulled down the microphone and began his spiel. She was a nervous wreck, but none of the turmoil she felt was apparent. For Jack's sake, she was putting her best face forward.

"In this corner, wearing blue trunks with red and white stripes down the sides . . . weighing two hundred ten pounds, with a record of thirty-four wins and one loss . . . from Dallas, Texas . . . the number two ranked heavyweight contender of the world, 'Poison' Ivy Stephens."

There was some polite applause, but mostly there were boos when the tall man with the shaved head came out of his corner and waved to the partisan crowd that filled Municipal Auditorium's huge Main Arena to capacity.

"And in this corner, in green trunks with a white stripe and shamrocks down the sides"—now the crowd began to cheer loudly and steadily—"weighing two hundred five pounds, with a record of seventeen KO's and one TKO . . . from Kansas City, Missouri . . . the former Golden Gloves Champion, Jack 'The Irish Terror' Ryan."

Maureen stood with the rest of the crowd when the hometown favorite, looking breathtakingly handsome with that white satin robe draped over his broad shoulders, stepped out of his corner to salute them.

His eyes scanned the ringside seats until he spotted her. If he noticed her parents standing on either side of her, he gave no indication. He simply smiled and nodded at her as if to say, "This one's for you," before turning and sauntering toward the center of the ring to receive final instructions from the referee and to shake hands with his old nemesis.

For the ten short seconds it had taken Jack to acknowledge her presence, Maureen was the star of the show. Necks craned from as far away as the cheap seats with people trying to figure out just who the slender redhead in that purple silk slip of a dress was. Why, with those amethyst earrings dangling to her sculpted shoulders, she looked more like a social butterfly who'd gotten lost en route to the Jewel Ball than a woman who'd come a great distance these last seven weeks.

Then the bell rang, signaling the beginning of the first round, and the fight fans returned their attention to the center ring as Jack and "Poison" Ivy came out swinging.

"Your father tells me he's a lawyer," Laura said, trying to make the best of things as she resumed her seat.

Maureen smiled lovingly at the woman who'd come such a long way herself. "Yes, Mom, he's a lawyer."

"Give him an uppercut!" Paul shouted at Jack then. It was hard to say just who the retired banker and refined gardener surprised the most—himself or his wife and daughter—when he got to his feet and shook his fist in the air.

The fight was every bit as brutal as Maureen had feared it would be. Her senses swam as the former champion and current contender slugged it out, round after round. She saw the fierce determination on both their increasingly battered faces. Heard every grunt and groan. Smelled the sweat and the blood, and breathed in the awesome possibility that Jack might really win.

She cupped her hand over her mouth in horror, stifling a scream, when "Poison" Ivy's mean right hook reopened the old cut over Jack's left eye.

Duck had the remedy, though. At the end of the round, he rolled up the sleeves of his shamrock green sweatshirt and went to work, wiping Jack's face with a towel and inspecting the damage. Then he pulled an instant cold pack and a small iron out of his bag of tricks and pressed it to the cut to stop the bleeding.

The petite Donna, dressed to the nines as usual, proved just how big a fight fan she was when she leaped to her feet at one point and screamed at Jack, "Stick him a good one!"

Her husband and four children had obviously never seen this side of their wife and mother before, because they gaped at her in amazement. Then the five of them stood in tandem and joined her in cheering him on.

By the beginning of the twelfth round, everyone in the Main Arena was on their feet. Though they'd both staggered a few times, neither Jack nor "Poison" Ivy had gone down even once for the count. And the crowd, sensing this was more a test of character than a grudge match, was openly rooting for Jack.

Maureen's heart was in her throat the entire final three minutes of Jack's last hurrah. She closed her eyes, afraid to watch. Then she opened them, afraid not to, and saw the kind of finish of which legends are made.

The bell finally ended the slugfest a few minutes before midnight, with both Jack and "Poison" Ivy still on their feet, so it was up to the judges to declare a winner. The fighters, hurt and exhausted, hugged each other before retreating to their corners to await the outcome. The crowd fell almost ominously silent while the judges tallied their scorecards.

Maureen couldn't stand the suspense. She looked

around her at all the people she'd come to know and love these past seven weeks—at Duck, cornerman extraordinaire; at Frankie, who was doing his time like a man; at Tammy, who was learning the meaning of self-respect; at Rocstar, who no longer had a gang but did have a job and a pretty new girlfriend; at the boys, who had the hope of the future written all over their multihued faces. And it dawned on her at the same moment the ring announcer declared "Poison" Ivy Stephens the winner by unanimous decision that Sully hadn't given her up after all. He'd given her an extended family.

Only one gloved hand was raised, but there were two winners in that ring.

Three, if one counted the beautiful redhead in that purple slip of a dress who leaped to her feet and rushed to the apron to raise her arms to the man who'd gone the distance.

Jack got rid of his gloves, then bent over the ropes and lifted Maureen into the air so that her head was higher than his. She hung there for a fraction of a moment, one shoe off and one shoe on, her radiant face tilted into the hot, overhead lights. And then, amid the ecstasies of joy and disillusion that raged around them, she kissed her fightin' man—soon to be her family man—with all the passion she'd saved just for him.

The neighborhood had their hero.

And the Lady had her Champ.

Many of today's most popular and successful writers of women's fiction began their careers writing short, contemporary romances. Like Nora Roberts, Sandra Brown, and Iris Johansen, the author of this book made her name and honed her craft on what people in the book trade call "category" romance. The category romance—as published by Bantam's LOVESWEPT—is a wonderful and engaging form of short fiction that concentrates on the love story between two average, contemporary people. Unlike the old-fashioned, formulaic rich-man-poor-woman romances that dominated the market years ago, today's category romances are very contemporary, timely stories, often dealing with the very issues that are important to you. The style is breezy, the love is real, and the passion is modern and intimate. Some LOVESWEPTs are more witty, some more passionate, some are laced with humor, some packed with emotion, but they are all well-written stories of true love by very talented authors. These stories will quickly entrance and then entertain you for a few hours.

The author of this book has written a brief account of her experience with LOVESWEPT, and she invites you to take a dip into the world of category romance. If you have never read a LOVESWEPT novel, the author and her publisher invite you to ask for one at your bookstore, and discover an entertaining reading experience.

True story: In February, 1979, on the Mexican Government Ferry (actually more of a chicken boat in those days) from Isla Mujeres to Puerto Juárez, I lost a book. Not just any book, mind you, but the first book I ever wrote. It was a category romance called *Prophecy of Love*, which I had *hand*written (meaning no copies) between carpools and court reporting assignments and because travel articles, short stories, and humorous essays weren't really satisfying my need to weave a longer, richer story.

Needless to say, I was devastated. All that hard work—gone! Both those wonderful main characters and those delightful secondary characters—vanished! And, vanity of vanities, the poor publishing world—deprived of the opportunity to discover this great new literary talent!

But writers are as stubborn a lot as they are strange. (Who else but a crazy woman would spend hundreds of hours alone, talking to—and answering!—herself, plotting romance, revenge, and revolutions?) Having already proved to myself that I could write a beginning, middle, and end, I *rewrote Prophecy of Love* (on the typewriter this time, with two copies . . . just in case I got the urge to climb on another chicken boat).

Through a friend in my critique group, I contacted an agent, Andrea Cirillo—a real, live *New York* agent, talking to word-swallowing, Midwestern me!—who said yes, she'd like to see what I'd written. Mercury never flew any faster than I did to the post office. And when the agent said she'd like to represent me . . . suffice it to say, I was pumped up long before Michael Jordan got his Air Nikes.

Well, *Prophecy of Love* never sold. It's still sitting in my file cabinet, in fact, and will probably stay there forever. But the second category romance (written between carpools, a political campaign, and court reporting assignments) was snapped up almost immediately. As was the third one.

Look out world, I thought, I'm on my way! I quit my day job (the court reporting, not the carpools) and went to work on a fourth category romance. Which didn't sell. Deservedly so, I admit now, but then—well, once again, I was devastated. Maybe I was a two-book wonder, I worried. A fluke. Maybe I'd never sell another book . . .

I wasted an entire year wallowing in self-doubt before I started a new category romance, a book from the heart, that sold almost immediately. Books six, seven, eight, and nine—all LOVESWEPTs—followed. And now, you hold in your hand the next, natural step for me—a FANFARE that is not only the fulfillment of my chicken-boat dreams, but which I hope will be the first of many still-longer, still-richer books to come.

See, what I finally realized during that year of introspection was that my first editor had done me a tremendous favor by rejecting the fourth book. Category romance readers are not only the most loyal audience a writer can have, they are also the most perceptive. If the writer doesn't believe in her story, neither will the reader; if the writer doesn't laugh or cry, feel a frisson of fear or grow a little warm at the appropriate moment, neither will the reader; if the writer doesn't love her book, neither will the reader.

Which brings me back to LOVESWEPT. As a mainstream writer who began her book career in category romance, I can tell you that selling a manuscript to LOVESWEPT is a real coup. Everyone from the editorial staff to the art department to the sales force cares deeply about the quality of the books they publish. And as a voracious reader whose husband says her nose ought to be covered with blisters from having it constantly buried in a book, I can tell you that their caring shows.

If you don't believe me, try one. I think you'll agree that it's an excellent line of category romance. And until we meet again, between the covers of my next book, happy reading!

Fran Baker

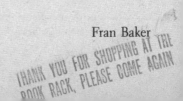

ABOUT THE AUTHOR

A former court reporter who's married to a judge, FRAN BAKER had numerous travel articles and humorous essays published in various newspapers and magazines before she took the "fiction plunge." Since then she has developed a great track record for producing top quality romance, and she says that next to giving birth, writing is the most soul-satisfying work she's ever done.

Don't miss these fabulous Bantam women's fiction titles on sale in March

ONCE AN ANGEL

☐ 29409-1 $5.50/6.50 in Canada

by Teresa Medeiros

Bestselling author of HEATHER AND VELVET
A captivating historical romance that sweeps from the wilds of an exotic paradise to the elegance of Victorian England. "Teresa Medeiros writes rare love stories to cherish."
— *Romantic Times*

IN A ROGUE'S ARMS

☐ 29692-2 $4.99/5.99 in Canada

by Virginia Brown writing as Virginia Lynn

Author of LYON'S PRIZE
A passion-filled retelling of the beloved Robin Hood tale, se in Texas of the 1870s. The first of Bantam's new "Once Upon a Time" romances: passionate historical romances with themes from fairy tales, myths, and legends.

THE LADY AND THE CHAMP

☐ 29655-8 $4.99/5.99 in Canada

by Fran Baker

Bestselling Loveswept author Fran Baker's first mainstream romance! The passionate story of a boxer/lawyer and the interior decorator who inherited his gym— and won his heart. "Unforgettable...a warm, wonderful knockout of a book."
—*Julie Garwood*